BLOOD MONEY

BLOOD MONEY

By

SCOTT PRATT

ISBN: 1494715228
ISBN 13: 9781494715229

This book, along with every book I've written and every book I'll write, is dedicated to my darling Kristy, to her unconquerable spirit and her inspirational courage. I loved her before I was born and I'll love her after I'm long gone.

PROLOGUE

1931
Carter County, Tennessee

T he moon was full, a liquid, orange ball rising steadily over the mountains to the east, when Hack Barnes heard the first rumblings of the trucks coming toward him. He gazed upward and wondered about the omen. His coon hound had howled earlier, before the moon appeared. Hack was smart but uneducated; he believed in many of the suspicions handed down by his ancestors. One of them was: *"If a dog howls before the moon rises, someone is going to die."*

As he sat waiting, listening to the sounds of the forest that surrounded him – the yelp of a coyote, the screech of an owl, the breath of the wind – Hack couldn't shake the feeling that he was about to become a part of something mysterious, something dangerous. He was no stranger to lawlessness, no stranger to the dark side of life, but something was making him uneasy. Hack ran a calloused hand across his thick beard, leaned his Winchester rifle against the side of the barn, spit out a long stream of tobacco juice and stretched his neck toward the sound of the trucks. Through the leaves, he could make out the dappled beams of headlights coming over the ridge to the southeast, less than half-a-mile away. The beams bounced wildly as the trucks made their way across the potholes and washed out crevices in what passed for a county road that led to Hack's place – five hundred acres of rugged, East Tennessee mountain land that had been handed down through three generations.

A few minutes later, the trucks rattled up near him and the engines went silent. Hack could make out the figures of two men in the first truck. One of them was familiar. Carmine Russo, head of the Russo family and the most notorious gangster in Philadelphia, was in the passenger seat, while the other was a stranger, most likely a bodyguard. The passenger door opened and Russo stepped out. He was wearing suspenders over a long-sleeved white shirt that was rolled up to the elbows, dark slacks and dress shoes. A black fedora sat at an angle atop his head. A leather shoulder holster was wrapped around his thick torso, the butt of a pistol visible beneath his arm.

"Hack," Russo said, extending a beefy hand. The gangster was a couple of inches taller than Hack and at least fifty pounds heavier. His face was as round as the full moon above, his eyes like black, shiny marbles.

"Mr. Russo."

The bodyguard climbed out of the other side of the truck and positioned himself at the back. Another man Hack had never seen got out from behind the wheel of the second truck and stood next to the bed. Both of them were carrying Thompson sub-machine guns. Introductions were neither offered nor desired.

"Ready?" Russo asked.

"I reckon," Hack said.

"Anybody else know?"

"Nobody."

"Good man." Russo clapped Hack on the shoulder. "I knew I could count on you. Let's get it unloaded."

The trucks were Ford Model AA flatbeds. Large, canvas tarps had been tied down over the beds, and the two bodyguards set about untying knots and pulling rope through grommets. Each truck carried five stacks of thin, wooden crates, five to a stack. Twenty-five crates on each truck, fifty in all.

"Where do you want it, Hack?" Russo asked.

"In the barn."

Hack and the bodyguards began unloading the crates. Each had two rope handles. They were heavy. Russo stood by and watched, chewing on a cigar and surveying the surrounding darkness. The crates were carried into an empty stall in the barn and stacked neatly. It took them nearly an hour. When the last crate was in the stall, Hack began to re-cover them with the canvas.

"What are you going to do with them?" Russo asked. He was standing inside the stall now. Two hanging oil lanterns cast flickering shadows across his face.

"I'll load them on the mules and start hauling them up the mountain at first light," Hack said. "Looks like it's going to take me a couple of days."

"You've got a good place to hide them?"

"Won't nobody bother 'em."

"Would you like to see what you're keeping for me? Hey boys! Come on in here. Let's show Hack what we brought."

"Don't much care what it is," Hack said. "You asked me for a favor and I said I'd do it. I'll keep my word."

"Did ya hear that?" Russo turned to his bodyguards. "Now *that's* a man I can trust. How long we been doing business, Hack? Ten years?"

"A while, I reckon."

"Ten years," Russo said. The bodyguards had retrieved their Thompsons. They were holding them loosely, the barrels pointing at the barn floor. "Hack and me have moved thousands of gallons of liquor up the roads and the rails. Never a disagreement over a single dime. We could have moved a lot more, too, but Hack cares about quality. And he cares about secrecy. This is a man who knows how to keep his mouth shut."

Hack saw Russo's right hand move in a blur. He saw the pistol, heard the sound of the hammer cocking.

"It's a shame I can't say the same about you," Russo said. The stall exploded with noise and light. Two shots. The bodyguards fell to the ground in a heap. Hack didn't move. The night had gone silent, save for the sound of Russo's breathing. The acrid smell of gunpowder filled the stall. Russo turned his face slowly toward Hack. Hack looked into the dark eyes, uncertain of whether he would take another breath.

"My trial starts in two weeks, which means I might be back in a couple of months," Russo said. "But if I end up going to prison, it might be five years or more. When I get out, my business in Philly will be gone, but with the help of what's in these crates, I'll get it back in a hurry. If it isn't here when I get out..."

Hack held Russo's cold gaze. "It'll be here," he said. "All of it."

"It better be, my friend. Because somebody will always be watching. Remember that. Somebody will always be watching."

PART I
PRESENT DAY

CHAPTER ONE

My name is Joe Dillard, and the young woman sitting across from me was lovely. Her name was Charleston Story, but everyone called her Charlie. Her hair was long and auburn, her eyes sapphire-blue and intelligent. Her skin was smooth and tanned, her smile perfect and easy. She was around twenty-five, fresh out of law school. I'd known her – not well, but casually – since she was a small child because I'd unsuccessfully defended her father on a marijuana production charge after the feds raided his farm over in Carter County more than twenty years earlier. It was one of my first cases as a defense lawyer in federal court and left me with a sour taste in my mouth. The girl's father, a young man named Luke Story, had been drafted into the army, sent to Vietnam, and had lost a part of an arm to a Viet Cong grenade before he was eventually caught growing dope. The federal judge who sentenced him was unsympathetic regarding the military service. He sentenced Luke to twenty-five years in prison for growing fifty marijuana plants.

"So what can I do for you?" I said after Charlie and I finished the obligatory small talk.

"I need a job," she said with a slight Tennessee lilt. "I finished at the top of my class in law school and interviewed with some of the best firms in the state, but as soon as they found out about Daddy being in prison, they all thanked me politely and showed me the door. I have to work under the supervision of a licensed attorney until I pass the bar and nobody else seems to want to give me a chance. I hate to spring this on you, Mr. Dillard, because I've heard about your wife and I know you don't take a lot of cases these days. It's probably asking too much, but is there any way you could help me out?"

"How is your dad?" I said, taken off guard by her directness and needing a moment to think. "How much longer are they going to keep him?"

"He gets out in a couple of months," Charlie said. "He has to spend six months in a halfway house in Knoxville after that, which means he won't be home for good until early spring, but at least we can finally see the light at the end of the tunnel."

I'd always admired people who were direct and got right to the point, but what Charlie was asking of me was something I'd never considered. With the exception of a few years I spent in the district attorney's office prosecuting criminal cases, I'd always practiced law alone. I'd never had an associate or a partner and didn't want one now. My wife was battling metastatic breast cancer and I was spending as much time with her as possible. My case load was light; I turned down far more cases than I accepted. I was renting a space in Jonesborough near the courthouse that consisted of a tiny waiting room, a half-bathroom, my office and two other rooms, one of which occasionally served as a conference room and another that was empty. I had no secretary, no paralegal, and no investigator, although I did have my son, Jack, who was home for the summer following his first year of law school at Vanderbilt. He'd set up shop in the conference room and was calling himself my law clerk, although I had no real need for a law clerk. Just as I was about to explain all of those things to Charlie, Jack's muscular frame materialized in the doorway.

"I'm sorry to interrupt," he said, "but can I speak to you in private for just a minute? It's important."

"Excuse me," I said to Charlie, "I'll be right back."

I got up and walked out of the office and down the short hallway to the conference room. Jack closed the door.

"You have to help that girl out," he said in a whisper.

"What? You were eavesdropping?"

"The walls are thin. But yeah, I was eavesdropping. You have to say yes."

"Why?"

"Because she's obviously bright. She said she finished at the top of her class. And it isn't fair that she's being blackballed because of her father. You're all about justice, Dad. It's unjust, an injustice, a travesty of justice, that that tremendously beautiful young lady in there can't break into the legal profession because her father is in jail."

"'Tremendously beautiful' being the key phrase, I suppose."

"I could learn a lot from her," he said. "We're about the same age. I think we'll become good friends."

"Inter-office romances are unhealthy and unwise—"

"Who said anything about romance?"

"So you're not planning to ask her out?"

"Of course not. Well, it might have crossed my mind, but maybe she already has a boyfriend."

"Do you want me to ask her for you? Better yet, why don't you go in there and ask her yourself?"

"Come on, Dad, *please*. She's a freakin' knockout. Even if we don't wind up dating, she's so easy on the eyes it'll make my summer much more pleasant. But don't do it for me, do it for her, or better yet, do it for justice. Nah, never mind that. Do it for me."

"You're a pain in the butt sometimes, you know that?" I said, and I turned and walked out.

"Sorry," I said as I sat back down behind my desk. "Do you have a boyfriend, Charlie?"

She blinked a few times. "What? Why?"

"Because my son seems to be quite enamored with you."

She smiled and her eyes twinkled.

"He's cute," she said.

"Great," I said. "He thinks you're cute and you think he's cute. A perfect basis on which make a sound decision and go forward in building a professional relationship."

"Wait," she said, "I didn't mean to—"

I held up my hand. "I was kidding, Charlie, but I can't give you a job. It doesn't have anything to do with your father. I just don't have a job to give. I don't take in enough work these days to be able to pay you a salary, and I don't have room for another lawyer here."

"You don't have to pay me a salary," she said. "I already have someone who is willing to pay me five thousand dollars to represent him. That should be enough to get me through until I pass the bar. I still live at home on Buck Mountain with my uncle so I don't have a lot of expenses. And as far as having a place to work, I have a cell phone and a laptop so I don't really need an office. I can work anywhere."

"You need somewhere to meet with clients," I said.

"What I need is someone to show me the ropes. The one thing they don't teach you in law school is how to actually practice law."

"You're right about that," I said, remembering how utterly helpless I often felt when I got out of law school and hung out my shingle. "If it hadn't been for the older lawyers around here when I was getting started, I would have wound up getting sued for malpractice every time I turned around. They really helped me out."

"Maybe it's your turn," she said as the smile returned to her face. "A little karma. What goes around comes around."

"Let me tell you a little about how this profession works," I said. "You start at the bottom of the totem pole. You have to take cases no one else will take, chase windmills no one else will chase. In a town this size, if you manage to stay with it, work hard, find a niche, and avoid all the pitfalls of substance abuse and greed that seem to plague lawyers, after ten years or so you'll be able to make a decent living. After twenty years, if you've managed to live within your means, you'll become somewhat comfortable, at least financially. After thirty years, you can start thinking about retirement, but you won't want to retire because you've worked so hard to achieve and maintain your station in the profession. After forty years, you'll be managing the health and personal problems created by constant stress and emotional turmoil. Sometime after that, you'll drop dead of a heart attack or a stroke and will soon be forgotten."

"I'll go ahead and slit my wrists now if you'd like," she said. "Do you have a razor I can borrow?"

I leaned back in my chair and couldn't help smiling back at her. She was so pleasant, and Jack was right about her being easy on the eyes.

"Where did you live in Knoxville while you were in school?" I said. "I spent three years down there. Both of my kids were born there."

"I didn't live in Knoxville. I commuted."

"You what? From Buck Mountain?"

"Five days a week for three years," she said. "I have a 75,000-mile law degree. My grandmother was sick and I didn't want to leave her alone, so I decided to make the drive every day. I'd leave at five-thirty in the morning and get back around six in the evening."

"And you still managed to finish at the top of the class?"

"I wasn't the valedictorian, but I was close."

The fact that she was so determined to become a lawyer that she was willing to drive roughly two-hundred and fifty miles round-trip every day to earn her degree impressed me. I changed my mind and decided right then to take her on board.

"What's the case?" I said. "The one that involves someone paying you five thousand dollars. Is it a criminal case?"

"No, it's civil. The client is a neighbor of mine named Roscoe Barnes. He's an elderly man and his son is trying to have him involuntarily committed to a mental institution. Roscoe is old, but he isn't crazy and he's in pretty good health."

"Is Roscoe wealthy?"

"I don't think so. He taught English at Cloudland High School for thirty-five years and his wife was a math teacher before she died fifteen years ago. He owns several hundred acres of land up on the mountain, but a lot of it is exposed rock. I don't see how it could be worth a lot of money, but Roscoe mentioned that his son – his name is Zane – wants his land. I get the sense that Roscoe isn't telling me everything, but he's mentally competent and he isn't a danger to himself or anyone else. That's the legal standard for involuntary commitment, isn't it?"

I nodded and said, "Has the son hired a lawyer?"

"Nathaniel Mitchell. They've already served the petition on Roscoe."

"Then the son has money. Mitchell is the most expensive lawyer in Northeast Tennessee."

"Zane is a developer," Charlie said. "Builds big houses in the mountains for the *nouveaux riche*. Maybe he's struggling because of the economic downturn in the housing industry, but I still don't understand why he would go after his own father's property."

"You should get an affidavit from an expert that says Roscoe is competent and file a motion to have the petition dismissed," I said. "Try to take them out of the game before it gets started. Once the discovery process gets underway, Mitchell will try to bury you in paper and he'll make things as expensive as possible hoping your client will run out of money and give them what they want."

"Roscoe won't give them anything. He's a stubborn old bird."

"I want to meet him and talk to him," I said. "If I'm going to help you out on a case, I want to know our client. Early Monday morning would be best for me."

Her eyes brightened.

"You'll do it, then? You'll supervise me?"

I nodded again. "We'll work something out as far as finding some space for you here."

"How much of the five thousand do you want?"

"Keep it. You need it more than I do."

Before I could say another word, she was on her feet and around the desk.

"Please let me hug your neck," she said.

I stood, bent over, and opened my arms. She squeezed me so tightly and for so long I started to feel light-headed.

"Whoa, whoa," I said. "I can't help you if you strangle me to death."

"Thank you, Mr. Dillard," she said when she finally let me go. "You won't regret this."

A minute later, she'd picked up her pocketbook and was walking toward the door. Just before she walked out she turned.

"By the way," she said. "The answer is no."

"I beg your pardon?"

"Tell Jack I said no. I don't have a boyfriend."

CHAPTER TWO

L ater that afternoon, my cell phone rang. I looked down at the caller ID and smiled. It was my wife, Caroline, probably calling about where she wanted to eat for lunch.

"You need to go over to the Sullivan County jail," she said when I answered, "and talk to a young man named Jordan Scott. I just got off the phone with his father. He's been arrested for murder."

"Murder? What murder?"

"It apparently happened this morning," she said.

"I don't want to get involved in a murder case, Caroline. I thought we talked about—"

"I know, I know," she said, "but this one is different. You need to get over there right away. He needs help."

The tone of her voice was urgent, which was uncharacteristic.

"Who did he supposedly murder?" I asked.

"A cop. He's black, Joe. Just a kid, and he shot a white police officer. I think it's going to be a bad one."

"Then why do you want me to get involved?"

"Trust me," she said. "I've been talking to his father for the past forty minutes. He's a good kid from a good family. There are circumstances, Joe. This is something you need to do."

"What circumstances?"

"I heard them from his father. If I tell you, then you'll be getting your information third-hand. It's better if you get it straight from him. If you aren't comfortable representing him after you talk to him, then fine, don't do it. But if half of what his father told me is true, you'll take the case."

"Which means I'll probably get caught up in another firestorm."

"Firestorms are what you do best, baby."

The door buzzed and clanged, and I walked into a small interview room walled by concrete blocks of gunmetal gray and floored in gray linoleum. The sights, sounds and smells of county jails were routine to me, but the nagging feeling of claustrophobia never quite left me once I walked through the first, locked door.

The young man sitting at the round, steel table was wiry and strong, with a long neck and a pair of the biggest hands I'd ever seen. His ebony skin seemed to have been stretched tightly over his body like shiny, black cellophane. His kinky hair was thick and cropped close, his jaws square, sturdy and muscled. His physical presence reminded me of my son – all muscle and sinew, nothing extraneous. His eyes were the brown of chocolate syrup and he had deep dimples in his cheeks. He was handcuffed, shackled and waist-chained, wearing the green and white, striped jumpsuit and rubber flip flops that were standard issue at the Sullivan County Jail. Of the many jails I'd visited over the years, Sullivan County was one of the worst. It was overcrowded and filthy. Toilets and showers were stopped up, wiring was corroded and exposed, and the guards were cynical and abusive. If you believed what Winston Churchill once wrote – that you could judge a society by the way it treats its prisoners – then Sullivan County was a cruel and unforgiving place.

I set my briefcase down on the table and took out a legal pad and a pen.

"My name is Joe Dillard," I said. "I'm a lawyer. Your father called and asked me to talk to you. Anything you say to me is strictly confidential, but I want you to know up front that I'm not your lawyer, at least not yet. I want to hear what you have to say before I decide whether I'm going to represent you. Are you okay with that?"

He nodded.

"Your name is Jordan Scott?"

"Yes, sir."

"Do you know what you're charged with, Jordan?"

"Murder."

"Did you kill someone?"

"Yes, sir."

"Do you know who you killed?"

"His name was Todd Raleigh. He was a deputy for the Sullivan County Sheriff's Department."

"Do you want to tell me why you killed him?"

"Because he deserved to die."

CHAPTER THREE

This is what I learned during my first conversation with Jordan Scott, who was well-mannered, articulate and intelligent:

Jordan had grown up in a middle-class home in Kingsport. His father worked as a machinist at Tennessee Eastman in Kingsport and his mother was a speech pathologist in the Sullivan County school system. Jordan had a sister named Della who was one year older and a brother named David who was three years younger and who suffered enough brain damage during a traumatic birth to be classified by those who make such determinations as "borderline mentally incapacitated."

Jordan said he was a straight-A student at Dobyns-Bennett High School and an all-state athlete. He was an all-state running back in football, an all-state shooting guard in basketball, and won the state championship in the two-hundred meter hurdles in track his senior year. He had athletic and academic scholarship offers from Division I college programs all over the country, including the University of Tennessee, Kentucky, Georgia, North Carolina and Duke.

But Jordan decided to stay close to home. He didn't want to leave David, and although he was big, strong and fast enough to compete at the Division I level, he knew he wasn't – and never would be – quite big enough, quite strong enough, or quite fast enough to compete with the freaks of nature in the NBA or the NFL. East Tennessee State University in Johnson City was only a thirty-minute drive from home. It was a Division I school with a decent basketball team, and it offered something else that appealed to Jordan – a medical school. There were only a handful of African-American doctors in the region, and Jordan believed he could be of some value to his community in that regard, so he chose ETSU over all the others and enrolled. His parents bought him a used car when he graduated from high school, and between the academic and athletic scholarship money he received, he was able to pay all of his school expenses, split an apartment with a teammate, and stick some money in his pocket each semester. Life was good.

During his freshman year, Jordan maintained a 4.0 grade point average and led the basketball team in scoring and assists. He was named to the Atlantic Sun All-Conference team and was selected as Freshman of the Year. He also fell in love with a green-eyed, brown-skinned, Tyra Banks look-alike named Holly Ross. Holly was from Ooltewah, a small town near Chattanooga. She was a volleyball player, a long, lean, reserved beauty who was studying biology and believed she was destined to help save the planet.

In May of Jordan's sophomore year, after a season in which Jordan struggled with hamstring and ankle injuries and still put up even better numbers than his freshman year, Holly went out for a jog alone. As she ran along a path through a stretch of woods at the Mountain Home Veterans Administration Center across the street from the ETSU campus, she was attacked, brutally beaten and raped at knifepoint, thus becoming the third victim of a serial rapist who terrorized the region for the next several months. The police had not released information about the first two rapes to the public, hoping to catch the rapist without causing a panic, but after Holly was attacked, they changed their plan and sounded the public alarm. Three women had been raped in three different counties: one in Sullivan County, one in Carter County, and Holly in Washington County. Over the summer, three more women, all younger than twenty-five, suffered the same fate as Holly. A multi-county task force was formed as the police searched desperately for the rapist.

Holly spent two weeks in the hospital following the rape, and Jordan was there every day and night. She went home for the summer and fell into a deep depression. Jordan drove to Ooltewah twice a week to offer whatever love, care and support that Holly would accept. He went with her to some of her rape counseling sessions, and, little by little, she seemed to come back from the abyss. By the end of August, when classes at ETSU resumed, she'd decided to go back to school and rejoin her teammates on the volleyball team, despite the fact that the rapist was still on the loose and still attacking young women. Jordan was inspired by her courage. He proposed to her on the fifth day of September and gave her a ring. It would be a long engagement – they planned to marry the day after they graduated – but Jordan said he knew he'd found his soul mate.

Nine months later, with the rapist still on the loose and still committing rapes, Jordan was stopped for speeding in Sullivan County as he and Holly were returning to ETSU from dinner at his parents' home. A Sullivan County deputy named Todd Raleigh walked up to the passenger window and leaned down. He recognized Jordan, and after giving him a short lecture on careless behavior, let him go. But as Raleigh spoke through the window, Jordan watched in horror as Holly broke down. Tears began to stream down her face and mucous ran from her nose. Her jaw muscles started to spasm involuntarily. She looked as though she'd come face-to-face with death. As soon as Raleigh went back to his cruiser, Jordan noticed the smell of urine. Holly had wet herself.

It took Jordan an hour to calm her down enough to speak. *It was him*, she said. *The voice, the eyes, the smell.* She was certain. Todd Raleigh was the man who had raped her.

What followed was a nightmare worthy of Dante. They called Holly's parents, and the four of them went to the sheriff's department together. They spoke to an investigator who immediately bumped them to the head of the investigative division, who bumped them to the chief deputy. What they were insinuating was ridiculous, they were told. Todd Raleigh was a dedicated officer with an impeccable service record. Holly's attacker had worn a ski mask, so she'd been unable to provide police with a detailed description. She knew he was white, she knew approximately how tall he was and approximately how much he weighed. He'd left semen in her, though. Why didn't they just get a DNA sample from Raleigh and either arrest him or eliminate him based on the results?

Not possible, she was told. To request a DNA sample from Raleigh would be akin to accusing him of rape. Besides, he had the same rights as anyone else. Without more evidence, they couldn't force him to give a sample. In fact, if it came down to it, they would advise him *against* giving a voluntary sample. The chief deputy, a fat, red-faced, bellicose, belligerent individual named Matthew Bacon, blatantly accused Holly of lying. Quite the lawsuit she'd have, he said, if a white cop was accused of raping a young black woman. A college woman, at that. Sensational lawsuit. Was she trying to get rich at this innocent officer's expense?

Jordan left the police department angry and frustrated. Holly was a mess. She retreated somewhere inside herself, into a psychological bunker where no one was allowed. He couldn't even get her to speak. That night, while Jordan lay on the couch in Holly's apartment, she went into the bathroom and slit her wrists with a razor blade. On the day she was buried, another young woman was raped.

Jordan became filled with a simmering rage. He also became obsessed with Todd Raleigh. He stopped going to class, didn't take his finals, and stopped going to basketball workouts. He believed what Holly had said about Raleigh and was consumed with the idea of making Raleigh pay for what he'd done. But he did so in a measured, calculating fashion. He began stalking Raleigh the way a lion stalks a wildebeest, patiently, hiding in the shadows. He borrowed cars from friends and teammates who were too concerned about his well-being to question. The cars served as both camouflage and shelter during long hours of surveillance. He bought a pair of binoculars, took a shotgun from his father's closet and kept it with him every time he followed or watched Raleigh. Within a week, he knew Raleigh's routines, and on the fourth day of the second week, he got what he wanted.

Raleigh left his apartment at 5:30 a.m. and appeared to be going for a run. Nothing unusual. Raleigh went for a run every day, but he never ran at the same place and the times varied depending on the shift he was working. On this day, he drove to the parking lot of an abandoned bakery about a mile from a park near the Holston River just outside the Kingsport city limits. The morning was gray and misty, the sun not yet up. Jordan hung back, watching as Raleigh got out of his car and jogged off toward the park. He waited ten minutes and drove past the park. He didn't see Raleigh, so he parked a couple of hundred yards down the road. He retrieved the shotgun from the trunk and slipped into a field adjacent to the park, moving low and slowly through the tall fescue. Jordan knew the park well – he'd run there many times in high school – so he worked his way to fence line on a rise that overlooked the southern end. Raleigh was nowhere in sight, and neither was anyone else. Jordan put his back against a poplar tree, laid the shotgun across his thighs, and waited. Just as the sun began to peek over the trees behind him, Jordan saw a small car pull into the parking lot. A solitary figure got out, walked to the rear of the car, and pulled a bicycle off a rack. It appeared to be a woman, though Jordan couldn't quite tell from where he was. The rider guided the bike onto the asphalt path that wound through the park and started pedaling.

The attack happened in an instant.

The biker had circled the far end of the park and had just started along the western border when a figure emerged, seemingly from nowhere, throwing a shoulder into the biker like a linebacker. The biker went flying, and a second later was being dragged toward the bushes. Jordan sprinted from his hiding place to the spot where he saw the biker disappear. He listened, and above his own breathing, could hear muffled sounds of struggle among the leaves and the underbrush. He flipped the shotgun's safety off and moved toward the sound.

The first thing Jordan saw were two sets of feet. Raleigh was grunting and cursing.

"Stop!" Jordan yelled, aiming the shotgun at the back of Raleigh's head. "Get off of her!"

The ski-masked man turned and locked predatory eyes onto Jordan, who was less than ten feet away. The girl – Jordan didn't even know her name – was bleeding from the nose and appeared to be half-conscious. Raleigh jumped up and tried to run, but the double-ought buckshot Jordan fired from the twelve-gauge blew half of his head off before he got ten feet.

Raleigh was dead.

Holly was avenged.

Jordan called the police and calmly waited for them to arrive.

After listening to what he had to say, I sat back and folded my arms.

"How much of this did you tell the police?" I asked.

"I didn't tell them anything other than I shot the man because he was raping the girl."

"They didn't question you?"

"They tried. I told them I wanted to speak to a lawyer."

"Do they have the gun?"

"Yes."

"Did the girl say anything to you before the police got there?"

"She was crying. I asked her if she was all right but she seemed to be afraid of me. I guess I can't blame her since she saw me shoot the man. Am I going to spend the rest of my life in jail?"

"I don't know, Jordan. It's possible. I have a pretty good idea how they'll come at you. They'll say you went vigilante, and there's no place for vigilantes in a civilized society. They'll say Raleigh was running away when you pulled the trigger, so the danger to the girl had passed and there was no danger to you. They'll say the amount of force you used was unreasonable, excessive under the circumstances. They'll talk to people at the sheriff's department and they'll find out about the accusation Holly made against Raleigh. Then they'll go back and talk to everybody you know and they'll find out you've been skipping school and basketball practice. They'll put it together, and when they do, they'll start screaming pre-meditation, especially since you were carrying the shotgun with you in a city park on a Monday morning. They'll say you were hunting Raleigh. They'll play up the pre-meditation to try to get a first-degree murder conviction. They probably won't ask for the death penalty, but you never know. If they convict you of first-degree murder, you won't be eligible for parole for fifty-one years. Did you see a weapon on Raleigh, by the way?"

"He had a knife."

"Did he make a move toward you? Were you afraid he was going to kill you?"

"I didn't know what he'd do. He was raping somebody. Was I just supposed to let him run away so he could rape somebody else?"

I shook my head. "I don't know what you should have done, but it doesn't matter now, does it? You did what you did. You shot him, you told them you shot him, and now you're going to have to deal with the consequences. Even if you're eventually found not guilty of murder, you're going to be in this place for months, maybe a year, probably in solitary confinement. You're also going to become the focus of a whole bunch of hatred, whether you deserve it or not. You think you killed a man, a rapist, but you also killed a symbol. Even if Raleigh was what you say he was, and believe me, we're going to have to find a way to prove it and find a way to get it admitted in court, you killed a representative of law and order, a *white* representative of law and order in a community that is dominated by whites. You've committed an act that flies in the face of their entire judicial system, and you're about to find out how brutal that system can be. If everything is the way you say it is, and *if* we can get a fair trial in front of an impartial jury, then maybe you can walk away from this, but even if you do, I want you to know you're going to pay a steep price."

Tears welled in his eyes and they took on a luminescent glow.

"I don't know you, Mr. Dillard, but I want to ask you a question."

"Go ahead."

"Have you ever been in love?"

I thought about Caroline and the many years we'd been together, the trials and tribulations, the joy and the pain.

"Yes, Jordan, I've been in love for a long, long time."

"That's what he took from me, and no matter what the judicial system does to me, I don't think the price could be any steeper."

CHAPTER FOUR

Charlie Story sat down on the couch in the day room. It was clean, almost sterile, like a lobby in a college dorm, Spartan in its décor and furnishings. The block walls were painted a glossy, pale yellow. The floor was covered with short-napped, indoor-outdoor, brown carpet. She'd been coming to this place every other Sunday since she was old enough to drive.

A man in a khaki uniform similar to those worn by janitors walked across the room, sat down next to her, and smiled. His hair was dark brown, short, and just starting to gray at the temples. He had green eyes flecked with gold, a high forehead and a sharp, angular face dimpled in the chin.

"Only a few more trips to the big house," Charlie's father, Luke Story, said as he kissed her on the cheek.

"I know. Finally."

"Finally? You mean you won't miss it?"

"I'm sure I will," Charlie said. "I'll miss the pleasing sights and sounds and the delightful people. Especially the guards. They're so charming, such wonderful conversationalists."

"Yeah, they'll miss you, too. They start drooling every time you walk through the door."

"It's hard to believe you're getting out, that it's almost over."

For twenty years, since Charlie was five, her father had been in federal prison. She knew his story well. He was open with her about what he'd done, and she'd read the transcripts from his trial and every newspaper account that was published. Luke had graduated from Cloudland High School in Roan Mountain, Tennessee, in 1967, was drafted in 1968 and sent to Vietnam in February of 1969. He wound up being assigned to the 101st Airborne Division as an infantryman, and in May, ten weeks after he arrived in country, his left arm was nearly blown off just below the elbow by a rocket pro-pelled grenade as he and his fellow soldiers tried to take a hill from the North Vietnamese Army. By September, he was home with a Purple Heart, a useless arm, and more than his share of bitter resentment.

Luke moved back in with his parents when he returned to Tennessee and invested some of the money from the disability check he received each month into marijuana seed and fertilizer. He started growing weed on his parents' land the following spring, got busted by the sheriff's department two years later, and spent a year in the county jail. As soon as he got out, he went back to growing weed, and within three years he'd earned enough to pay cash for his own place, a run-down, hun-dred-acre farm a couple of miles from his parents. He lived in a breezy old farm house, grew tobacco and corn along with the marijuana, and started a herd of Black

Angus beef cattle. By the time he was thirty, he'd learned to bribe the locals, and the marijuana had made him a millionaire. He later took a wife, Ruth Ann, whom he'd met during a trip to the West Virginia mountains to visit one of his old Army buddies who was also in the marijuana business.

The demand for weed was booming, Luke was conscientious about improving his product, and the money continued to roll in. So he bought another two hundred acres adjacent to his property, completely remodeled the old farm house and the barn, and Ruth Ann started a greenhouse business that quickly became profitable. Five years later, after two miscarriages, Ruth Ann finally gave birth to a daughter. She was conceived during a trip to Charleston, South Carolina, so her parents named her Charleston.

It was a warm, August morning when the inevitable happened. A small army of federal agents descended on the farm like locusts. Charlie was only four years old, but she remembered the incident vividly. Large men in dark jackets, all carrying guns, broke through the front door just before sunup. Charlie was sitting in a booster chair at the kitchen table. Her father was drinking his coffee across from her. The men screamed at him and threw him to the floor. They did the same to her mother. One of the agents picked Charlie up and carried her outside as though he was rescuing her from a fire. She tried to fight him, but it was useless. He put her in a car with two women who drove her away. Her grandparents picked her up several hours later. She didn't see her father for almost a year, and she never set foot in that house again.

Luke Story had intended to get completely out of the marijuana business by then, but he couldn't resist experimenting with cross-breeding and had planted fifty plants that spring just to see what the yield would be. The agents found them hidden among corn stalks in a field about two hundred yards from the house. They cut down the plants and seized everything in sight. The federal drug laws allowed them to eventually take Luke's land, his house, his livestock and all of his equipment and vehicles. The agents padlocked the greenhouse business and seized all of the money in every bank account Luke and Ruth Ann owned. They tore the house and the barn apart looking for cash, but found very little. Ruth Ann had never actively participated in the marijuana business, and the agents knew it, but they arrested her and held her in jail until Luke told them where he kept the bulk of his cash. They dug up a fifty-five-gallon oil drum behind the barn containing nearly a million dollars.

Luke was charged with manufacturing marijuana, conspiracy to distribute marijuana, tax evasion, and, because he had a shotgun in his closet, they added a charge of being a convicted felon in possession of a weapon. He was too stubborn to plead guilty, so he went to trial a year after he was arrested and was convicted. His prior marijuana conviction was used against him at sentencing, as was the weapons charge. The judge added everything up, thanked him for his military service, expressed regret that he'd been wounded in combat, and sentenced him to twenty-five years in prison. The judge also ordered that his disability checks be discontinued. The next day, Charlie's mother, Ruth Ann, who'd been forced to take Charlie and move in with Luke's parents, left early in the morning and never came back. No one had seen or heard from her since. Charlie suspected she'd gone back to her native West Virginia, but by the time Charlie was old enough to look for her, she'd lost the desire.

The federal government had finally eased the sentencing laws regarding non-violent drug offenders, so Luke would be getting out a little earlier than he'd expected. Charlie was looking forward to having her father home. She had some concerns about how well Luke would get along with his brother, Jasper, about how he would adjust to life outside of prison, and about their financial situation, but Charlie had taught herself to be an optimist. She'd figure it out. She always had. They'd get by somehow.

"How's the job hunt going?" Luke asked. "Any prospects?"

"I'm going to work with Joe Dillard," Charlie said, knowing what would come next.

"Dillard! He's worthless," Luke said. "He's the reason I've been rotting in this hell hole for more than twenty years."

"That isn't true and you know it. He didn't grow marijuana and he wasn't a convicted felon when he got caught growing marijuana. He didn't bury his money in a barrel and evade paying taxes. You're the one who did all of those things. I've read all the transcripts, daddy. He did the best he could; there just wasn't much he could do for you. But he's the best criminal defense lawyer around and everybody knows it. I can learn more from him than any other lawyer in the state. So I don't want to hear another word out of you about Joe Dillard."

Luke scratched his head and contemplated his shoes for a minute. He reached over and punched his daughter lightly on the shoulder.

"You've got a lot of your momma in you, girl," he said.

"I've got a lot more of my daddy in me, I'm proud to say. I can't wait until you get out of this place. It'll be so good to finally have you home."

Luke picked up Charlie's hand and squeezed it.

"I know you don't need it," he said, "but I'm looking forward to finally taking care of my little girl."

CHAPTER FIVE

At 7:30 a.m. on Monday, Jack and I watched through the front door as Charlie Story and our new client, Roscoe Barnes, walked through the parking lot toward the office beneath a threatening, slate-colored sky. Charlie was wearing jeans, an orange, University of Tennessee hoodie and a pair of old-school Converse high-top basketball sneakers. Roscoe was wearing blue denim overalls, a red flannel shirt, and work boots. I was wearing a suit and had insisted that Jack do the same since we were meeting a new client.

"We're overdressed," Jack said.

I shrugged. "Nothing wrong with a little professionalism," I said as I reached out and pushed the door open.

Charlie introduced everyone and we walked back to my conference room. The table was big enough to accommodate six people. Jack and I sat on one side, Charlie and Roscoe on the other. After the introductions, I got down to business.

"Charlie sent me a copy of the petition your son filed, Mr. Barnes," I said. "It makes some pretty alarming allegations."

"Yeah," Roscoe said. "It says I'm too crazy to be left alone."

"Are you?"

Roscoe glanced at Charlie and then looked me straight in the eye.

"I'm no crazier than you or anybody else," he said. "I might be a little eccentric, but I'm old enough to have earned the right. I get out of bed every morning at the same time, go through pretty much the same routines every day. I feed myself and bathe myself and take care of my place as best I can. I take the medicine the doctors say I should take and I don't run around naked and howl at the moon."

"There's a sworn affidavit attached to the petition signed by a psychiatrist named Frederic Heinz," I said. "I checked him out and he has impeccable credentials. He also specializes in treating elderly patients. Tell me about the examination he did."

"There wasn't any examination," Roscoe said. "Zane showed up unannounced about a month ago and had this man with him that he introduced as his buddy Fred. I didn't think anything about it other than it was unusual for Zane to come around since I only see him a couple of times a year. I fixed supper for them and they stayed for an hour, maybe an hour-and-a-half, and then they left. Couple of weeks later a sheriff's deputy knocks on my door and handed me a copy of the petition. Made me mad enough to spit."

Roscoe was a retired English teacher. Charlie had been his student at Cloudland High School for two years. They also happened to be neighbors on Buck Mountain and had known each other for most of Charlie's life. Roscoe was in his mid-seventies, a slight, stooped man with a sharp nose and, I soon found, a tongue to match. I'd done some research over the weekend and learned that the legal process of taking over an elderly person's life wasn't all that complicated, but the law made it difficult nonetheless. Tennessee law required that "credible" medical evidence be presented to the court in order to have a person declared mentally incapacitated. That evidence also had to be "clear and convincing," one of the highest standards in the legal profession.

"I understand these allegations make you angry," I said to Roscoe, "but we have to talk about them and we have to file a written answer. So I'm going to ask you some questions and I'd appreciate it if you wouldn't spit on me."

"Fire away, counselor," Roscoe said. "I'll try to mind my temper."

"They allege that you set your house on fire several times in the past year. Is that true?"

"I get a little absent-minded sometimes and leave a hamburger patty on the stove. I've started a couple of grease fires, but they stayed in the pan. I told Zane and Fred about it because I thought it was funny. Didn't think they'd use it against me to try and have me locked up in the looney bin."

"They say you left a dead dog in your bed for three days and your son practically had to get into a fist fight with you to get the dog out of the house."

"That happened during Christmas when he came to visit. My old retriever, Dixie, died in her sleep. I loved her dearly and couldn't bring myself to accept that she was gone. It wasn't three days; it was a day and a half. And he didn't have to fight me to get her out of there. I finally wrapped her in a blanket and carried her out by the barn and buried her myself. I may not have done it quickly enough to suit him, but I did it."

"They say you talk to yourself sometimes."

"Don't you? Doesn't everybody?"

"They say you forget to take your prescribed medications."

"Once in a blue moon I forget, but it hasn't hurt me. He wouldn't have known that, either, if I hadn't told him."

"They say you served them food that was inedible and that your house is – and I'm quoting here – 'unfit for human habitation.'"

"All I can say to that is that they ate the pork chops and the potatoes and the corn and the bread and I didn't see any gagging or puking going on. The house isn't as clean as it once was, but I keep it up pretty good. I do the dishes every day and I do the laundry and I vacuum and dust once a week. I even clean out the bath tub and the toilet every ten days or so. It isn't as spic and span as a military barracks, but it isn't filthy, either."

"Dr. Heinz's report says you're 'disaffected' and 'incapable of sustaining a line of thought' most of the time. Why do you think he would say something like that?"

"Because that's what my son paid him to say."

I pushed the papers away from me, folded my arms across my chest, and leaned back in my chair.

"Why, Mr. Barnes?" I said. "Why is your son doing this? I'm not a doctor, but I have to admit you seem fine to me. So I'm having trouble understanding why this is happening."

"I can't tell you," he said.

"Can't or won't?"

"Won't."

"Why not? Why won't you tell me?"

"You'll find out soon enough."

"I'd rather find out right now, from you, straight from the horse's mouth. Why is your son trying to have you committed?"

"He wants something I have, but don't even bother asking me what it is, because I'm not going to tell you."

"It's difficult for a lawyer to represent a client who won't be open and honest with him."

"But you've done it before, haven't you? Charlie tells me you've done a whole bunch of high-profile criminal cases and that you were a prosecutor for a few years. You should be used to people being less than open. I'm not being dishonest with you, Mr. Dillard. I'm just not going to tell you everything. If you can't live with that, then I guess Charlie and I will have to find someone else. And like I said a minute ago, you'll find out soon enough what Zane wants so badly. Or at least Charlie will find out. If she chooses to tell you about it after she finds out, then so be it."

"Are we talking about something illegal?"

"Not illegal. Dangerous, maybe, but not illegal."

I looked around the table. Charlie was typing notes into a laptop. Jack was suppressing a smile. I couldn't imagine what he found amusing, but I knew him well enough to be able to read his facial expressions. Roscoe was sitting ramrod straight in his chair, a look of defiance in his brown eyes.

"Okay, Mr. Barnes, have it your way," I said. "But this is what has to happen immediately. We need to get you examined by another psychiatrist and have him write a report that we'll submit to the judge. Once that's done, the judge will appoint a lawyer of his choosing to act as a *guardian ad litem*. It's required in all conservatorship cases in Tennessee. The *guardian ad litem* is supposed to be neutral. He or she will talk to all the witnesses and will probably request an independent psychiatric examination. Then the guardian will submit a report to the judge and make recommendations. The judge doesn't have to follow the recommendations, but from what I've been able to gather, the judge usually does what the guardian recommends. You'll have to pay for the psychiatrist we use, but the court will pay for the guardian and any examinations the guardian requests. Do you have a psychiatrist in mind? Someone you know and trust?"

"I don't know any psychiatrists," Roscoe said. "Never talked to one in my life outside of that nimrod that Zane brought to the house."

"Then Charlie will find one for you. It'll probably cost you between three and five thousand dollars. Can you afford that?"

"Will my health insurance cover it?"

"If it was a routine exam, I suppose it would," I said, "but this isn't routine. We're hiring an expert and we want him to be on our side. Money talks, Mr. Barnes, as much as I hate to say it. It's just the way the system works."

"I have a little money stashed away," he said. "I ain't too happy about wasting it on something like this, but I'll do it if I have to."

"Maybe we can get it back for you if the judge dismisses the petition, but if he doesn't, you're in for a long, difficult journey through the court system. Are you prepared for that?"

Roscoe nodded his head slowly.

"I think you'd be surprised at how well prepared I am, Mr. Dillard. As a matter of fact, I'm certain of it."

CHAPTER SIX

Charlie arrived home that night a little before seven. The sun was dropping steadily toward the mountain peaks to the west. Buck Mountain had finally awakened fully from its winter sleep. Bright green leaves covered the trees that encircled Charlie's home; the laurel bushes and undergrowth were thick and lush. A stiff, cool breeze rustled through the canopy as she walked toward the back porch. She heard her mare, Sadie, whinny in the barn.

Sitting in a chair on the back porch was Jasper, Charlie's uncle. His dog, a massive, Irish wolfhound named Biscuit, was lying at his feet. Jasper was whittling a branch down to a sharp point. He was three years younger than Charlie's father, a quirky man whose daily attire consisted of green coveralls that zipped up the front, an Atlanta Braves baseball cap and a pair of black work boots. He was tall and gangly with closely-cropped, black hair and hazel eyes.

Jasper had been married once, for two days, to a red-haired girl of Irish descent named Rachel Dearring. He kept a photograph of her on a bureau by his bed. After a weekend honeymoon in Boone, North Carolina,

Jasper was driving back toward Buck Mountain when he lost control of his car on a rain-slicked curve near the Tennessee - North Carolina border. The car tumbled down a slope into a ravine and came to rest on its top in a creek. Jasper crawled out of the car without a scratch, but his eighteen-year-old wife, his Rachel, was killed. Jasper moved back in with his parents and never left. Both of his parents had since died, leaving just Charlie and Jasper on the small farm.

"What's gonna be on the table this evenin', Peanut?" Jasper said as Charlie approached. Some people called her Charleston. Nearly everyone else called her Charlie. Jasper was the only person who called her Peanut. He said it fit her – a little salty with a tough shell.

"I've got a couple of those trout you caught thawing in the refrigerator," Charlie said. "Thought I'd fry some potatoes and onions, boil some greens and make some hushpuppies. How's that sound?"

"Like a little piece of heaven. I fed and watered that nag for you."

"Thank you, Uncle."

Jasper didn't often feed and water Sadie. If he'd done so, it usually meant he'd done something else, something Charlie wouldn't be pleased about. She walked past him, through the screen door and the mud room and into the kitchen. She set a bag of groceries and a gallon of milk on the counter near the sink and looked around. As soon as she spied it, she understood why Jasper had fed the horse. Sitting in the middle of the kitchen table was a plastic, green, round-bellied Buddha about eighteen inches high.

"Uncle! Come here!"

The door opened and Jasper sauntered in with a sheepish look on his face.

"What's this?" Charlie pointed at the Buddha.

"That there is a far-Eastern religious artifact," Jasper said.

"It looks like molded plastic to me. Where did it come from?"

"Found it at a garage sale in Hampton this morning."

"Have you converted to Buddhism?"

"Don't reckon I have."

"Then why is it here?"

"Just kind of struck me. You know I've always been interested in the different ways the human race expresses spirituality."

The statement was dubious. Jasper had hundreds of "artifacts" around the house that he'd collected over the years: wooden angels, plastic crosses, ceramic statues of Christ, prints and images of God and Satan, and dozens of bibles. He also had copies of the Koran, books about Hinduism, the Mormon faith, Catholicism and the religions of American Indian tribes. He even had books on astrology and scientology. He had statuettes of cows, statuettes of patron saints, statuettes of Nordic gods, Greek gods, and Roman gods. He also had stacks and stacks of old *National Geographic* magazines, *Life* magazines, and newspapers. He claimed to have read everything, but Charlie didn't believe him. He didn't read very often, and when he did, it was usually trade magazines about one of his other obsessions – taxidermy. Jasper was a master taxidermist; he'd been doing it since he was a boy and made a decent living at it. People came from hundreds of miles away to have him preserve and mount their deer and bear and fish and fowl. He was part mortician, part sculptor and part painter. He spent hours every day in his shop, which was housed in an old chicken coop near the barn that Jasper had expanded and remodeled. He never allowed anyone else to go in there. The only time Jasper had ever spoken harshly to Charlie was one day when she was very young. She walked unannounced into his shop, stood marveling at his creations, and was greeted with anger. Jasper had yelled at her about privacy and his right to practice his craft free of the prying eyes of children. He'd shoved her out the door. She hadn't set foot in his shop since, and to her knowledge, neither had anyone else. Jasper did business with his customers on his cell phone – he was a throwback, but he loved gadgets – and kept the door to his shop padlocked when he wasn't working. A large sign on the door said simply, "Keep Out."

"You're going to have to find another place for Mr. Buddha," Charlie said. "I'm not going to look at that green belly every time I sit down to a meal."

Charlie picked the Buddha up off the table and handed it to Jasper.

"Where else am I gonna put it?" he asked.

"I don't know. Put it in your room, in the den, in your shop."

"Ain't much room in any of those places."

"Your hoarding is getting out of control, uncle. The house looks like a junkyard. You won't throw anything away. Pretty soon we're not going to be able to move in here."

"You're exaggerating, Peanut. It ain't that bad."

"Really? Where are we going to put Daddy when he gets out of jail? You've already filled Grandma's room up with junk, and she's only been gone for three months."

"It ain't junk."

Charlie felt her face flush. "It's all worthless! What you call religious artifacts I call trinkets! And all these old magazines and newspapers? What good are they? You go to garage sales and you bring all this mess in here, but nothing ever goes out. You barely have room on your bed to sleep. The place is closing in on me. I feel like I can't breathe."

"It ain't junk," Jasper said quietly. He was looking at the floor. "Everything I bring in here means something to me."

Charlie was immediately ashamed for raising her voice. Jasper was one of the most unusual people she'd ever known. He was an obsessive-compulsive, pretty much a recluse, and he skinned and mounted animals for a living, but at his core, he was decent and kind. He'd always been good to her.

"I'm sorry," Charlie said. "I didn't mean to yell at you."

"It's okay, Peanut. I just can't help myself sometimes."

"I'll get supper started."

Charlie opened the refrigerator and bent down to retrieve the trout from the meat drawer. She heard Jasper shuffling off through the kitchen. She unwrapped the fish and pulled a frying pan from the drawer beneath the oven. She set it on top of the stove and walked to the pantry for some flour. When she turned back toward the stove, she glanced at the table.

There, sitting in the same spot from which she'd removed it a few minutes earlier, was the green Buddha.

CHAPTER SEVEN

J ohnny Russo looked around the parking lot nervously.
It was a little after ten at night, a light drizzle was falling,
the street in front of the restaurant was quiet. Johnny
was sitting in a two-year-old Cadillac Escalade that had
been rebuilt entirely from stolen parts and was untrace-
able. The New Jersey plates had been stolen off of a Toyota
parked in a lot in Camden, just across the Delaware River
from Philadelphia, two hours earlier. In the passenger
seat was Johnny's best friend, Carlo Lanzetti. At twenty-
three, Carlo was the same age as Johnny. He was a giant
of a young man, almost six-and-a-half feet tall, two-hundred fifty pounds of human-growth-hormone-induced
muscle. Johnny and Carlo spent two hours in the gym
every day and an hour in the tanning bed. Johnny didn't
like the steroids that Carlo called "juice." He'd tried HGH,
but it made him irritable and made his testicles shrink. He
was five-feet-eleven, a hundred and eighty pounds, plenty
strong, but Carlo was massive. Carlo was a beast.

"What's he doing in there?" Carlo asked. He was
nervously tapping his fingers against the dashboard.

"Don't ask stupid questions."

"Don't start with the stupid."

"The man walks into a building," Johnny said. "There's a big sign up there, all lit up, see it? Boticelli's *Restaurant*. You know it's a restaurant. I know it's a restaurant. What do people do in restaurants? They eat. You know this. So why do you have to ask a question like that? If you don't already know the answer, you're stupid. And if you do already know the answer, then why ask the question? It's stupid."

"But why is it taking him so long? That's all I'm asking. Why is it taking him so long to eat?"

"Maybe he doesn't eat like you. Maybe he eats with a fork and a spoon instead of a shovel. Maybe he doesn't suck the food up like a vacuum cleaner. Maybe he actually chews it."

"And maybe you should shut your mouth before I crush you like a bug."

"You see, Carlo? There you go again. That's what I'm talking about when I say you got no social skills. That's your problem. Any time there's some little argument or somebody disagrees with you in any way, the first thing you want to do is resort to violence. How many times have I heard you say, 'I'll crush you like a bug? I'll cave your skull in. I'll break every bone in your body.' You just can't go around saying stuff like that all the time. You can't do business that way. People are scared of you."

"You got that right. People are scared of me and they should be. *You're* scared of me."

"Nah. You know I ain't scared of you."

"Now you're lying. You're sitting there and you're telling me a big, fat lie. You lie to me all the time. If your lips are moving, you're lying."

Johnny's cell phone buzzed and he looked down.

"It's Mucci," he said. "Leonetti just gave the waiter his credit card. He'll be out soon."

The man they were waiting for was Anthony "Skinny Tony" Leonetti, a forty-five-year-old associate in Philadelphia's Pistone family. Leonetti was a small-time drug dealer and a hopeless gambler.

"I don't want to end up like this guy," Carlo said. "Almost thirty years he's been on the streets humping and he's never been made. A guy like that? They oughta show him a little respect, at least make him a soldier, give him a couple of rackets."

"I know, but he's a thief."

"Yeah, but what I'm saying, if they would've given him a racket or two, helped him make some decent money, maybe he wouldn't have stolen from them."

Two weeks earlier, someone had broken into a stash house and stolen two kilos of pure heroin owned by Pistone capo Andrew Mangione. It didn't take the wise-guys long to learn that Skinny Tony was suddenly putting out significantly more product than usual, and that he hadn't purchased any product recently. Skinny Tony was the thief. Three days later, a contract was given to two upstarts, Johnny Russo and Carlo Lanzetti, on the recommendation of Pistone soldier Robert "Bobby Big Legs" Mucci, who also happened to be Johnny Russo's second-cousin on his mother's side. Mucci was inside the restaurant, two tables away from Leonetti, and was keeping Johnny and Carlo updated via text messages. It was nothing unusual. Both Leonetti and Mucci were regulars at Boticelli's.

Johnny watched as Carlo got out of the Escalade and walked to the dumpster in the corner of the parking lot. Leonetti's red Buick was parked less than ten feet from the dumpster, one of only six cars left in the lot. Carlo disappeared into the dumpster's shadow. Johnny knew he was pulling a black ski mask over his face, pulling the hood up on his black sweatshirt with "Temple" emblazoned across the front, tying the string tightly beneath his chin. Johnny knew Carlo was carrying a pistol, a clean, silenced piece that would soon be cut up into pieces and resting at the murky bottom of the Delaware River.

Less than five minutes later, Leonetti walked around the corner of the building with his wife. Johnny started the Escalade's engine, left the lights off, and slowly pulled out of the spot he'd backed into. He saw Carlo, a shadow emerging from a shadow. Carlo covered the ten feet in three steps. Leonetti's left hand reached for the door handle on the driver's side. Johnny heard two dull *pops* and saw the muffled flashes. Leonetti dropped. Johnny reached across and opened the passenger door. A few seconds later, Carlo climbed in.

Johnny could hear Leonetti's wife screaming as they pulled out of the lot. Carlo pulled the ski mask off.

"Let's drop off the car and the gun and go to Mario's," Carlo said. "I'm craving a calzone."

CHAPTER EIGHT

I t only took a short time for the news to get around that I was supervising a new lawyer, which resulted in a telephone call from the General Sessions Court judge's office. The judge wished to appoint Charlie to a criminal case, his secretary told Caroline. The public defender's office had already represented the client once and did not feel they should represent him again, so they needed a private lawyer to fill the void. The judge felt that Charlie, under my supervision, would be perfect. I called Charlie and asked her to accompany me to the courthouse in Jonesborough. The secretary told Caroline that the case was a "run of the mill stalking case, nothing too serious." The defendant's name was Clyde Dalton. We walked into the courtroom and sat down at the defense table just as the bailiff was saying, "the Honorable George Lockhart presiding."

Judge Lockhart was elderly – seventy-eight to be exact. The sleeves of his black robe were frayed and he had the sleepy-eyed, droopy face of a porch hound. He sat down in the high-backed chair behind the bench, folded his hands in front of him, and closed his eyes, just as he always did. Everyone else went on about their business. A group of lawyers crowded around the prosecution table. The buzz in the room always reminded me of a hornet's nest.

A serious-looking woman with thick glasses and black hair was sitting next to us. She was in her mid-thirties, and she had a stack of manila files in her lap. Her name was Martha Moore. She worked for the probation office and was wearing the same indifferent look on her face that all probation officers wore in court.

"Know anything about a defendant named Clyde Dalton?" I asked her.

"The stalker?"

"Yeah, that's the one."

"I've never supervised him, but one of my colleagues has in the past. I know enough to tell you with some confidence that he's crazier than an outhouse rat."

"Crazy how? Are we talking legitimate mental illness or redneck crazy?"

"Paranoid schizophrenic crazy. Manageable with medication, but without it he tends to cause problems."

"What kind of problems?"

"He's mainly a pest. Fixates on women and sends them love letters scribbled on toilet paper, envelopes, brown paper bags, anything he can find to write on when the mood strikes him."

"Is he violent?"

"Not that I know of."

Charlie was looking toward the bench. Judge Lockhart's head was in his hands. She leaned toward Martha and me, nodded her head at the judge and said, "What's he doing?"

"Dying slowly," Martha said.

The door to the holding area opened and a lean, skin-headed man wearing an orange, jail-issued jumpsuit walked in. A bailiff was at his shoulder. He was cuffed and shackled and looked like he had no idea where he was. The bailiff stood at the podium next to the skin-head and cleared his throat loudly, but Judge Lockhart didn't move. The bailiff did it again, and the judge's eyelids separated so slowly they appeared to have been glued together.

"That's him," Martha said to me. "That's your boy."

I tapped Charlie on the arm and we got up and walked to the lectern "Excuse me, judge," I said. "I understand you've appointed my young associate to a case. She's here if you'd like to do the arraignment."

"Ah, yes, Mr. Dillard," Judge Lockhart said. "And this young lady is ... who is she?"

"Charleston Story."

"Yes, yes, Charleston Story. Good morning, Miss Story. Welcome to my world."

"Thank you, your honor," Charlie said. "Glad to be here."

"Wish I could say the same. Let's see, I have just the case for you."

He turned and leaned toward his clerk and said something I couldn't hear. The clerk reached into her stack and pulled out a warrant.

"The public defender has a conflict of interest so I have to appoint a private attorney to represent this man," the judge said. "Since you're the new kid on the block, it goes to you."

Several of the lawyers in the room snickered.

"Are you up to it, Miss Story?"

"I hope so," Charlie said.

"Clyde Dalton," the judge said in a loud voice. "You are charged with aggravated stalking. This pretty young lady here is going to be your lawyer, and since she's new to the profession, this handsome gentleman standing next to her is going to help her with your case. Do you understand that?"

"Does she work for the CIA?" Dalton said.

"I think a mental evaluation might be in order, judge," I said.

"Ah, the voice of experience," Judge Lockhart said. "Mr. Dalton, have you been taking your medication?"

"It gives me headaches," Dalton said.

"We've been through this before," the judge said. "When you don't take your medication you do things that cause you to wind up standing here in front of me. This time it's more serious, though. Now you're charged with a felony instead of a misdemeanor."

"It's the waves," Dalton said. "The microwaves they send at me. The CIA and the NSA keep trying to—"

"That's enough!" the judge said, raising his voice and holding up his right hand like a traffic cop. "I'll order another mental evaluation, Mr. Dillard. You set it up, the state will pay for it. What it will tell you is that if Mr. Dalton doesn't take his medication he will be unable to comprehend the charges against him and will be unable to aid in his defense. Therefore, without his medication, he will be unable to stand trial. However, if he *takes* his pills, he becomes perfectly able to understand and to aid in his defense and therefore become competent to stand trial."

"I take it this isn't his first rodeo," I said.

"Third," the judge said. "I'm also ordering Mr. Dalton to stay away from Veronica Simpson, the victim in this case. He may not go within a thousand yards of her. He may not contact her or communicate with her in any way, shape, form or fashion. If he does, he goes to jail, and I don't necessarily think jail is the best place for him. Mr. Dillard, Miss Story, I will leave it to you to insure that your client complies with my order. He has family, although my understanding is that his family has become so frustrated with him that they've pretty much washed their hands of the entire situation."

"What about bond, judge?" I said. "If he can't afford a lawyer he probably can't afford to post bond. Are you going to keep him in jail? We ask that you release him on his own recognizance."

"I suppose we need to hear from the prosecutor regarding bond," the judge said. "What say you, Mr. Garland? Mr. Garland? Are you paying attention?"

Ramey Garland was the assistant district attorney in this particular division of General Sessions Court. He'd been with the DA's office for thirty years, suffered from a degenerative eye disease, and was nearly blind. I knew him. He'd actually worked for me when I was the district attorney general. I'd heard complaints about his ineffectiveness, but he was such a nice man that I simply hadn't had the heart to get rid of him. He was sitting at the prosecution table, surrounded by lawyers, studying warrants with a magnifying glass. Someone leaned down and whispered into his ear.

"Beg pardon?" Ramey said from the table.

"Clyde Dalton," the judge said. "Stalking case. He probably can't post bond. Are you opposed to me releasing him pending a mental evaluation?"

"Nah, go ahead," Ramey said.

"Brilliantly expressed," Judge Lockhart said. "Very well, Miss Story is appointed. Mr. Dalton will be released on his own recognizance pending a mental evaluation and subject to my prior order. Anything else?"

"No, sir," I said.

"Bailiff, take him back and bring in the next one," the judge said, and Charlie and I turned and walked out the door.

CHAPTER NINE

Two days after they whacked Skinny Tony Leonetti, Johnny Russo and Carlo Lanzetti walked in through the back door of a small deli called Poppa's on South Broad Street. Both of them were wearing their favorite designer brands: skin-tight Under Armour wife beaters and Nike sweat pants and shoes. Their hair was black – Johnny's had blonde highlights – short, and spiked. Their bodies were bronzed by tanning beds. Their legs, chests, and underarms were freshly shaved. Johnny wore an Italian horn on a gold chain around his neck. Carlo wore a large cross on a silver chain. There was no particular significance in the symbols to either of them; they just liked the bling. Johnny led the way down a short hall and pushed a button on the wall. A couple of minutes later two deadbolts slid and they were face to face with Bobby "Big Legs" Mucci.

"You're late," Mucci growled as he stepped back so they could enter.

"You said three," Johnny said.

"It's four minutes after. When I tell you three, it don't mean four minutes after. It means three. You guys look like a couple of mopes, you know that? And you smell like French whores."

Johnny walked past Mucci without responding. He liked Mucci okay for an old-school guy, but the constant insults got on his nerves. Who was Mucci to judge his appearance, anyway? Mucci wore solid-colored golf shirts with logos and khaki slacks and loafers. He looked like a bulldog dressed up as a golfer. He was in his late forties, shy of six feet tall with short, brown hair and a pock-marked face. His upper body was a little pudgy, but his butt and thighs were distinctly disproportionate – they were huge. "Big Legs" was a small-time sports bookie and controlled a dwindling numbers game that encompassed ten city blocks. He'd been made a member of the Pistone family for eighteen years and had done a six-year bit for aggravated assault. He talked the talk and tried to walk the walk, but like all of the other older wiseguys that Johnny knew, Mucci seemed defeated.

Mucci walked behind a desk in the run-down office. The place smelled of rat piss and cigar smoke. There was a monitor on a table with a split screen that showed the hallway outside the dead-bolted door. Two computers that Mucci used to handicap ball games sat on another table next to the desk. There were no pictures on the beige walls, only jagged cracks in the ancient plaster. Johnny and Carlo sat down on a dusty, overstuffed couch. Mucci reached down and turned off the two cell phones that were on top of the desk.

"I got good news and bad news," Mucci said. "The good news is you guys did okay. Clean hit. Nice work. Everybody thinks so. The bad news is the books are still closed and they're gonna stay that way for now."

Johnny looked at Carlo, then back at Mucci. "I don't think I heard you so good."

"Yeah, you did. The books are closed."

"That ain't what you told me when we took this contract," Johnny said. "You said—"

"I said I'd talk to them about it, and that's what I did."

"So we clipped a guy for nothing? No money, and now we don't get made? This ain't right."

Mucci shrugged his shoulders and lifted his hands, palms up. "What can I say? Business isn't so good these days. It's tight, *capisci*? Not the way it used to be. The government is offering millions in the lottery and every schmuck with a buck is playing. It kills the numbers racket. The sports bettors go online now. It's a crime, all that money going to offshore companies. The drug trade is risky – too much competition and cops everywhere. It's tougher to make money, so they don't let many people in anymore. They open up the books, next thing they know the money is spread so thin there isn't enough to go around."

"We make money," Johnny said. "They take it every week."

"You gotta pay your dues."

"When was the last time somebody got whacked?" Johnny asked. He felt betrayed, anger coursed through him. He and Carlo had taken a huge risk, and now ... "I mean here in Philly. Before we did our thing the other night. When was the last time the family ordered somebody gone?"

"Been awhile," Mucci said. "Since Sal went to jail."

"More than five years. That's why you guys ain't making no money. You're soft. People don't fear you. A little heat comes down from the feds, and all of a sudden everybody's a rat. They don't respect you anymore."

Mucci pointed a thick finger at Johnny. "Watch your mouth, punk."

"What are you gonna do?" Carlo said, his face pink with anger. "Whack us? Johnny's right. You guys don't do that anymore. I tell you what *we're* gonna do, though. We're gonna quit paying. If you ain't gonna let us in, we ain't gonna pay. Why should we? What are we paying for? Protection? We don't need your protection. Me and Johnny can take care of ourselves. Connections? You don't have any connections, and if you do, you ain't sharing them with us. Do you and your wiseguy brothers support our business? Help us in any way? No. You just sit around with your hands out and wait for your tribute. You're welfare gangsters, you guys."

Mucci narrowed his eyes and looked at Johnny. "What about you? That how you feel?"

Johnny nodded. "Yeah. That's how I feel. Screw you guys. We ain't paying no more."

Carlo stood and took a step toward Mucci's desk. He looked like the grizzly bears Johnny had seen on National Geographic and the Discovery Channel, hovering over his prey, panting, about to attack.

"How about I just snap your neck like a twig?" A vein in Carlo's forehead was protruding, a sure sign he'd gone into a steroid-induced rage and was about to do something violent. Johnny stood and put a hand on Carlo's bicep while Mucci stared up at Carlo.

"I'll give you both a little time to think about this," Mucci said. His tone had changed. It was less aggressive, lighter, not so self-assured. "Maybe change your minds. You're young. You need to be patient."

"Patient? For what?" Carlo waved his hand and looked around the room. "So some day we can have all this?"

A couple of minutes later they were on the sidewalk.

"Short and sweet," Johnny said.

"Yeah. I'll bet he pissed himself."

"He's on the phone right now, ratting us out to the bosses. We just spit in their faces. They'll do something. They'll come at us."

"I hope so," Carlo said. "I'll make 'em wish they was never born."

CHAPTER TEN

ike I told Roscoe Barnes the day I met him, money talks in the legal system. In this particular case, the amount had been five thousand dollars in cash, and it was paid to a well-qualified psychiatrist in Johnson City named Dr. Leland Holmes. Charlie had chosen him and made the initial contact, and once he received the money, the doctor became extremely accommodating. He'd set up an appointment for Roscoe immediately and had written a report that said exactly what we needed it to say. Roscoe was mentally competent. He was not a danger to himself or anyone else. As soon as I received a copy of the report, I called Nathaniel Mitchell – Roscoe's son's lawyer – and asked for a meeting.

At 9:00 a.m. on a Wednesday, Roscoe, Charlie and I approached the front door of Mitchell, Skaggs, & Ward, the oldest and largest law firm in Northeast Tennessee. Charlie was dressed in a royal blue business suit and carrying a briefcase. Her hair was pulled back into a pony tail and she was wearing a pair of dark-framed glasses that gave her the look of an attractive, studious young lawyer. I'd asked her to persuade Roscoe to wear something at least semi-formal, but he'd stubbornly refused and was decked out in his bib overalls and red flannel shirt.

Nathaniel Mitchell's firm's offices occupied the entire top floor of a gleaming, ten-story bank building in Johnson City. The building sat at the top of a hill, the centerpiece of the city's high-rent district. I'd been there a couple of times before, and I always felt as though I was entering a fantasy world, a world where, at least on the surface, everything seemed clean and perfect. Crystal chandeliers sparkled overhead, varnished cherry wood molded gleaming marble floors, expensive paintings and tapestries covered freshly-painted walls. Even the people seemed unreal, all scrubbed and expensively dressed and utterly efficient. Charlie had told me that Mitchell, Skaggs & Ward was one of the law firms that had told her they just couldn't have the daughter of a convicted drug dealer on their roster.

We checked in with one of the receptionists and were accompanied to a conference room that offered a panoramic view of Buffalo Mountain to the south. As we walked into the room, Charlie spotted a large, glass bowl filled with small candy bars: Snickers, Milky Way, Baby Ruth and Butterfinger. She walked over, fished two Butterfingers out of the bowl and sat down. She offered one to Roscoe, who shook his head. She wolfed one down and just as she was opening the second candy bar, the door opened and two men walked in, both wearing tailored, navy-blue suits, starched, white shirts and maroon ties.

"Must be the uniform of the day," I heard Charlie mumble. I stifled a chuckle, because I was wearing the same damned thing they were wearing.

"Beg your pardon?" The older man was Nathaniel Mitchell. He was in his early sixties, tanned and fit, with a head of thick, meticulously-groomed, silver hair, a lantern chin, strong jaw, and lovely, ivory-colored teeth that were perfectly aligned. Mitchell was a mouthpiece for the rich and powerful in Northeast Tennessee. I'd met him at bar association meetings back when I used to attend and was well aware of his reputation as a shark. He always drove a brand new, silver Jaguar and carried himself with an arrogance that surrounded him like aerosol spray.

"I was just admiring your suit," Charlie said.

The other man was Mitchell's client, Zane Barnes, short and thin, in his early fifties with salt-and-pepper hair that had receded to the crown of his head. His face was pale and drawn, his nose ridged, his mouth small and tight. Zane Barnes was Roscoe's son and his only living relative.

We went through the introductions while Nathaniel Mitchell and Zane took their seats at the table. Once everyone was settled in, I slid a copy of Dr. Holmes's report across the table to Mitchell along with a document I planned to file in court asking the judge to dismiss the case. Mitchell slid a pair of reading glasses onto his nose and scanned the documents.

"My, my, you've been busy," he said.

"Just wanted to give you a heads up," I said. "It appears you may have been misled by your client. You have no case."

Mitchell removed the glasses and smiled.

"All this tells me is that we're going to have a swearing match between experts," he said, "and my expert is as well-qualified as they come."

"His examination was a fraud," I said. "Once the judge hears the circumstances, I don't think he'll look too kindly on Dr. Heinz."

"I'm aware of your reputation in the criminal courts, Mr. Dillard, but I don't believe I've ever seen you in civil court. I bring that up because I'm sure, considering your many years of experience, that you understand how important relationships can be. You've spent a career building relationships with judges and attorneys and clerks in the criminal courts, and I've done the same in the civil courts."

"Are you trying to tell me that you have the judge in your pocket?"

"I said no such thing, and I resent the implication. Although I will say that Judge Beckett and I go way, way back. He was a member of our law firm for ten years before he took the bench and we've remained very close over the years."

"Good for you," I said. "Maybe I should ask him to recuse himself since the two of you are such good buddies. Might interfere with his ability to remain impartial."

"I've been practicing in his court for fifteen years and there has never been even a hint of impropriety. As a matter of fact, I feel certain that Judge Beckett would be outraged by any suggestion or insinuation you might feel compelled to make in that regard. You might even earn yourself a contempt citation."

"Wouldn't be the first time I've gotten sideways with a judge," I said. "Probably won't be the last, either."

"Listen to us," Mitchell said with a smug smile, "fencing like a couple of first-year law students at a beer bust.

I assume you asked for this meeting so that we might attempt to find some common ground, some resolution that allows all of us to walk out of this room feeling that we've accomplished something worthwhile."

"There is no common ground," Charlie blurted. It surprised me, because I'd asked her to let me do the talking.

"There is always common ground, Miss Story," Mitchell said. "Zane is willing to negotiate. *I'm* willing to negotiate. We're willing to give something as long as we get something in return. That's how this works."

"Don't patronize me," Charlie said. "I may be a rookie, but I know when someone is being railroaded."

"You act like this is personal," Mitchell said. "I'm representing a client, that's all, and he has a *case*. Your client is clinically depressed and suffers from dementia. He's a danger to himself, and we have an expert medical opinion to back up the claim. What you need to understand is that the stakes are high for your client. If he loses, if the judge rules against him at trial, everything changes for him. He'll end up in a long-term care facility."

"That isn't going to happen."

"I wouldn't be so sure. We have a solid case, compelling evidence, which we will continue to build during the discovery process."

"So far your only witness is a prostitute, just like you."

Mitchell's eyes narrowed and his nostrils flared. I turned to look at Charlie, but she was so locked onto Mitchell that she didn't even notice me. Mitchell put both hands on the table and stood. He nodded at Zane Barnes, who did the same.

"I see that I made the right decision in not hiring you, Miss Story," he said. "Sometimes people just can't overcome their genetic predispositions. Go ahead and file your motion to dismiss, Mr. Dillard. Schedule the hearing as soon as possible so we can get in front of Judge Beckett and see what he has to say."

And with that, Mitchell turned and walked out of the room, followed closely by his client. The three of us – Charlie, Roscoe and I – remained seated while an awkward silence hung around us like a thick cloud. After a few minutes, I said, "Did I just hear a young lady who hasn't even passed the bar exam call Nathaniel Mitchell a prostitute to his face?"

"I'm sorry," Charlie said. "He was just so ... so ... *holier than thou.*"

"Do you drink beer, Charlie?"

"What?"

"Beer. Hops and barley. Alcoholic beverage. Do you drink it?"

"Not very often. Occasionally, I guess."

"Good. Meet me at The Purple Pig at seven o'clock tonight. I want to buy you one."

CHAPTER ELEVEN

The Purple Pig was a honky-tonk sort of place in Johnson City, about a mile from the East Tennessee State University campus. Good bar food, cold beer, a jukebox and reasonable prices, karaoke on Friday nights. The same people telling the same stories at the bar night after night. It was like an old friend, one that's dependable and never seems to change.

Charlie showed up right on time. Jack and I were sitting in a booth near the jukebox. We'd already ordered a beer and were talking baseball when she walked in. I noticed several heads turn at the bar as she passed by.

I'd asked Jack to come along for a couple of reasons. First, I wasn't really comfortable meeting a beautiful, young woman at a bar, and second, I thought it might give them a chance to get to know each other a little better. Jack had ribbed me about playing matchmaker on the ride into town, but he didn't say anything about not wanting to go.

The encounter between Charlie and Nathaniel Mitchell had jostled some kind of toggle inside me that caused me to want to find out what was driving her, what she wanted out of life, what she thought about the world and the people around her. Part of it was just curiosity, but there was also a more serious element. At some level, I knew I was sizing her up, taking stock of whether I thought she might make a suitable companion for my son.

Charlie ordered a Coors Light and I told Jack about our visit to Nathaniel Mitchell's office.

"She called him a prostitute," I said. "You should have seen the look on his face. If he'd had a gun and been able to get away with it, he would have shot her dead on the spot."

"I apologize for that," Charlie said. "I've thought about it all day and I'm really sorry. I should've kept my mouth shut. All I did was make things worse for Roscoe."

"He wasn't going to give us anything anyway," I said. "He bills by the hour. The longer the case runs, the more money he makes. He might be a little more inclined to be nasty from now on, be a little more difficult to deal with, but the bottom line hasn't really changed. In the end the decision about Roscoe will be made by a jury."

"Do you really think it will go that far?" Charlie said. "You don't think the judge will dismiss it?"

"I've been doing this for a long time, Charlie, and I can tell you one thing that is certain in the practice of law. You never know what a judge will do."

"You don't care for judges much, do you?" she said.

"Nah, don't trust them. Just the fact that someone would want to be a judge is a character flaw as far as I'm concerned. Most of them are just educated bullies. So what about you, Charlie? We haven't really gotten into why you wanted to get into law and what you plan to do once you pass the bar."

"She's an idealist," Jack said. "Same as me. Same as you, too, without the cynicism. She's going to do criminal defense and civil rights cases."

I turned and looked at him, raised an eyebrow. "And you're basing that opinion on?"

He looked over at Charlie and winked. "We've talked a few times," he said.

"Really? At the office? On the phone?"

"We've texted some."

"We had dinner together a couple of nights ago," Charlie said.

"Is that right?" I said. "So you guys are dating already?"

Jack cleared his throat and sat up a little straighter.

"Not dating. That isn't the way it works these days. We're still in what you'd call the talking phase."

"She just said you went to dinner. Wasn't that a date?"

"Not really," Jack said. "It was more like getting to know each other in a social setting, you know?"

"That's a date."

"No, it isn't. I guess it used to be a date, but not anymore. The whole ... I don't know, I guess you'd call it protocol, of dating has changed. First you talk, then you date, then you agree to be exclusive, then become boyfriend and girlfriend, and then you're in a relationship."

"Ah, I get it," I said. "It isn't really official until it's announced on Facebook."

"Exactly," Jack said. "If it ain't on Facebook, it ain't legit."

"So is that where you guys are heading? Toward an official Facebook proclamation?"

Jack shrugged his shoulders and looked at Charlie. She was smiling back at him, but I could tell I'd managed to make both of them uncomfortable.

"Charlie?" I said. "Is that what's going on here? Do you intend to make my son your exclusive boyfriend and announce it to the world on Facebook?"

She took a sip of her beer and set the bottle back down on the table. The waitress had brought her a glass, but she wasn't using it, which reminded me of Caroline. No glass for her, either. I liked that.

"We'll just have to wait and see," Charlie said.

I cut them some slack after that, and we spent the next hour talking about law and judges and Roscoe Barnes. Charlie was a delightful mix of intellect, beauty and country common sense. I kept thinking about how much she reminded me of my wife. I even found myself thinking at one point in the conversation that the two of them would make beautiful babies together. My next thought was, "Damn, Joe, you're getting old and soft."

Jack and I drank two beers, Charlie one, and we shared a pizza. I went to the bathroom, and when I came back, Jack had moved to the other side of the booth.

"We better head out of here," I said. "Another beer and my blood alcohol count will probably be over the legal limit. You ready, Jack?"

"I think we're going to catch a movie," he said. "Charlie says she'll drop me off at the house later."

"Another date that isn't a date?"

"Something like that."

The check was sitting on the table. I picked it up and said, "I'll take care of this and the tip. You kids have a nice night." I walked out of the bar and was getting into my truck when Jack came jogging up.

"Hey, dad. You're not mad, are you?" he said.

"Mad? Why should I be mad?"

"I didn't mean to spring all this with Charlie on you. I probably should have told you on the ride in."

"You're a big boy, Jack. You can date whoever you want."

"We're not officially dating, but I'm glad you're not mad."

I reached into my pocket and pulled out my wallet. "You need money?" I said.

"Nah, dad, I'm good."

"You sure? Movies are expensive."

"I'm sure." He reached out and gave me a hug. "I love you, man," he said. "I'll see you tomorrow."

CHAPTER TWELVE

S heriff Leon Bates pulled into my driveway the next morning at precisely seven o'clock. I'd called Leon the day before and asked him to come out and have a cup of coffee. Leon was an immensely popular and effective sheriff as well as being a consummate politician. We'd become close friends during my short tenure at the district attorney's office. We'd gone through one particularly rough patch, but had renewed our friendship during a search for a young girl who had been kidnapped the previous year. Leon had helped me find and recover the girl and had gotten himself shot in the process. His wounds had healed quickly, however, and he'd climbed right back into the saddle.

We went through the ritual of allowing Rio, my German shepherd, to sniff Leon at the door. Nobody came through that door without the dog's approval, and anyone who came to the house regularly knew the routine. Leon's khaki uniform was draped over his gangly frame, and he was carrying his cowboy hat in his hand. He walked through the kitchen and sat down at the table while I poured two cups of black coffee.

"Where's the missus?" he said as I handed him a cup.

"She sleeps later than she used to," I said.

"She doing all right?"

"Yeah, she's okay. Bad day every now and then because of side effects from medication, but for the most part, she's doing really well right now."

"Glad to hear it," Leon said. "So what can I do for you, brother Dillard?"

I sat down across from him and took a sip of the coffee.

"I'm sure you heard about the shooting over in Kingsport. Jordan Scott? Killed the rapist?"

"Course I've heard about it. I read in the paper that you were representing him. Surprised me a little, to tell you the truth. I thought you were cutting back, what with your wife's illness and all."

"She insisted that I take it."

"You're in for a hard road, brother. That's a rough bunch over there."

"That's why I called you. What do you know about them?"

"Probably more than I should. Certainly more than I'd like to. This deputy that was shot, Todd Raleigh. You know who his daddy is?"

"I know his name is Howard Raleigh and that he's a county commissioner. That's about it."

"He's a real peach, that one," Leon said. "Comes across as a community leader type and an entrepreneur, owns several businesses in the county, convenience stores and a car wash and a couple of used car lots, but that's mainly how he launders his real source of income, which is cock fighting. Owns a big farm in a remote part of the county, been fighting and breeding roosters there for almost twenty years. Big operation, big money."

"Let me guess," I said. "The reason he's been able to operate for so long is that the sheriff is in his pocket."

"Owns him lock, stock and barrel. Back about ten years ago, a few years before I became sheriff over here, they had a sheriff in Sullivan County named Rufus Seale. Big ol' beer-bellied, red-headed man who liked to beat on inmates at the jail and always had a half-chewed stogie in his mouth. Got himself elected on an old school law and order platform, but everybody that knows about such things knew that he was taking graft from Howard Raleigh to protect his bird fighting operation. The problem with Rufus was that he got arrogant about it. I've heard it told more than once that Rufus started showing up at the cockfights, in uniform, and passing his hat. He'd walk out of there with three, four thousand in cash, which didn't sit too well with Howard Raleigh since Howard was already paying him a tidy sum of cash every month. About three months after Rufus started showing up and passing his hat, he went deer hunting up in Johnson County and wound up getting shot through the heart. It was eventually ruled a hunting accident."

"But you don't think it was an accident?"

"Howard Raleigh either shot him or had him shot," Leon said. "I'd bet my life on it. Enter Raymond Peale, a roofing contractor with no previous law enforcement experience. Howard Raleigh nominates Peale to replace Rufus Seale at the next county commission meeting, and lo and behold, he has the votes to get 'er done. So Peale becomes Raleigh's hand-picked sheriff, Raleigh's son winds up becoming a deputy, and the rooster fighting continues on unmolested by the evil hand of law enforcement."

"What about the feds?" I said. "If you know all of this, surely they must know it, too. Why haven't they gone in and busted it up?"

"Because they've been focused on counter-terrorism for the past ten years. A cockfighting operation in rural Tennessee hasn't been at the top of their priority list. But just between you and me and that German shepherd, they're on it now. Peale and one or two of his deputies have taken to selling drugs that they steal from the evidence locker and there's been some cash from drug busts go missing. There'll be an arrest or two sometime in the not-too-distant future."

"And you know all this how?"

"Because I'm a friend to all, brother Dillard. I get along with everybody, and it serves me well."

"I need someone on the inside at the sheriff's department over there," I said. "If this Todd Raleigh that Jordan Scott killed really was a serial rapist, then I'm betting he had some problems at work. A rapist with a badge and a gun can't be a good combination. My guess is that there have been complaints filed against him for misconduct. I'd love to get my hands on them, because if I can sucker the prosecution into putting on testimony about his character, then I can attack him and flip the focus of the trial from Jordan Scott to Todd Raleigh. Do you think you might be able to help me out with that?"

Leon reached up and started pulling at his ear lobe with his left hand. With his right, he took another sip from the coffee cup and set the cup back on the table.

"Let me just stew on this a second," he said. "What you're asking me to do is to help you gather information that will eventually lead to the character assassination in a public trial of a fellow law enforcement officer who recently had half his head blown off."

"While he was committing a rape. That's an important detail, don't you think?"

"You're positive he was a rapist?"

"I've already talked to the young woman he was raping in the park when Jordan shot him. She's the daughter of one of Raleigh's best friends, an old high school buddy. Raleigh had been at her house the night before. That's how he knew she would be in the park early the next morning. He knocked her off of her bike, dragged her into the bushes, and was raping her when Jordan told him to get off of her and then shot him. So yeah, I'm sure. I'm hoping to get DNA samples from Raleigh and have them compared to samples that were taken from some of the other rape victims so I can prove he was a serial rapist, but I'm not too optimistic about it. My understanding is that Raleigh was cremated. The pathologist should have samples from the autopsy, but I doubt the judge will allow me to test them."

"There ain't gonna be any samples," Leon said. "If Todd Raleigh was a serial rapist, Peale and Raleigh's daddy will have destroyed the samples by now."

"Sounds like a fine, upstanding bunch of folks they've got running the show over there," I said.

Leon pointed a long finger at me. "You listen to me, brother Dillard," he said. "I know when you set your mind to something you ain't afraid of the devil himself, but you be careful messing with those boys. Sticking your nose in the middle of their business will be like crawling under a rock to catch a rattlesnake with your bare hands. The chances are good that you'll wind up getting bit."

CHAPTER THIRTEEN

Zane Barnes entered his father's house quietly through the kitchen door. It was just after dark, the night outside quiet and still. He could hear the television in the den where he knew Roscoe would be sitting in his recliner, either sleeping or watching the Atlanta Braves play baseball.

Zane had been a millionaire until the recession and the credit crunch started bleeding him dry. He'd been building upscale houses in the western North Carolina mountains for years, but when the economy went suddenly and unexpectedly into the toilet, he was unprepared for the fallout. He had four houses under construction when George Bush announced, near the end of his term, that the federal government was about to embark on a massive bailout of the Wall Street financial industry. The credit crunch that ensued shut down the real estate market. All four houses were still vacant. Building them had cost him nearly two million, and he'd been paying interest on that money for so long now that even if the economy turned around and he was finally able to sell them, he wouldn't turn a profit. His stock portfolio lost sixty percent over a six-month period in

2008 and still hadn't recovered. His gold-digging wife had taken his two teenaged children and left him a year ago when she realized how much trouble he was in. Between the alimony, child support and mortgage payments, he was paying out more than thirty thousand a month and nothing was coming in. Another year and he'd be broke.

But back in January, Zane had discovered, completely by accident, what he hoped would be his ticket out of the financial morass. He'd gone to Buck Mountain hoping to talk to Roscoe about borrowing some money, although he wasn't sure how much money Roscoe had. Zane rarely saw the old man, despite the fact that he lived less than an hour away. He'd never cared much for his father. He thought Roscoe a simpleton, a lazy redneck content to squat on the land he'd inherited and waste his life teaching English to teenagers who didn't give a damn. Since his mother had died, Zane had made only perfunctory visits at Christmas, and those had been brief.

He was desperate, though, and he thought he might be able to use Roscoe to get him past his financial woes if he could talk him into either selling his land or, at the very least, pledging it as collateral so Zane could borrow enough money to get him through another year or so until the economy made a complete recovery. Roscoe's land was also home to large stands of valuable trees: white and red oak, hickory, walnut and elm. The timber rights alone would probably be worth a hundred grand. Maybe he could talk him into selling the timber. He'd walked into his father's house that day and found him fully clothed and fast asleep in his bed. When he reached down to wake him, Zane noticed a glow, almost a sparkle, coming from beneath the pillow where his mother's head used to lay. He pulled the pillow up and his jaw dropped. He shook his father awake.

"What's this?" Zane had demanded.

Roscoe, bleary-eyed and groggy, sat up slowly. "What are you doing here?"

"I said what's this?"

"Something I found."

"Where?"

"At the end of the rainbow."

"Is there more?"

"None of your business."

Zane had grabbed Roscoe's shirt and shaken him: "*Is there more?*"

The old man smiled and nodded: "Lots more."

"How much?"

"You'll never know."

"Where is it?"

"I already told you, at the end of the rainbow."

Zane had threatened, harangued, pleaded, and begged, all to no avail. Roscoe refused to tell him anything. He finally left and devised a plan the next day to gain control of Roscoe's property. The lawsuit that followed, however, had done nothing but cost Zane more money. Even the possibility of losing his freedom had failed to loosen Roscoe's tongue. And now, with the first hearing in front of Judge Beckett only twelve hours away, Zane had decided to make one final attempt. He walked into the den. Roscoe was exactly where he thought he'd be – in the recliner. He was wide awake.

"You shouldn't be here," Roscoe said.

Zane turned off the television. He sat down on the couch across from Roscoe.

"I've had a change of heart," Zane said. "I want you to come and live with me. I have plenty of room. It's a great place, beautiful, right on the river. I know you've never seen it, but I think you'd like it. I have a cook and a few other people who help around the house. They'll wait on you hand and foot. I have an indoor swimming pool and a whirlpool, a sauna, you name it. You'll eat good food, and I'll make sure your medical care is the very best available. You can live out your life in luxury. You won't have a worry in the world."

"I believe I'll stay put."

"I'm sorry, Father," Zane said. "Really, I'm sorry. I've behaved very badly. You're old and you're sick and you need help. It's my place to help you. Let me help you."

"I'm not sick and I don't need help. From you or anybody else. Why don't you grow some balls for once in your life and just come out and say what you really want?"

"I'm your son. I love you. I've always loved you. Just let me help you."

"You love two things, boy. You love yourself and you love money, and the only reason you're here right now is that you're afraid you might lose in court tomorrow. All you really want is for me to tell you where the rest of it is, and that ain't gonna happen."

Zane kept his tone steady. "Please, let's not fight. I'm not here to argue or bring up the past or cast aspersions."

"I'm going to watch my ballgame," Roscoe said. "Feel free to leave any time." He pushed a button on the television remote and the set came back to life.

Zane stood.

"Fine," he said. "You're a fool, always have been. You're going to rot in the worst nursing home I can find. And as soon as the jury finds you incompetent, I'm going to hire a crew and clear this mountain. I'll bulldoze every building, sell every tree. I'll find it. Believe me, I'll find it. And as soon as I do, I'm going to divide this place up into little pieces and sell it off a bit at a time."

"You wanted to know how much," Roscoe said.

"What? What did you say?"

"There are a hundred of them. You took one; that leaves ninety-nine. But you'll never get your hands on it. Not in a million years. Now get out."

CHAPTER FOURTEEN

Roscoe Barnes, clad in the same black suit he'd worn when his wife and daughter were buried, crawled out onto the brick ledge beneath the courthouse clock. His balance wasn't what it had been when he was a youngster, back when he could stand in the bow of his little row boat, the one in which he stalked smallmouth bass along the banks of the Nolichuckey River. Sometimes, when the water was calm, he would climb up onto the edges in the bow, shift his weight gently from right to left with his arms outstretched, and imagine he was floating above the cool water. But that was then. This was now.

He made it out onto the ledge, sat and let his legs dangle, craning his neck so he could read the time on the clock behind him. It was 8:15 a.m. The hearing was supposed to start in at nine. Charlie Story and Joe Dillard had already gone inside. Now he was waiting for Zane. Roscoe had a message for him.

A couple of good things had come out of the lawsuit Zane filed against Roscoe. One was that Roscoe had gotten to know Charlie much better. He'd always thought a great deal of her, but now he felt as though he knew her heart. She was a special person, he believed, someone who cared about others, someone who held strong convictions about right and wrong and who wouldn't compromise those convictions. He believed she would become an excellent lawyer and would one day make some lucky man a fine wife.

Roscoe smiled to himself. Wouldn't Charlie be surprised when she received the gift he was giving her? She deserved it. Her father was in prison and her mother had abandoned her. Her grandparents were dead and she was living with her uncle Jasper, a man Roscoe believed to be border-line insane. She'd worked her way through law school, and now it was high time that fortune smiled on her. Roscoe intended to make it happen.

The other good thing that had come from the lawsuit was that Roscoe had gone to see his doctor. Roscoe didn't much care for doctors and rarely submitted himself to examination, but at Charlie's suggestion, he'd gone in for a complete physical a couple of weeks before he'd gone to see the psychiatrist. What Roscoe found out was that he had lung cancer and, without treatment, would be dead in less than six months. Even with treatment, the prognosis was grim. He'd kept the diagnosis to himself, but it had allowed him to make some decisions and some plans. One of his decisions was about to become very, very public.

Roscoe spotted his son's black Mercedes as it pulled into a space near the courthouse. Zane got out and started walking toward the front steps. Roscoe stood on the ledge. More people were walking in and out of the courthouse beneath him now, others were moving slowly up and down the sidewalk, dressed in their brightly colored clothes. He could hear the gears clicking steadily behind the clock face, the pigeons cooing softly in the rafters. His legs were trembling; he was a little light-headed.

Lord, don't let me slip. Don't let me fall.

Someone spotted him. Voices began to call up to him from the crowd that was gathering below.

"Hey! What are you doing up there?"

"Have you lost your mind?"

Zane looked up. He was almost at the top of the steps. He began pointing and shouting. Uniformed men began to appear beneath Roscoe along with men in suits, women in smart dresses and business attire, young people, middle-aged people, old people, all of them staring at the spectacle forty feet above. Someone was banging on the door that closed the clock tower off from the stairs. Roscoe had locked it, but he knew they would soon come with a key. Then they would be in the clock tower, trying to talk him into coming back inside. They might even try to grab him. A siren wailed in the distance.

Roscoe looked upward. The sky was a hard, icy blue, his favorite color. The sun above the mountains was brilliant. A soft breeze washed over him. The clock clicked again. A dove flew past and he watched as it went higher, toward heaven. He thought of his daughter, Lisa Mae, run over by a drunk driver, and of his wife, Mary Beth, a victim of cancer, knowing they'd be waiting on the other side. He looked down at Zane – ungrateful, contemptuous, greedy. He didn't see Charlie or Dillard and was relieved.

It's a beautiful day to die.

Roscoe bent his knees, braced his backside against the clock, and spread his arms like wings.

Then he locked eyes with his son and launched himself toward the concrete below.

PART II

CHAPTER FIFTEEN

The stunning news that Roscoe Barnes had leaped off the courthouse clock tower was delivered to Charlie and me by a bailiff as we were sitting in an anteroom, going over the file one last time before the hearing. I told Charlie to stay put, got up and walked to the front door, and looked out. Roscoe had landed at the top of the concrete steps about fifteen feet away. He was lying face down and twisted on the steps; a large pool of dark blood had formed around his head. Zane was still standing there, absent-mindedly wiping blood from his suit. Roscoe had landed within inches of him, and the blood from Roscoe's shattered skull had apparently sprayed over Zane like a fountain.

I looked upon the body like it was a hallucination. I didn't know what to do, didn't know how to feel. I'd known Roscoe for such a short amount of time and the relationship had been strictly professional. I thought about Charlie and turned to walk back inside. I knew she'd be devastated, and she was.

A half-hour later, Charlie and I stood at the table in front of Judge Beckett. Nathaniel Mitchell and Zane Barnes were at the table next to us.

"We move for default judgment, your Honor," Mitchell said. "The defendant has failed to appear."

The judge looked at him incredulously.

"Of course he's failed to appear," the judge said. "He's dead."

"I think it makes our point," Mitchell said. "He was obviously mentally incapacitated. The conservatorship should be granted."

"Don't be ridiculous, Mr. Mitchell," the judge said. "There is no conservatorship. There's an estate. Did he have a will?"

"We don't know, your Honor," Mitchell said. "We'll investigate."

"Mr. Dillard? Do you have any knowledge of a will?"

"No, sir. He didn't mention anything to us."

"For the record, the conservatorship case is dismissed," the judge said. "The costs will be taxed to Mr. Barnes' estate, if there is one. If a will shows up and is submitted, the case will proceed through probate. Otherwise, his assets will be distributed according to statute. Court is adjourned."

I was numb. The judge's voice sounded far away, like an echo off a distant cliff, while the image of Roscoe's shattered body lingered in my mind. I put my hand on Charlie's arm and led her out of the courtroom. She hadn't said a word since the bailiff had broken the news to us. I took her out the back of the courthouse and around the side, avoiding the spot where Roscoe had landed. We drove back to Jonesborough in silence. Once we arrived, Charlie went straight into the bathroom while I told Jack what had happened. We could hear her crying, and the sound of the sobs broke my heart. About ten minutes after we'd walked through the door, a young man wearing a jacket and tie showed up carrying a large envelope. He said he was a courier and the envelope was for Charleston Story. She was the only person who could sign for it. I went to the bathroom and knocked lightly on the door.

"Charlie, there's a courier here. He says you're the only person who can sign for the package he's delivering."

She came out a couple of minutes later, red-eyed but composed. She walked into the lobby and signed the courier's receipt and stood there looking at the envelope.

"It says it's from an attorney named Gerald Benton," she said without looking up.

"Never heard of him," I said.

"Greeneville address," Charlie said.

She opened the envelope and pulled out a thin sheaf of papers along with another sealed envelope.

"There's a cover letter," she said. "Please find enclosed documents for your review. I will be submitting Mr. Barnes' will for probate before close of business today. Call me if I can be of assistance. Sincerely, Gerald Benton."

She moved the cover letter to the bottom of the sheaf and began reading. Her eyebrows arched and her mouth opened.

"What is it?" I asked.

"A will," Charlie said. "It's Roscoe's last will and testament," she said. "It makes me the sole beneficiary of his estate."

CHAPTER SIXTEEN

harlie asked for some privacy and retreated into Mr. Dillard's conference room. She seated herself at the table and opened the second envelope. It contained a letter and what appeared to be some kind of old map. Charlie's fingers trembled as she read the hand-written words:

My Dearest Charleston,

If you're reading this, it means that I have accomplished my goal this morning and that I no longer exist on this plane. Whether I exist at all remains to be seen. Please do not waste your time grieving. I learned recently that I have lung cancer. I would have been dead soon anyway.

The things that I've accumulated over my lifetime stay behind. There is a house, personal belongings, some land, vehicles, a little money. As I write this letter, all those things seem so insignificant. But I want you to take charge of them, to "own" them, as we say. You are well aware of my feelings toward my son, so the fact that I do not wish him to inherit my property should come as no great surprise. I've grown tremendously fond of you over the years, and especially the past few weeks, and there is no one to whom I would rather leave these worldly possessions.

One of my possessions will require special attention. It is something that is incredibly valuable, something that will change your life. My hope is that the change will be for the better.

I don't know whether you've heard the stories about my great-grandfather. His name was Hack Barnes. He was a moonshiner, a bootlegger, back during Prohibition. He lived on the land I'm giving to you, and he apparently did business with a gangster from Philadelphia named Carmine Russo. The story I always enjoyed the most was that just before Carmine Russo was convicted of tax evasion and sent to prison, he entrusted my great-grandfather with something valuable, something my great-grandfather promised to keep until Russo was released from jail. Some people said it was money, some said it was jewels, some said it was gold.

Russo never got out of jail. He died less than a year after he was convicted. My great-grandfather was murdered around the same time, along with his wife and two of his children. I've read old newspaper accounts of the murders. Reporters called it the "Buck Mountain Massacre." My grandfather, James Barnes, was a teenager at the time. He was visiting a cousin in Indiana and was the only surviving family member. After the murders, a story began circulating that just before Russo died, he told his wife about what he had entrusted to my great-grandfather. Russo's wife sent some men to Tennessee to collect it. My great-grandfather refused to give it to them or even acknowledge its existence, and a fight ensued. One of the gangsters started shooting, and before they realized what they were doing, they'd killed everyone. They went back to Philadelphia empty-handed.

I never put much stock in the story. After all, there was never any real proof that Hack Barnes and his family had been murdered by gangsters from Philadelphia. They could have been killed by a business rival or someone who believed my great-grandfather had cheated them. They could have been killed by thieves. Hack Barnes was a criminal himself. He dealt with unsavory characters. No one really knew, and to be honest, I never gave it much thought.

But then I made a discovery. Back in late December, I carried a box of Christmas decorations up to the attic. When I got to the top step, I tripped and the box went flying. It banged into an old dresser. There was a photograph of Hack Barnes in a frame on top of the dresser. It was taken in 1929, a few years before his death. I'd seen it many times, but had never paid it any attention. The box knocked the photo to the floor and I heard glass break. I picked the photo up. Both the glass and the frame had been broken. As

I examined it, I noticed that there was something between the matting and the back of the photo. I took the frame apart and found what turned out to be a map. I don't know who drew it; I can only assume that it was Hack Barnes. The map is enclosed with this letter. It now belongs to you.

I followed the map, Charleston, and I'd like you to do the same. It leads to a cave on the mountain near the southern border of my property. The cave is almost impossible to find, so you must look very carefully. Inside the cave, there are two large chambers. When you enter the lower chamber, keep going and you'll find a stream. Downstream leads under the rock wall and out of the cave, but upstream leads to my gift.

There is only one person in the world, other than you, that knows this thing exists. That person is my son. He does not know where it is, but he knows its value and he knows it's somewhere on the property. He knows because I made the mistake of taking one item out of the cave. Zane found it, and he took it. He desperately wants the rest.

I trust that you will see to it that Zane's desire is never fulfilled. I also trust that you will take what I am giving you and use it to your greatest benefit. I wish you peace, Charleston. May this gift help you live a long, happy and prosperous life.

Roscoe

P.S. Do you remember the story of Prometheus and the fire, Charlie? Read it again, and take heed.

Charlie set the letter down and looked briefly at the map. She folded everything and slid the papers back into the envelope. Her hands continued to tremble; she could feel her heart beating inside of her chest. Her mind was racing. Was this really happening? Had Roscoe really left her everything he owned? A map? A cave? Gangsters? Was this someone's idea of a sick joke?

Charlie picked up her cell phone and dialed the number on Gerald Benton's letterhead. She identified herself to the person who answered the phone, and within a few seconds, Benton came on the line.

"I thought I'd be hearing from you," he said in a deep baritone. "Is Mr. Barnes gone?"

"Yes ... you knew?"

"I'm sorry," Benton said. "He expressed deep affection for you."

"I'm not sure I understand," Charlie said. "Can you explain any of this?"

"How did he die?"

"He jumped from the clock tower at the courthouse."

"My goodness. I had no idea he was planning something so spectacular."

"But you knew he was planning something?"

"I assumed. He came in two weeks ago and asked me to draft a will. He said he'd been diagnosed with lung cancer and had decided to end his life on his own terms. I advised him against it, of course, but I suspected that he was going to take his own life. He didn't say anything about *how* he was going to do it, but he had obviously planned it carefully."

"Did you know him well?"

"Not well, necessarily, but I've known him for quite some time. I met him under difficult circumstances. I represented the man who killed his daughter. He said you reminded him of her."

Charlie swallowed hard. She knew Roscoe's daughter had been killed twenty years earlier by a drunk driver. The man lost control of his car and drove onto the sidewalk in the middle of the day in downtown Greeneville. Roscoe's daughter – her name was Lisa Mae – was walking back to work from lunch. She was pinned against a light pole and died the next day.

"Mr. Barnes came to see me after the criminal case was concluded and asked me to tell my client that he had forgiven him. He was a genuinely decent man."

"Yes," Charlie said, "he was."

"He called a couple of days ago and gave me very specific instructions on how and when to deliver the documents to you. He wanted them delivered by courier at precisely 11:00 a.m. this morning."

"Did you read them?"

"Just the will. The other envelope was already sealed when he delivered it."

"So this is legitimate? I mean, he was okay?"

"He seemed perfectly normal. As a matter of fact, he seemed ... how should I put this? At peace. He was at peace."

"Did he say anything about his son?"

"Very little."

"Did he tell you that his son had filed a petition to have him declared mentally incapacitated and was asking for a conservatorship?"

"No."

"If he had, what would you have thought?"

"I would have thought it ridiculous. And I'd be happy to say that under oath if it comes down to it."

"Did he leave instructions for his funeral?"

"He did. Now that his death has been confirmed, I'll be taking care of everything. I'll give you the particulars once the arrangements have been made."

A few minutes later, Charlie thanked Benton and hung up the phone. She walked out of the conference room and into Mr. Dillard's office.

"I think I'm going to take the rest of the day off," she said. "Maybe the rest of the week."

Mr. Dillard got up and walked around his desk. He put his hands on her shoulders.

"That's a good idea," he said. "Is there anything I can do? Anything at all?"

"I don't think so."

"Do you need to talk?"

"Not right now. I just need some time to think."

CHAPTER SEVENTEEN

Charlie drove home in a semi-daze, unaware of the colors, shapes and textures of the beautiful, rugged country that surrounded her. She went into her bedroom and changed clothes. She took her laptop out of her briefcase, sat down on her bed, and Googled "Prometheus." As she read, the story came back to her. Prometheus was a mythical Titan. He'd molded the first man from clay, and in order to help his creation survive, he'd stolen fire from the gods and given it to man. But while Prometheus' intentions were noble, Zeus, the king of the Olympians, was furious. Prometheus had given man the ability to survive, but he'd also given him the ability to destroy himself. Zeus was so enraged that he ordered Prometheus chained to a rock for eternity. Each day thereafter, a great eagle would fly down and eat his liver. Each night, the liver would regenerate.

The ability to survive, and at the same time, the ability to destroy himself. Charlie considered the irony.

Fire. So valuable, yet so dangerous.

A gift, and at the same time, a curse.

Charlie took the envelope out of the briefcase next. Jasper was out in his shop; she was alone. She read the letter a dozen times, studied the map. She'd been to Roscoe's house many times. She'd been riding her horse on Roscoe's property for nearly a decade. She believed she could follow the map, but she was hesitant. Zane might be there, and there could be legal complications. Since she'd represented Roscoe in the conservatorship, there was no doubt in her mind that Zane would contest the will by claiming that Charlie had a conflict of interest, that she'd somehow coerced Roscoe into leaving his property to her. Zane seemed to have plenty of money. He and his lawyers would most likely tie up the estate for years.

But the map beckoned. Roscoe's letter had said there was something "incredibly valuable," something that would change her life.

"I have to go," she said aloud. "Right now."

She walked out to the barn and saddled Sadie, an eight-year-old Palomino quarter horse that Charlie had bought when she was seventeen with the tips she earned as a waitress at Buddy's Diner in Roan Mountain. Biscuit stood by watching, his long tail wagging like a buggy whip. He loved to accompany Charlie and Sadie on their mountain excursions. As she led Sadie out of the barn, Jasper emerged from his shop.

"What are you doin' home so early, Peanut?" he called.

"Hearing got cancelled."

"Where you going? It's gonna rain like pouring piss out of a boot. I can smell it."

Charlie looked to the southwest. The wind had freshened, and a huge bank of dark thunderheads was rolling over the mountains in the distance.

"I'm going on a treasure hunt. It looks like Biscuit wants to come along."

Jasper laughed. "I'm partial to gold doubloons myself," he said. "Bring me a few, would ya?"

Charlie climbed into the saddle. "I think I'll take a ride up around Roscoe's place," she said. "If I'm not back by dark, sound the alarm."

"Will do," Jasper said. He waved and walked off toward the house.

Charlie had changed into a pair of jeans and a bright orange T-shirt with the University of Tennessee logo across the front. She'd stuck a flashlight and the map in one of the saddlebags. She clicked her tongue and Sadie took off at a trot with Biscuit trailing close behind. Her grandparents' property, fifteen acres which she owned jointly with Jasper, abutted Roscoe's five hundred acres just to the north. In twenty minutes, she was sitting atop Sadie on a knoll overlooking Roscoe's house. Zane's black Mercedes was parked in the driveway.

Charlie felt a pang of anger as she looked down at the car. Zane was probably inside rummaging through Roscoe's belongings. She thought about riding to the house and confronting him with the will but decided against it. Confrontations would occur in the future, she was certain, but for now, she wanted to try to follow the map.

She reached down and took it out of the saddle bag. It was brittle and yellowed, obviously very old. The drawing had faded, but she could make out the words "House," "Road," "Tempest Creek," "Sinkhole," "Teardrop Island," "Eyeball Rock," "Oak Split By Lightning," "Hourglass

Rock," and "Cave." Arrows indicated the direction she should travel. She felt a twinge of excitement as she oriented the map to the property. Tempest Creek originated at the top of the mountain and wound through Roscoe's property like a long, emerald-green snake. She knew where the giant sinkhole was.

Charlie turned Sadie southwest into the breeze and rode until she reached Tempest Creek. She turned due south and followed it through a draw for about a quarter mile. Just before a bend in the creek, she spotted the first landmark – "Eyeball Rock." It sat atop a small bald, one that Charlie had passed before. The boulder was almond shaped, about twelve feet across, and exposed to the weather. As Charlie stared at it, she could make out what looked like a pupil at its center. She looked to her right, to the west. Down a gentle slope, about a hundred feet away, was a small island in the middle of Tempest Creek. It rose out of the creek like a turtle shell and was shaped like a teardrop. The map told her to cross at "Teardrop Isle."

On the other side, five minutes due west of the creek, was the giant sinkhole. Charlie skirted the southern edge and began a steady climb through another stand of trees. At the top of the ridge, the creek came into view again on the other side. Charlie rode down the far side, crossed the creek again, still heading west, and came to another steep slope, this one bare, rocky and treacherous. Charlie was in unfamiliar territory now. She'd never ventured this far up the mountain. It just didn't seem safe.

Sadie picked her way carefully to the top of the slope behind the sure-footed dog. Charlie pulled on the reins and removed the map again. She looked at it, looked ahead. The creek wound through a small valley three hundred feet below. On the other side was another rock face, massive and sheer. About ten feet above the creek, a large boulder jutted out of the mountain, this one shaped like an hourglass. Charlie's eyes moved through the midline of the hourglass to the top of the face. Perched at the top, in a place where it had no business, was one of the biggest oak trees Charlie had ever seen. Its canopy was shaped oddly, like an umbrella. It had to be the "Oak Split by Lightning." The entrance to the cave should be on the other side of the hourglass-shaped boulder. Charlie looked at her watch. She'd been riding for less than an hour.

"Let's go," Charlie said, and Sadie began the descent through the rocks. At the bottom, just before they were to cross the creek a third time, Sadie spooked. She threw her head back, whinnied, and reared her front hooves off the ground. Charlie grabbed the saddle horn, barely managing to keep from going over backward.

"Easy, now," she said, patting the horse on her thick neck. "Just a little ways to go."

But Sadie refused to cross the creek. Charlie pleaded and cajoled, she even dismounted and tried leading Sadie into the water, but the horse would not budge.

"Coward," Charlie said.

She walked Sadie fifty yards downstream to a laurel bush, tied the reins to a branch, retrieved the flashlight from one of the saddle bags, and walked back upstream with Biscuit beside her. She waded across the creek and climbed up next to the boulder. She stared, uncertain at first, but then her eyes widened.

The mouth loomed before her, a narrow ellipse about three feet wide and perhaps eight feet tall, almost entirely covered by crawling vines, inviting and repulsive at the same time. Charlie stepped to the mouth and stood there, breathing deeply, calming herself and screwing up her courage.

"You ready?" she said to Biscuit. The dog hung back; he wasn't going in first.

She shined the beam inside. It penetrated several feet and then seemed to die out. She heard Sadie whinny. She took another couple of steps, now inside. She looked up. Slick, rock walls rose twenty feet on both sides, forming a tunnel. She looked down. No sign of animal waste, which meant, hopefully, no bears. More rock, shiny and hard, stretched out before her beneath her feet. She took a few more tentative steps. Biscuit was right behind her. The tunnel curved to her right. The blackness ahead was thick, impenetrable. She turned and looked back toward the light.

The tunnel sloped downward slightly. Ten feet inside, the temperature dropped at least twenty degrees. Ten feet farther, it dropped some more. The darkness was cool and utterly silent. Charlie stopped. She was sure she'd never experienced this kind of complete silence, complete darkness, complete stillness. The only sound was Biscuit's panting.

"If I keep going," she said to the dog, "I'll know what it's like to be dead."

Another ten feet and she would be so far around the curve that the entrance would disappear. The thought of being unable to see the light terrified Charlie. She didn't want to go back, but like Sadie, she didn't want to go forward.

Don't be a sissy. It's just a cave. The human race started out in places just like this.

More uneasy steps. Biscuit panting. The mouth was out of sight now, leaving Charlie wrapped in a cocoon of darkness. She thought about the batteries in the flashlight. Were they fresh? If they died … she wouldn't think about that right now. Just a little farther. The grade beneath her feet steepened downward.

Another step. Another. The dog growled.

Charlie sensed something frightening. The rock wall on her right ended suddenly and she moved the light in that direction. The cave opened into what looked like a giant, sprawling, eerie, gothic cathedral. Layers of rock, rounded cones of rock, webs of rock, as smooth as if they'd been polished, hung from the ceiling and rose from the floor. Some of it sparkled in the beam of the flashlight. Charlie cast the light around slowly. The cave seemed endless.

You need a bigger light. A much bigger light.

Biscuit growled again. Charlie's breath began to come in short bursts. Her mind conjured sharp-toothed beasts with shiny eyes crouching behind the rock formations, waiting for her to come closer. Then another image, this one of thousands of vampire bats, hanging upside down just beyond her light, ready to fly out, sink their fangs into her flesh, and suck all of the blood from her body. She suddenly felt surrounded, overwhelmed. She began to feel as though the walls of the cave were closing, that the rock ceiling above was collapsing. She tried to take another step, but her foot caught a rock and sent her sprawling onto her stomach. The flashlight clattered against the floor and rolled away. She crawled forward and reached for it.

"Please don't go out," she gasped. "Please don't go out."

Her fingers wrapped around the tube and she climbed to her feet. Terrified, she turned and scrambled back toward the entrance.

Back to the world.

Back to the light.

The thunderstorm Jasper had predicted began to rage just after Charlie returned home and finished tending to Sadie. She fixed supper for Jasper and herself and spent the rest of the evening doing laundry. Jasper puttered around the house, happily unaware that Roscoe Barnes had committed suicide earlier in the day. Charlie went to bed at midnight, determined to go back to the cave the next morning. She finally drifted off an hour later. She dreamed that she'd been chained to the hourglass-shaped boulder outside the cave. A huge eagle soared down out of the sun and landed on the rock behind her head. Charlie believed the eagle to be an angel from heaven, sent to rescue her from bondage. It wasn't until she felt the sharp pain of the great bird's beak tearing into her flesh that she realized she was being punished.

She awoke when the eagle tore out her liver and flew off into the clouds.

CHAPTER EIGHTEEN

At ten o'clock the next morning, Charlie was back in the saddle. Jasper had gone to town and taken Biscuit with him, so she and Sadie were on their own. The storms from the night before had moved northeast, but a thick cover of puffy, gray cumulus lingered and a fine mist of fog hovered over the mountain like damp gauze. The weatherman on the radio had said more storms were on the way. She'd gotten out of bed early and driven into Elizabethton to pick up some things at Wal-Mart. Charlie had made up her mind. If there was really something in the cave, she was going to find it.

There was a high-powered, battery-operated searchlight in one of the saddlebags along with extra batteries. She was wearing a hooded sweatshirt, and she had gloves and a stocking cap to keep her warm in the cave. She had a lighter in one pocket and a small can of pepper spray in another. She had enough food and water to last an entire day tucked into a backpack, along with two dozen small, cylindrical wax candles. The labels said they would burn for at least three hours.

The morning was unusually still, the forest chilled and misty. Charlie rode slowly, watching and listening for anything that seemed out of the ordinary. She expected Zane Barnes to spring from behind every tree and rock she passed. She strained to see as she topped ridges and rounded bends. She stopped often and turned to look behind her.

When she got to the creek across from the cave entrance, Charlie walked Sadie back to the same laurel bush where she'd tied her before. She wrapped the reins loosely around a small branch and pulled the searchlight out of the saddlebag.

"You can get away if you need to," she said, stroking the white patch between Sadie's eyes. "There are black bears up here, but they won't bother you. The bobcats and the coyotes are too small. You'll be fine."

Charlie looked back at Sadie as she stood at the mouth of the cave, took a deep breath, turned on the light, and walked inside. The difference between the piddly flashlight she'd used on the first trip and the spotlight was amazing. She'd decided she would spend as much time as she needed familiarizing herself with the cave. She wanted to know its scope, its depth, its dimension. She wanted to know if there was more than one entrance. She'd spent a great deal of the previous night trying to convince herself that this could be an adventure. Exploring a cave could be *fun*.

The temperature inside the cave was cooler than it was beneath the cloud cover outside. Again, the only noise Charlie could hear was the sound of her own breathing. Her eyes moved constantly, following the beam of light up the walls on both sides, across the ceiling, and back down to the floor. She reached the spot where the tunnel opened up into the cathedral. The size of it reminded her of the basketball arena on the University of Tennessee campus. Charlie stood there looking, marveling at the formations. She knew enough about caves to know that the formations had grown over thousands, perhaps millions of years and were still growing. She wondered how anything could grow in total darkness. How could a rock grow? It was fascinating, and so, so frightening.

This time, she kept going. Something like a path, about two feet wide, wound its way down through the rock. She kept moving the light, surprised at the colors that surrounded her: splotches of deep red, walls of tan and brown, the sparkle of crystallized oxide. She made her way deliberately, scanning the walls and ceilings, hoping she wouldn't encounter anything too terrifying.

When she got to the bottom, to what appeared to be the floor, Charlie took a candle from the backpack, lit it, and placed it on the ground. If she could get back to this spot, she knew she could find her way out. So, like Hansel and Gretel dropping bread crumbs, she started lighting candles every twenty steps and working her way along the wall around the cathedral floor.

Five candles in, Charlie's light illuminated a round opening in the rock about thirty feet ahead of her. It looked very much like the elliptical opening at the mouth, but it was much larger. When she reached it and shined her light through, it appeared to be another tunnel, angling sharply downward. She set another candle down and forged ahead.

Sadie entered her mind. How long had she been in the cave? She took her cell phone out of her pocket. No signal, of course, but it told her the time. She'd been inside about thirty minutes. She kept going.

After twenty-seven steps, the tunnel opened onto yet another space, not as long and wide as the cathedral, but still huge, with a ceiling that was much, much higher, maybe eighty, ninety feet. There was a small crack in the rock almost straight above her through which oozed the faintest bit of daylight. She looked around; something to the left caught her eye. The beam had passed over something that definitely didn't fit, but it was far enough away that she couldn't quite comprehend the shape. She held the beam, hesitant. It wasn't conical or funnel shaped like so many of the rock formations. It didn't seem to belong. She moved toward it carefully, staring, and she came closer, she realized what it was.

A still.

There was a vat to the right, large and made of wood, shaped like a barrel that had been cut in half. Just to the left of the vat was a pile of neatly-stacked firewood. To the left of that was a cooker, jacked up on columns of flat rocks. It looked like the fuel-oil tanks Charlie had seen sitting on metal stands outside of people's homes. She wondered how many gallons it held. Beneath it was a fire pit, full of burned coals that glittered like black diamonds under the flashlight. A shiny, spiral copper tube rose from the top of the cooker and descended to another metal container, this one much smaller than the cooker, but still twenty-five gallons or so. A pipe that looked like an outdoor water spigot came off the bottom of the container. Charlie realized she was standing on the spot where Roscoe's great-grandfather made his liquor. She flashed the light around nervously, feeling, like yesterday, as though someone, or something, was watching her.

She stood for several seconds without moving, heard a sound, a small splash like a fish breaking the top of the water. The light from the candles flickered off the cave walls. She took a few steps toward the sound, shining the light along the cave floor. The stream came into focus after her next step. The cave, at that spot, was about sixty feet wide. The stream itself was less than ten feet across. Charlie walked carefully down a short slope and shined the light onto the water. She could see the water moving, slowly, from her right to her left. It disappeared beneath the rock face to her left. Roscoe's letter said that direction led out of the cave. She moved the light to her right to another rock face, but there was a little clearance, maybe eighteen inches or so, between the top of the water and the bottom of the rock. She walked close to the spot, knelt and shined the light beneath. There was clearance between the water and the rock for as far as the light would penetrate, but there was only one way to see what was in there.

Charlie removed her backpack, took everything out of her pockets and set it all on the rock floor. She took a deep breath and waded into the water.

It took a few seconds for the water to seep through her boots and jeans, but when it did, it nearly took her breath. The water was freezing cold. She slid her feet along the bottom until she was in the center of the stream. It was above her waist, just a few inches beneath her chest. She held the flashlight at chin level, bent over just a little, and moved beneath the rock.

She tried to count the number of steps she was taking, but the freezing water made it impossible. She turned her head to make sure she could still see the spot where she'd gone under the rock. When she turned back and took another step she heard a sound like a fountain, water falling into water. The sound grew louder and two steps later, she found herself in another chamber, this one about the size of her bedroom. About fifteen feet ahead and above her, an underground stream bubbled through the rock face and fell into a pool. She shined the light around ...

There.

Right there.

Charlie's heart almost stopped. On a wide ledge to her left was a line of stacked, wooden crates. Charlie scrambled out of the water and stood. Could this be it? Could it?

The crates were small, about sixteen inches long by eight or ten inches wide, maybe four inches deep. They were stacked ten high, five stacks, fifty crates in all. Charlie forgot about the cold, the darkness. Nothing existed except what might be inside the crates. She lay one of the flashlights down on the stack on the far right. The top crate looked as though its top had been removed. The others were nailed shut. She hooked her fingers beneath it, lifting slowly.

Sawdust.

How could that be?

She removed the glove from her right hand and reached down, began brushing the sawdust away. The pad of her finger touched something solid and cold. She leaned down, pursed her lips, and blew. The particles of wood separated like fairy dust. Charlie straightened.

Beneath the light, a brilliant, lustrous glow appeared. Charlie's eyes widened. She reached down again. Her hand wrapped around the hardness, the coldness. She had trouble lifting it with one hand, so heavy. She reached down with her other hand and lifted a bar of gold from the crate. It had to weigh twenty-five pounds or more.

There was a small circular imprint on the top of the gold bar, about the size of a wedding ring. Charlie bent closer, focusing the light. The words "Johnson and Matthey" were stamped around the top of the ring. At the bottom: "London." In the center of the circle were the words, "Poured by."

Charlie put the bar back in the crate, straightened and took a step back. She stood motionless, her eyes wide, her mouth open. The gold, illuminated by the flashlight, glowed like fire in the night.

"I found it, Roscoe," Charlie whispered. "I found Prometheus's fire."

CHAPTER NINETEEN

I walked into Perkins Restaurant at eight-thirty on Saturday morning and spotted the man I was meeting immediately. Pete Sams was sitting in a booth by a window against the far wall. He waved and I walked over.

Pete was a reporter for a little weekly in Carter County called *The Carter County Comet*. I wasn't sure of his exact age, but my guess was he had to be mid-to-late sixties. He was a slim, jovial man with long teeth and thinning, silver hair. I'd talked to him a couple of times about cases over the years and had always found him to be cordial. He wasn't overly aggressive, didn't lean toward sensationalism, and had never misquoted me or tried to play me. He was just one of those small-town newsmen who popped up on the grid from time to time. He'd called late in the afternoon on the day Roscoe Barnes took his plunge from the courthouse clock tower and had asked if we could meet Saturday morning. He said he wanted to talk about Roscoe. I told him I didn't think there was much I could tell him, but he was insistent, so I finally relented.

I slid into the booth and ordered a cup of coffee, hoping the conversation wouldn't take too long. Caroline and I were planning to take our grandson and niece to Dollywood that afternoon and I wanted to be back home by ten. Pete was already munching on a muffin and sipping from a glass of milk. He smiled and offered his right hand across the table.

"Appreciate you taking the time to talk to me," he said.

"Are we on or off the record?" I asked. "I always like to get that straight on the front end."

"How about we just have a discussion and then if I want to quote you on something, I'll ask."

"Sounds good," I said. "What do you want to discuss?"

"Have you ever heard of Russo's gold?"

"Russo's gold? I don't think so, Pete."

"It's one of those legends that might actually have some truth to it," he said. "Starts back in the thirties. This Philadelphia mobster named Carmine Russo supposedly did a lot of business with a local moonshiner named Hack Barnes. Hack Barnes was Roscoe Barnes's great-granddaddy, and the story goes that he and Russo became pretty tight over the years. He lived on the property Roscoe owns, or owned until he killed himself. Carmine Russo was the top mobster in Philadelphia and finally got himself arrested by the feds. He was looking at five, maybe six years in jail for tax evasion, and he knew he wouldn't be able to hold onto his rackets from inside prison. He also apparently didn't have anybody in Philadelphia he could trust, so the story is that he converted a bunch of his cash to gold and brought it down here to Hack Barnes so Hack could hide it and hold it for him until he got out of jail. His plan was to retrieve the gold when he got out and buy his way back into power on the streets, but his plan didn't work out because he wound up with pancreatic cancer and died a little over a year after he went to jail. Right around the same time Russo died, Hack Barnes, his wife and two of his children were murdered in their home. The old news stories called it the Buck Mountain Massacre. Nobody was ever arrested for the murders, but a Thompson sub-machine gun was used in the killings and there was a lot of speculation that mobsters were involved. The scuttlebutt has always been that Carmine Russo – or his wife – sent some of Carmine's boys down here to get the gold back from Hack Barnes since Carmine knew the cancer was going to kill him. Hack wouldn't give it to them so they killed him."

"And the gold stayed put wherever Hack Barnes hid it," I said.

"Exactly."

"Nice story. You planning to print it and somehow tie it to Roscoe's death?"

"I was hoping you might be able to help me out with that. You were representing Roscoe in a lawsuit that was filed by his son. Did he say anything about finding any gold?"

"If he did, I wouldn't be able to tell you, but what I can tell you, with complete honesty, is that Roscoe Barnes didn't say a word to me about any gold."

"Was he crazy?"

"Not that I could tell. Seemed like a normal person to me. A little rough around the edges sometimes, maybe a little eccentric, but nowhere near crazy."

"Then why did his son try to have him committed?"

"Your guess is as good as mine."

"Well, here's my guess. My guess is that Roscoe found the gold and Zane somehow found out about it, or at least Zane *thought* Roscoe found the gold. Zane wanted it and Roscoe wouldn't give it to him. Everybody who knows anything about Zane and Roscoe knows they couldn't stand each other. I think Zane filed suit to have Roscoe declared mentally incompetent so Zane could take over his property and eventually wind up with the gold. Roscoe was so enraged that he splattered himself all over the courthouse steps right in front of Zane. On the surface, it appeared that Roscoe may have cut off his nose to spite his face because he didn't have any heirs besides Zane, which would mean that Zane would wind up with the property anyway. But then I got a phone call from a clerk in the probate office who said a will had been filed. I got my hands on a copy of the will, and it leaves everything Roscoe owned to a neighbor of his, a young girl named Charleston Story, who also happens to be a brand new lawyer working under your supervision and who was also representing Roscoe in the commitment proceeding. Interesting, don't you think?"

"Interesting? Maybe. Also a little far-fetched for a news story."

"It isn't really a news story. More of a feature. It's got a little history, some violence, gangsters, gold, intrigue—

"Speculation."

"Nothing wrong with that in a feature story. Were you aware that Roscoe willed everything to Miss Story?"

I nodded. I didn't see anything improper or unethical about telling him the truth.

"The lawyer who filed the will had a courier bring it to Charlie at my office a few hours after Roscoe died," I said. "Roscoe had apparently planned things very carefully."

"I know," Pete said. "I talked to the lawyer, Gerald Benton. Nice guy. He said there was a sealed envelope in the packet with the will, but he said he didn't know what was in it. Do you?"

"No. Charlie is the only person who knows what was in that envelope. She didn't offer to tell me, and I didn't ask."

"I guess I need to talk to her. Would you mind giving me her cell number?"

"I don't think I should do that without asking her first."

"I'll figure out a way to talk to her, you know. Even if I have to show up at her place unannounced."

"When are you planning on running this story, Pete?"

"We publish every Thursday. I should have it ready by then."

"Have you considered what might happen if you run a story that says there might be gold somewhere on Roscoe Barnes's property? That's what you're planning to imply, isn't it? Crackpots and criminals will come crawling out of the wood work. Or what about this? What if Carmine Russo has living relatives who think they have some kind of claim to it?"

"I guess they'll file their own lawsuit."

"What if they're mobsters? Mobsters don't file lawsuits. You could get someone hurt, Pete. Maybe even killed. How much gold is supposed to be up there on the mountain?"

"I'm not sure. I've heard it was worth a million dollars back when Russo brought it down here."

"Which would make it worth what today? Twenty million?"

"You don't follow the price of gold, do you, counselor? If it was worth a million back in the thirties, it's worth about fifty million today."

I shook my head and breathed deeply. Fifty million dollars? I'd seen people do terrible things to each other over fifty dollars, let alone fifty million. The chances of Pete's conjectures actually being fact were slim, but the entire situation with Roscoe had been bizarre from the beginning.

"Do me a favor," I said. "Hold off until I can talk to Charlie about this. She's just a kid, a sweet, naïve kid. I'd hate to see this blow up in her face and get out of hand, especially if there's nothing to it."

Pete picked up the last piece of his muffin and stuck it in his mouth.

"How long have you been practicing law, Joe?" he said.

"Let's see ... more than twenty-five years, I guess."

"Well sir, I've been sticking my nose in other people's business for more than forty years," he said, "and I'm here to tell you there's something to this one. This is the best story I've ever run across, and I'm going to write it. I'll give you until next week."

CHAPTER TWENTY

When Charlie emerged from the cave, she looked up to see another bank of black thunderheads boiling out of the west like flying tidal waves. The wind was howling across the mountain. A storm was almost on top of her. Sadie was wide-eyed, and Charlie was grateful she hadn't pulled away from the laurel bush and bolted. One bar of gold was all Charlie had managed to get out, and even that had been a struggle. The bar was heavy, and only seemed to get heavier the closer she'd gotten to the mouth of the cave. She tucked it quickly into one of the saddlebags. Heavy drops of rain began to pelt her face. The storm was upon her. Charlie jumped into the saddle and Sadie took off at a gallop.

The first crack of lightning exploded so close behind them that Charlie felt the shock wave. The wind was roaring like a wild animal and the day had turned to near-darkness. The rain began to pour about a mile from the barn, and by the time they reached it, Charlie was drenched again. She removed the bar from the saddlebags and put it in the bottom of a trunk in which she kept her grooming tools and some tack. She covered it with a couple of old saddle blankets and closed the lid.

She took off her backpack and set it aside, unsaddled Sadie, replaced Sadie's bridle with a halter, and groomed her while the lightning flashed and the thunder crashed outside. Biscuit was cowered in Sadie's stall, whining and shivering. The dog was normally fearless. He slept in the barn with Sadie – Jasper had never let him in the house – but thunder terrified him.

When she was finished, Charlie covered herself with a saddle blanket and trotted through the rain down the path to the house. Jasper was sitting at the kitchen table, eating a cookie.

"How was your ride, Peanut?"

"It was great. Really great."

"Great? You look like a drowned rat."

Charlie walked past the table and down the hall to her bedroom. She peeled her wet clothing, dried off, and pulled on a bath robe. She picked her laptop up off the dresser, went to the Google search engine, and typed in "price of gold."

Fourteen hundred dollars an ounce.

She typed in "gold bars" and read for a little while. She discovered that the bars she'd found weighed four hundred troy ounces each, around twenty-seven pounds. She'd opened another crate before she left the cave – there were two bars in it. Fifty crates. Ninety-nine bars. She pulled up the calculator on the computer screen. Thirty-nine thousand, six hundred ounces of gold. She punched more numbers into the calculator.

"Oh ... my ... god."

The number was staggering. She did the math again. If the gold was real, each bar was worth five hundred and sixty thousand dollars at the current market price, which meant there was more than fifty-five million dollars worth of gold in the cave.

Fifty-five million dollars!

She started to jump around the room like a little girl, her hands in tight fists against her sides. She sat on the bed and bounced. She put a hand over her mouth and giggled. Should she tell Jasper?

No. Don't tell anyone. Not yet. Not until ...

She'd found it! She'd found gold!

The first thing she'd do would be to buy a car. She'd been driving her little Ford pick-up for six years. It had almost two hundred thousand miles on it. What kind of car? What color? She could fix up the place, add on and give Jasper all the space he needed for his junk. She could buy a new place if she wanted. A place for her dad. And she'd travel. She'd never been more than a hundred miles from home; had never ridden on an airplane. Europe was a must, and Hawaii, and the Caribbean, and New York City. She'd stay at five star hotels and see everything there was to see. She'd shop in the best shops, eat in the best restaurants, visit the most interesting places on earth. She'd do all the things she'd only been able to dream about. She'd learn to snow ski and water ski, scuba dive, maybe even to sail. She'd buy another horse, maybe two, maybe ten. She could buy a ranch if she wanted.

Fifty-five million dollars!

Charlie suddenly stopped bouncing as the enormity of the situation hit her. Who could she tell? Who could she trust? Who could help her? How would she get the gold out of the cave? There was so much of it. It was so heavy. The cave was deep and huge and in a rugged, remote location.

She couldn't allow anyone to find out. If the news got out, every thief and beggar and con man within five hundred miles would descend upon her. How would she turn it into money once she got it out? Was it really hers? *Legally* hers?

She got off the bed and walked into her bathroom. Closed the door. Stepped in front of the mirror and looked at herself.

"Okay, you've found it," she said. "Now all you have to do is figure out a way to keep it."

CHAPTER TWENTY-ONE

Johnny Russo walked into the row house on South Bancroft that had been home to his parents for thirty years. The first floor had a unique feel – unlived-in Italian was how he would describe it every day but Sunday. His mother was a clean freak; the whole house was spotless. The marble tile in the foyer shined, absent of footprints or dust. The glass teardrops hanging from the small chandelier above sparkled like diamonds in a jewelry store display case. The furniture in the den was covered with plastic.

The smell on Sunday, however, was incredible: the aroma of garlic, onions, oregano and basil sautéing in olive oil floated through the air along with the smells of freshly baked bread and oven-roasted chicken. As he moved through the den, Johnny thought back, as he always did, when he was a kid. The family gathering early in the afternoon after Mass. Silverware clinking against china, Pops at the head of the table, Ma to his right, Johnny next to her, his twin sisters, Isabella and Donata, five years older, sitting across the table. The girls' voices light and silly. Pops drinking red wine.

Johnny's father, Nico Russo, was a made man, just as his father and his father and his father and his father had been. Johnny worshipped him. Nico's great-great-grandfather, the legendary Carmine Russo, was the boss of Philly in the twenties and thirties. The wiseguys called the Prohibition era the golden years. Nico told his son that during Carmine Russo's heyday, he took in millions each year from his various "business" ventures. He also paid out tens of thousands of dollars in bribes to politicians, judges, police officers and railroad workers to insure that his booze made it to Philadelphia unmolested and on time from suppliers in the south. Carmine had the mansion in Bella Vista, the fancy cars, the tailored suits. When Carmine was sent to prison, his sons were too young to take over the business, and a bloody war ensued for control of the rackets. Carmine died in prison within a year, and the Russo family was pushed aside. They'd been fighting unsuccessfully to get back to the top ever since, and Johnny's father was full of resentment. He made a decent living loan-sharking, brokering truckloads of stolen property, and extorting business owners out of protection money, but he drank too much and often ranted about how he would run things if he were boss.

"Money is the key," he often said to his son. "You'll hear them talk about respect and *omerta* and *our way*, but when it all gets boiled down, what's left is the meat, and the meat is money. In this country, in every country, money is what matters. Money is what takes care of you, takes care of your family."

Johnny pushed through the swinging door that led to the kitchen. His mother, a short, proud, black-eyed woman named Tessa, was straining pasta over the sink.

She looked over her shoulder and smiled. Johnny leaned over and kissed her on the cheek from behind.

"You look so tired," she said.

"I was up late. How's Pops?"

"The same. Go on up and say hello. I'll call you when it's ready."

Johnny climbed the steps to the second floor. As he neared the landing, he could hear the steady rhythm of the heart monitor. His father lay in a hospital bed, just as he had for the past eleven years. He was pale and emaciated, the skin on his face drawn so tight that his face looked like a skull with eyes. The eyes were closed right now, but they opened occasionally. When they did, they saw nothing. Pops' hair had turned gray.

"Hey Pops," Johnny said as he sat down in the chair by the bed. "How's it going?"

Eleven years earlier, Johnny Russo was one of the best twelve-year-old baseball players in the city. He'd been recruited by a man named Mark Giamatti to play on a South Philly all-star team called the Heat that traveled all over southeastern Pennsylvania and western New Jersey. Johnny was the shortstop, the team's best pitcher, and he led the Heat in every offensive category. Giamatti called him a "five-tooler" and the "real deal." He had speed, a great arm, he could hit for power and average, and had incredible hands. Johnny's best friend, the powerful Carlo Lanzetti, was the first baseman.

On a Saturday in August of that year, a team from Collingswood, New Jersey, came across the river to play the Heat at one of the fields at FDR Park. Coach Giamatti said the boys from Jersey were good, they'd have their hands full, and he was right. The first game of the double header started at noon, and it was close. Johnny pitched well, got two hits, and the Heat won, 3–2. In the middle of the second game, beneath a scorching August sun, Johnny heard his father's distinctive voice coming from the other side of a chain-link fence along the third base line. Johnny was surprised. Nico didn't often come out to watch him play. Nico was a nocturnal creature; he usually got home about the same time Johnny was getting out of bed. He slept until three or four in the afternoon, ate, and went out to work. He was constantly tired, and Johnny had noticed that he was drinking even more than usual. From the tone and volume of his voice that day, Johnny knew he'd been in the bottle.

In the bottom of the final inning, Johnny came up to bat with the bases loaded, two out, and his team trailing 5-4. There were thirty or forty people watching and yelling, most of them players' families. The Collingswood pitcher was a stocky left-hander with a good curve ball who had come in after the fourth inning and kept the Heat hitters off balance. Johnny took the first pitch, a fastball that he thought was a little inside, but the ump called it a strike. He heard his father curse. The next three pitches were curve balls, all of them out of the zone. The count was 3-1, a hitter's count. The next pitch was another fastball, this one belt high on the inner half, and Johnny roped it down the left field line. He thought it would go into the corner for a game-winning double, but it hooked at the last second and landed about a foot foul. Johnny got back into the box, expecting another fastball. Instead, the kid threw him a back-door curve. It looked high and outside. It *was* high and outside, and Johnny took it.

The ump rang him up. Strike three. Game over.

The next few minutes were like a dream. Johnny remembered turning to look at the ump, but he'd already spun around and was walking away. There were cries of joy from the Collingsworth fans, protests from the South Philly fans. Johnny was disappointed, but he'd made outs before, lost games before. It wasn't the end of the world. He was walking back to the bench when he saw his pops come around the fence. Nico grabbed Johnny's aluminum bat out of his hand and sprinted straight toward the umpire, who was heading toward the parking lot. Johnny yelled at Nico when he realized what was happening, but it didn't matter. Nico was drunk and angry, bellowing about his kid being screwed. He beat the umpire savagely with the bat right there in the park, in front of everybody. When he was finished swinging – sweaty, panting and muttering – he dropped the bat on the ground, walked slowly to the parking lot, got in his car and drove away.

The cops picked Nico up that night at a bar on Tenth Street. He'd broken both of the umpire's legs and one of his arms. Since he didn't hit the ump in the head, the cops charged him with aggravated assault instead of attempted murder. Nico made bail before sunrise, but the next morning his picture was on the front page of the *Philadelphia Inquirer*, along with a story about the violent nature of mob life and the need for accountability. It named Nico as a soldier in the Pistone family and even mentioned the boss, Salvatore Pistone. Two nights later, Nico was found on the same ball field where he'd beaten the ump with two bullets in his head. The doctors removed the bullets and managed to keep him alive, but so much damage had been done to his brain that he went into what the doctors called a "persistent vegetative state." His heart beat, his lungs worked, but he was completely unaware of his surroundings. He was a dead man living, maintained entirely by Johnny's mother, who fed him through a tube, changed his diapers, shaved him, bathed him and turned him to prevent bedsores. Johnny and his sisters had pleaded with their mother to remove the feeding tube, but she steadfastly refused. When God wanted him, she said, He'd take him.

The shooting of his father ignited a fuse in Johnny that had been smoldering for more than a decade. He knew Salvatore Pistone had put out a contract because of the unwanted publicity and scrutiny caused by Nico's drunken behavior. The fact that Nico had been earning money for Sal and doing dirt for Sal for almost twenty years didn't matter. Sal was embarrassed, so he accused Nico, tried him, convicted him, and sentenced him to death, all in a matter of forty-eight hours. When he realized that his father would never be a man again, that he was a vegetable, Johnny swore to himself that he would one day get even with Salvatore Pistone. His plans were on hold for now because Pistone was in jail, but he'd be out in a few months. Johnny intended to kill him.

Neither Johnny nor Carlo ever set foot on a baseball field again. Instead, they began selling pot to their classmates in the seventh grade. They got their product from a friend of Nico's, a wiseguy named Tommy Maldonado. Carlo quickly learned to either beat up or shake down any competition, and within a year, the boys were splitting two thousand a week. They branched out into ecstasy in the eighth grade. Both of them quit school in the tenth grade and moved into an apartment on Passyunk Avenue. Johnny knew his mother was frustrated and angry with him, but his sisters had both already moved out, leaving just him and his mother and the constant beep, beep, beep from the heart monitor in the bedroom. Night after night after night. It unnerved Johnny. He couldn't stand it, so he left.

Two weeks after they moved into the apartment, Tommy Maldonado, their drug supplier, showed up unannounced.

"Two things," he said. "You're growing too fast, stepping on people's toes. Slow down. And if you're gonna keep doing business in this neighborhood, you gotta start paying tribute. They've let you operate this long because of what happened to your father, but now you gotta pay."

So much for the mob's rule against drug dealing. They paid three hundred a week to Maldonado, who passed most of it up to his capo, who took his cut and passed it on to Pistone. It stayed that way for two years, until Pistone went to prison for racketeering. The mobsters upped the tribute to five hundred a week. Then last year, they bumped it again to eight hundred a week. By that time, Johnny and Carlo were veterans of the street. Carlo was so good at extorting other drug dealers that he didn't have to find them to collect. They came to him. Johnny and

Carlo had runners who were fixtures at raves and bars in South Philly. Carlo was such an intimidating figure that nobody stole from them. They were splitting more than three hundred grand a year after the tributes and after expenses, big enough to keep them and the bosses happy but small enough to stay under the feds' radar.

Johnny was telling his father about the meeting he and Carlo had with Big Legs Mucci when he heard his mother call from the bottom of the stairs.

"Okay, Pops, I gotta go now." He bent down and kissed his father on the forehead. "I'll see you next week."

He went back downstairs to the kitchen and sat at the table. The food was delicious, as always. He listened half-heartedly as his mother prattled on about church and the neighbors and a scheduled visit from his sisters, Isabella and Donata. Isabella was married and living in Atlanta, which she said she hated. Donata was also married, working as an executive chef in a high-end restaurant in Baltimore. They were planning to visit at the same time, in three weeks.

When he was finished eating, Johnny helped his mother clear the table.

"Go," she said, just as she did every Sunday. "I'll take care of the dishes."

Johnny stopped by the front door. On a small, round table was a shiny, navy blue porcelain vase in which his mother kept fresh flowers. He'd been setting cash next to it every Sunday since he moved out. He reached into his pocket, laid down a stack of hundred-dollar bills, and walked out into the gloomy afternoon.

CHAPTER TWENTY-TWO

Light rain popped against the windshield, the wipers shoving the water aside again and again as Charlie drove down the mountain toward Jonesborough. The afternoon light was dull, the cloud cover thick. The brilliant greens and golds of early summer were muted to browns and grays.

Charlie had decided that Joe Dillard was the most logical person to approach. She already regarded him as a friend. He was mentoring her. He'd helped her start making money, and he'd done it without asking for a dime.

This, however, was different. Fifty-five million dollars. The lure of that much money, the thought of it, had had such an impact on her that she was certain it would do the same to Mr. Dillard. Would he want to take charge of it? Would he want a percentage? How much would he want?

She let her mind wander again as she wound through curves and over hills. She must learn about investing, first thing. Stocks, bonds, commodities, utilities, real estate, all of it. She would immerse herself in the world of money, read books, subscribe to magazines, attend seminars. She didn't know a prospectus from a balance sheet or a put from a call, but she would learn. If she could learn to make the money earn just ten percent a year, she could make millions and never touch the principal. *Millions.* She couldn't really fathom the idea of that much wealth; money had always been tight and she'd been raised to be frugal, but the thought of being fabulously rich gave her goose bumps.

She'd called Joe Dillard's cell to see if he could meet her and talk. He said he'd been planning to go to Pigeon Forge with his family, but the thunderstorms had forced him to cancel the trip. Could they meet at the office? He had agreed. She found him behind his desk, doing some work on his computer. He greeted her warmly and she sat down. She'd decided to gauge Mr. Dillard's responses to her questions and then decide how much she would reveal.

"I may need to hire you, Mr. Dillard," she said.

Mr. Dillard raised his eyebrows. "Have you committed a crime?"

Charlie smiled. "I'm not sure."

"You're joking, of course. And please, Charlie, call me Joe. You make me feel so old calling me Mr. Dillard all the time."

"Okay, Joe. Can I ask you a hypothetical question?"

"I love hypothetical questions," he said. "They allow me to give hypothetical answers."

"Let's say you found something that was extremely valuable, something that's been hidden for a long time. Legally speaking, would it belong to you as soon as you found it or are there hoops you'd have to jump through?"

"Funny you should ask. I got a call from a newspaper reporter a couple of days ago and met with him this morning. The meeting made me curious about some legal issues and I was just doing some research on that very subject. I suppose the answer to your question would depend on what I found and where I found it."

Charlie took a deep breath. She didn't want to give her secret away, but she desperately wanted an opinion from someone she trusted.

"Let's say you found a bunch of silver in a cave."

"A cave? And to whom does this cave belong?"

"Let's say that's up for grabs."

"Up for grabs is a bit ambiguous, Charlie. Are you saying there might be some dispute over the ownership of the land – the cave – where I found this silver?"

"Exactly."

Joe leaned forward and folded his hands on the desk.

"What have you gotten yourself into, young lady?" he said.

"Nothing. I'm just curious."

"You lie poorly, Charlie. This is the first time I've seen you attempt it, and I have to say you're not good at it."

"Humor me. Please."

"What you're describing is called treasure trove. Treasure trove means treasure found. Most courts define treasure as money, jewels, or precious metals. The common law says that found treasure belongs to the finder. But Tennessee law is different. Hold on one second."

Joe turned to his computer and started clicking away. A few seconds later, he said, "Here it is. *Morgan versus Wiser*, nineteen eighty-five. Some men with a metal detector found a bunch of silver coins on another man's property. When the landowner found out about it, he sued. The appellate court ruled that since the men who found the silver were on the land without permission, they were trespassers. The court said if they allowed the finders to keep the silver they'd be encouraging trespassing, so they gave the coins to the landowner. It's the last reported case on treasure trove in Tennessee, so it's the law that controls. It's the precedent. So if you ... excuse me, if *I* was trespassing when I found this silver, I wouldn't be allowed to keep it."

"But if you weren't trespassing ... ?"

"Finders keepers. May I ask how much silver I found?"

"Let's say you found a lot."

"Would this sudden curiosity of yours have anything to do with Roscoe Barnes and his will?"

"Probably not."

"Don't ever try to sell used cars. You'll starve."

Charlie was struggling to contain her excitement. She wanted to blurt it out, to tell him about the gold, to beg him to help her. She could certainly afford to pay him. She had a gold bar worth half-a-million dollars in a trunk in the barn. She wanted to unburden herself, but instead, she asked another hypothetical.

"So if I ... if *you* found a bunch of silver buried somewhere and you got to keep it, what would you do with it? I mean, how would you turn it into cash?"

"I guess I'd shop reputable silver buyers and brokers to find the best price," Joe said.

"And what? You just sell it to them? Just like that?"

"Just like that."

"Do they write you a check? Hand you cash?"

"I don't have a lot of experience with this type of thing, but I suppose it would depend on how much money you're talking about. I'd think they would analyze the silver to ensure its authenticity and purity and then they would either mail you a check or wire transfer the money to an account of your choosing."

Charlie opened her mouth to ask another question but caught herself. Joe's eyes had turned into laser beams. She suddenly felt as though he knew what she was thinking, that he could see into her soul. He'd been trying cases in front of juries for twenty-five years and she'd heard him speak of a sixth sense he'd developed, what he called "the art of detecting bull crap." Charlie squirmed under his gaze, re-crossed her legs.

"What if ... ?" she stammered, "What if ... ?"

"Spit it out, Charlie. You've gone this far."

"What if you wanted to hide the money so nobody knew you had it? How would you do it?"

Joe took a deep breath, leaned back and laced his fingers behind his head. The laser beams emanating from his brown eyes grew brighter, more intense.

"Charlie, I'm going to ask you a simple question, and I want an honest answer. Have you found gold on Roscoe's property?"

Charlie remained silent, but her chin, almost involuntarily, dipped and rose, dipped and rose.

"So it's real. The legend is true. Do you know the story? Do you know the story about Carmine Russo?"

"Roscoe wrote me a letter and told me about it. He left me a map."

"How much did you find?"

"Ninety-nine, I think."

"Ninety-nine what?"

"Bars."

"What kind of bars? How big?"

"I think they're four hundred ounces each."

A long, slow rush of air escaped Joe's lips. She watched him closely as he silently multiplied quantity by value. He turned to his computer, punched in some numbers, let out a low whistle, turned back.

"And you found this on Roscoe's property?"

"In a cave. But isn't it my property now?"

Joe shook his head.

"Not until a court says it is. If the will turns out to be valid, then I suppose it's yours, but you know as well as I do that Zane Barnes and his lawyers aren't going to just stand by and let you take fifty million dollars right out from under their noses. Did Roscoe's letter say anything about Zane? Does he know about this gold?"

Charlie nodded. "It said he knows about it, but he doesn't know where it is."

"Then you can count on him and Nathaniel Mitchell being a part of your life for the next several years, and I'm afraid that's only going to be the beginning. A newspaper reporter from Elizabethton is going to write a story about the gold, Charlie. Once it hits the paper and the internet, all hell is going to break loose. It could even get dangerous for you. You're going to need to take some steps to protect yourself and to protect the gold, and you're going to need to take those steps as soon as possible."

"What kind of steps?"

"You should probably turn the gold over to the court. Happens all the time with money. If there's a dispute over money, the parties turn it over to the court and the court deposits it in an interest-bearing account until the dispute is resolved. Once the trial and the appeals are over, the court gives the money to the winner, or if a settlement is reached, the court splits it up according to the agreement. There is obviously going to be a dispute over Roscoe's will, so that's probably what you should do."

Charlie was silent for a few minutes.

"But what if I don't?" she said. "What if I don't want to turn it over to a court? I talked to the lawyer in Greeneville that drafted the will and he said he didn't have any doubt about Roscoe's mental state. He even said he'd testify in court. And Roscoe's letter said he didn't want Zane to have any of the gold. He wanted me to have it. If I turn it over to the probate court or the chancery court or whichever court this ends up in, there's a chance I'll never see it again. Or like you said, by the time the case goes through a trial and the appellate process, it could be five years, maybe even ten years, before I can touch any of it. I don't want to wait that long."

"I understand," Joe said. "Well, to be honest, maybe I don't. Fifty million dollars is probably more temptation than I can fathom. But my concern is that if you try to keep all this gold and convert it to cash without going through the court system, you'll wind up with nothing but trouble. You can't keep something like that a secret, Charlie. Word will get out, and when it does, bad things will happen. You could wind up a victim of your own good fortune. And if you decide to take the gold out of the cave and turn it into cash, you'll have to pay tax on it. Income tax, which means you'll have to explain how you got the income to the IRS. If you don't, you could wind up in jail. My advice – and I assume you came here for advice – is to hire the best probate lawyer you can find, turn the gold over to the court, and let the system sort it out. It'll take a long time, but just keep on doing what you've been doing – study for the bar exam, learn to practice law, get ready to bring your father back into your life. If everything goes well, you'll be a multi-millionaire before you turn thirty and life will be sweet."

"If I decide to turn the gold over to the court, will you represent me?"

Joe shook his head. "There's too much at stake. You need someone experienced in probate law, a specialist. If you'd committed a murder, it would be different, but I'm not the guy you want for a case like this."

"I have a lot to think about," Charlie said.

"You certainly do. I know you've been through a lot in the past few days and I know the thought of being instantly rich is alluring, but please, please think this through carefully. I've thought about it a great deal this morning, and I have to tell you there's one thing that really bothers me."

"What's that?"

"If this gold came from Carmine Russo, it has to be blood money. Men like him were glorified thieves and murderers, Charlie. They terrorized people, tortured people, killed people, and they did it all for money and power. I'm not particularly superstitious, but you mentioned karma the first day you came in here to talk to me. What goes around comes around? If that gold is the result of terror and corruption and murder, I don't think I'd want any part of it. So just think about it carefully, okay? I'd hate to see anything bad happen to you."

Charlie stood to leave. She was suddenly exhausted and spoke quietly: "Bad things have already happened to me. My father has been in prison since I was a small child. My mother abandoned me the day after he was sentenced. I've lost both of the grandparents who raised me in the past year. Maybe Roscoe giving me this gold is a sign. Maybe it's my turn to be happy."

"Money won't bring you happiness," Joe said. "It might make your life easier in some ways, but it will bring its own set of problems."

"I think I'm willing to take a few risks," Charlie said, and she turned and walked out the door.

CHAPTER TWENTY-THREE

On Sunday morning, Caroline and I loaded up Rio, our German shepherd, and Chico, our teacup poodle, and drove to Winged Deer Park just outside of Johnson City. We'd walked hundreds of miles along the trails there over the years, but because of her breast cancer, Caroline had gone through several periods during which she was simply unable to tolerate the strain of sustained exercise. Her latest bout with the disease had been a particularly intense one, so intense that there had been times when I didn't believe she would make it through another month, but through a powerful combination of medication and determination, she had rebounded once again and was able to walk a mile or so three or four times a week without too much discomfort.

We parked near the lake and started up the trail beneath a clear, azure sky. I'd always enjoyed walking with Caroline, spending time with her, but her sickness had changed my perception of, and appreciation for, time. I savored time more, was much more aware of it each day. I had become more patient, sometimes to the point that I surprised myself. Small inconveniences bothered me less, and small pleasures brought me more enjoyment than they had in the past. I'd always been aware that I tended toward intensity, and I don't think that had changed all that much, but the focus of my intensity had definitely changed. It had turned away from my legal career, away from murderers and thieves and judges and cops and politicians, and I was now focused much more on my life with Caroline and the rest of my family.

"Am I becoming a bore?" I asked Caroline as we walked past a pavilion while the dogs wandered nearby in search of squirrels.

"A bore?" she said. "Why would you ask me a question like that?"

"Because I'm starting to feel like a bore. I'm afraid I'm getting old and boring."

"How can you think you're getting old and boring? Look at you. You're still gorgeous and sexy and vital. You can still run five miles and barely break a sweat. You're big and strong and have one of the sharpest minds imaginable. You remind me of the ancient Greeks, Joe, maybe Leonidas. A citizen-soldier, an everyman who is capable of great things when the need arises. A tremendous combination of mind, body, and spirit."

"Wow," I said. "Leonidas, huh? I guess that makes you my Gorgo."

"Don't call me Gorgo. What a terrible name. It sounds like some kind of slimy monster."

"But she was a strong woman. A queen."

"Who wound up with a dead husband after he marched off to Thermopylae and got himself killed by the Persians."

"She was the daughter of a king, the wife of a king and the mother of a king. Now *that's* a woman who lived a full and adventurous life."

"I like my life better. My father wasn't a king and my husband and son may not be kings, but I wouldn't trade my life for hers or any other woman's."

We walked in silence for a couple of minutes before I said, "You're right. It's been good, hasn't it? Ups and downs, ins and outs, joys and tragedies, but all in all, it's been good."

She nodded and smiled at me. "And it isn't over. We still have a long way to go."

I reached out and took her hand. "I know we do, baby. How do you feel?"

"Good. I feel pretty good. So good, in fact, that I don't feel like talking about how I feel, so let's talk about something else."

"Okay, what do you want to talk about?"

"Jack and this new girl."

"Jack and Charlie? What about them?"

"He's in love, Joe."

"In love? He barely knows her. What makes you think he's in love?"

"I can see it on his face, hear it in his voice when he talks about her. And he actually said the words to me. He said, 'Mom, I know it sounds silly, but I think I'm in love. I've never felt this way about a girl before.'"

"Of course he hasn't felt that way before. He's just a kid. He doesn't know anything about love, what it feels like, what it means. He's too young."

"He's older than we were when we fell in love. In fact, he's older than we were when we got married. He's older than we were when we had our first child. Have you forgotten?"

"I suppose I have, or maybe I just choose not to think about it. Do you really think she might be the one for him?"

"I don't know. I haven't even met her yet, but I plan to change that very soon."

"You might want to hold off for a little while."

"Why?"

"Because there's a ... there's a bit of a ... complication that you don't know about. Jack doesn't even know about it, or at least I don't think he knows about it."

"What complication? What are you talking about?"

"I'd rather not get into it right now, Caroline, but it's serious. Could be a huge problem for both of them."

She stopped, pulled her hand away from mine, and folded her arms.

"What is it?"

"C'mon, don't do this. Let's keep walking and talk about something else. I'll tell you about it some other time."

"You'll tell me now, Joe Dillard. Right now. We've been through this a hundred times. You always promise not to keep things from me, and then you go right back to keeping things from me. I want to know what this complication is."

"It may not be that—"

"You said huge problem for both of them. That's what you said, just a second ago."

"But I—"

"Spill it, mister. I'll stand here until dark if I have to."

CHAPTER TWENTY-FOUR

Later Sunday evening, after she had fed Jasper, cleaned the dishes, showered and dressed and put on a light dusting of makeup because she was expecting a guest, Charlie walked out onto the back porch. Thick, dark clouds had moved in earlier and hung low over the mountains. It was chilly, and a slight breeze was blowing. She saw a flash of movement in the trees about fifty yards in front of her. She stared at the spot and saw the twitch of a long tail.

"There you are," she said. She went back inside to the refrigerator and took out a small bunch of white grapes. She sat down outside and fixed her eyes on the edge of the woods, tossed a grape out into the grass. A minute later, a red fox appeared, stepping cautiously into the fading light.

"C'mon," Charlie said. "Don't be shy. You know they're not sour."

Charlie had noticed him lurking about early in the spring and had started tossing food in his direction: grapes, slices of apple, boiled eggs. Biscuit had seen him a couple of times, but paid him absolutely no attention. She'd named him Reynard after a fabled fox her third-grade teacher had read about in class.

"I haven't seen you in two weeks," Charlie said. "Where have you been?"

He was a beautiful animal, the size of a small dog, with golden eyes and a bushy tail that made up a third of the length of his body. He moved gracefully, and when startled he could run as fast as Sadie. And when the wind was right, Charlie could detect a distinctive odor. Reynard smelled very much like a skunk.

"That's it," Charlie said as Reynard picked up the grape and swallowed it. She tossed another, this time much closer to the porch. He ignored it. She longed to pet him, but she knew he would never allow it. Fifty feet was his limit.

"Some things just aren't meant to be touched, are they?" she said.

Charlie tossed another grape, closer to him. He picked it up and appeared to smile.

Charlie heard the sound of tires traveling over gravel, coming up the driveway. Reynard bolted into the trees. Charlie turned to see Zane Barnes's Mercedes crawling toward her. She shivered involuntarily; Roscoe wasn't yet in the ground, and here was Zane. She heard Jasper banging away at something in his shop and took comfort knowing he was nearby. She braced herself for what she knew would be an unpleasant conversation.

Barnes cut the engine and got out of the car. He was alone, wearing a brown pullover and khaki pants. It was the first time she'd ever seen him in anything but a business suit. He walked stiffly toward the porch. Charlie stood still, the bunch of grapes still dangling from her left hand.

"Good evening," Barnes said. He stopped about ten feet from the porch.

"What can I do for you?" Charlie's tone was neutral, neither friendly nor hostile.

"I just thought we should have a little talk."

"About what?"

"I'd like to make you an offer."

"You're wasting your breath. I'm not interested."

Barnes' shoulders rose and fell. He spread his feet a little, squared his shoulders. Charlie smiled to herself. He was taking on the posture of a gunfighter. A very short gunfighter.

"My father had five hundred acres of land. Some of it, a lot of it, is worthless. But the timber is worth some money. I'm prepared to offer you three hundred thousand to sign a release and a deed. There's no need for us to fight over it, no need for a long court battle. We can settle this right here, right now."

"Like I said, not interested."

"Make a counter offer."

Charlie thought about the bar of gold in the trunk in the barn, about the fortune in the cave. Zane probably wasn't certain that Roscoe had told her, but he had to suspect it. She decided to have a little fun. "Why do you want it so badly? Roscoe said you didn't really care about him or the land."

"That isn't true at all. I cared deeply about my father, and I care deeply about my heritage. That land is part of my heritage; it's part of me."

"Not anymore."

"I don't intend to let you take it."

"I'm not taking anything. Roscoe gave it to me."

Barnes snorted. "That will is a joke. My lawyer will tear it apart, piece by piece. You'll be left with nothing."

"Then I won't be any worse off than I am right now, will I? You, on the other hand, will be paying Mitchell four hundred dollars an hour plus expenses. How much did he stick you for on the conservatorship? Twenty thousand? Thirty? Whatever it was, this will cost you a lot more."

"Do you think I care about how much it will cost? I'll keep you locked up in court for twenty years if that's what it takes."

"I'm young. I have time."

The lines in Barnes' face were tight and deep. Behind him, Charlie saw Jasper walk out the door of his shop with Biscuit at his heels. He secured the padlock and started walking toward them. Barnes didn't notice.

"I want you to listen to me, young lady, and I want you to listen closely," Barnes said. His voice was growing harder, edgier with each word. His lips barely moved when he spoke. "I'm willing to make it worth your while to walk away from what rightfully belongs to me. You've gotten lucky. You're looking at a three-hundred thousand dollar windfall you don't deserve. But I'm warning you, it would *not* be wise to push me. You need to think about how much it really means to you to own that land. Because if you insist on acting in an unreasonable manner, the cost is going to be much, much higher than you can imagine."

Charlie didn't respond. She watched as Jasper passed close behind Barnes, who was so startled that he jerked visibly.

"You remember Zane Barnes, don't you, uncle?" Charlie said as Jasper climbed the concrete steps onto the porch.

Jasper squinted at Barnes and spit a stream of tobacco juice onto the ground a few feet from Barnes' shoes. Biscuit let out a low growl.

"Sure do," Jasper said. "Went to school with him. Never did care much for him, though."

"Zane was just threatening me."

Jasper straightened and his eyes hardened. "Threatening you? How do you mean?"

"Roscoe had a will that left all his land and property to me. Zane isn't happy about it. He was just saying something about the cost is going to be higher than I can imagine. Isn't that what you said, Zane? Higher than I can imagine?"

Barnes' chin dropped slightly. He suddenly looked like a child caught in a lie.

"That right, Zane Barnes?" Jasper said. "You threatening my niece?"

"No," Barnes said, "of course not. I was just talking to her, trying to reason with her, that's all." The edge was gone; his voice had taken on a higher pitch.

"So you're saying she's lying? You're calling her a liar, right here to her face?"

"I'm not calling her a liar. There's just been a misunderstanding. It's a complicated situation."

Jasper moved back down the steps, his dog beside him. He stopped a few feet from Barnes, pointed a spindly finger at him. Charlie had never thought of Jasper as an intimidating figure. The overalls, the cap, the sneakers. It didn't really fit. But his posture was one of aggression. The atmosphere was almost electric. There was an aura of danger in the air.

"I've known you all your life, and there ain't a bit of good in you," Jasper said in a tone that frightened even Charlie. "There ain't an ounce of truth in you, either. What you need to do right now is haul your sorry carcass back to that fancy car of yours and get on out of here. If I catch you here again, I'll skin you and mount you on a mannequin."

Barnes needed no further prodding. He turned without saying a word and hurried toward the Mercedes. Ten seconds later, he was gone.

Charlie stood silently as Jasper climbed the steps again. She didn't know what to say.

"Ain't nobody gonna mess with my Peanut," Jasper said as walked past her. "Not while I'm breathing."

CHAPTER TWENTY-FIVE

About half-an-hour after Zane Barnes left, Charlie heard another vehicle. Her stomach fluttered because she knew it would be him. She looked out the kitchen window and saw Jack Dillard's red Jeep. She had texted him earlier and asked him to come visit her on the mountain. He'd said he would, so she had texted him the address and he'd found the place.

In her mind, Charlie likened her history of dealing with men to the history of the lost colony of Roanoke Island – brief and uncertain. She could count the number of men (both of them were boys, really) she'd slept with on two fingers. As a teen, she'd been tall and bony and awkward and flat-chested and smart, a combination that didn't exactly attract the attention of boys. She was a classic ugly duckling, didn't fill out until she was a junior in high school at the age of seventeen. When she returned to school after the summer, she noticed a distinct change in the boys' attitudes toward her, but by that time she found them silly and boring. She'd dated a boy named Dustin Hanks during her freshman year in college and lost her virginity to him, but as soon as she slept with him he became possessive and abusive and she ended it shortly thereafter. She kept her distance from boys after that, although she sometimes fantasized and often dreamed about them. The only other time she'd slept with a man was two nights before she graduated from law school. She'd gone to a party at a bar in the Old City in Knoxville and wound up taking her first shots of tequila. A blurry night followed, memories of flirting and dancing with a second-year law student, awakening in his apartment the next morning naked with him lying next to her and no memory of anything that occurred after midnight.

Jack Dillard was unlike any man she'd ever met. He was beautiful – tall and muscular and dark haired and dark eyed with a chiseled face, deep dimples and an easy, honest smile – but more than that, much more than that, he was funny and intelligent and unassuming and had a gentleness about him that made her feel safe and comfortable in his company. She knew the romance, if it really was a romance, was in its early stages and that they had much more to learn about each other, but even with everything else that had happened to her recently, she'd found herself thinking about him constantly. They'd been to dinner, they'd been to a movie, and they had texted back and forth hundreds of times already, and she had yet to find a single thing about him that she didn't like. He was a perfect gentleman, almost chivalrous, and Charlie found that endearing.

Charlie went out the back door onto the porch and down the steps while she watched Jack get out of the Jeep and start walking. He was wearing blue jeans and a black T-shirt with "Vanderbilt Baseball" written in gold across the front.

"Hey," Charlie said as Jack approached.

"Hey yourself," he said.

She wanted to drape her arms around his neck and hug him, but she restrained herself. Jack reached out with both hands and she took them in hers.

"Nice place," he said.

"I told you I lived in the boonies."

"I like it. It's beautiful up here. It smells fantastic. And so do you."

Charlie felt herself blushing.

"You look nice," she said.

"Really? Thanks. You look ... you look ... like you always do. Incredible."

Charlie held onto Jack's right hand and started pulling him toward the back porch.

"I want you to meet my uncle," she said. "He's a little different, okay? Don't freak out."

"Different how?"

"You'll see. I'd invite you into the house but I'm a little ashamed of how it looks in there right now. My uncle is a bit of a hoarder."

"I think you mentioned that."

"Hang on, stay right here."

Charlie walked up the steps to the door, opened it, and yelled, "Uncle? Uncle! Will you come out here for a minute?" She walked back down the steps and a few seconds later Jasper stepped onto the porch followed by his massive wolfhound. The dog came down off the porch and sniffed Jack's pants for a few seconds, then wandered off toward the barn.

"I'd like you to meet someone," Charlie said. "This is my friend Jack Dillard. Jack, this is my uncle, Jasper Story."

To Charlie's surprise, Jack walked up the steps and offered his hand to Jasper. "It's nice to meet you, sir," Jack said. The two men were about the same height, although Jack was much broader.

Jasper shook Jack's hand and Charlie was pleased to see just a hint of a smile cross his lips. "Good to meet you, too, young feller," he said.

There was a brief silence before Jack said, "Charlie has told me a lot about you."

"Has she, now? She ain't mentioned you to me."

"That isn't true and you know it," Charlie said.

"Must have slipped my mind," Jasper said. He turned his gaze back to Jack. "You courtin' my niece?"

"Yes, sir, I am. Well, I'm trying anyway."

"Say your name is Dillard?" Jasper looked at Charlie. "Ain't that lawyer you're working for named Dillard? Is this him?"

"His son," Charlie said. "Jack is Joe Dillard's son."

"You a lawyer?" Jasper said.

"Not yet," Jack said. "I'm in law school. Working on it."

"I ain't never had much use for lawyers."

"Uncle!" Charlie said. "*I'm* a lawyer. Well, almost."

"Didn't mean nothing by it, Peanut," Jasper said. "I'm just sayin' I ain't never used a lawyer in my life."

"Everybody hates lawyers," Jack said. "Until they need one."

"You gonna give him a tour of the place?" Jasper said to Charlie.

"I was planning to. Everything but the house."

"Ain't much else to see other than the barn and my shop. You ain't planning on showing him my shop, are you?"

"No, uncle, I wouldn't dream of it."

"Good. Nice to meet you, young feller." With that, Jasper turned and disappeared back inside the house.

"C'mon," Charlie said. "I'll give you the grand tour."

They walked slowly around the edge of the property for the next half hour, holding hands, taking in the beautiful views of the mountains. The cloud cover had started to thin and streaks of light from the setting sun slipped through and bounced off the distant peaks. Eventually they made their way to the barn where Charlie introduced Jack to Sadie.

"Do you ride?" she asked.

"I used to," Jack said. "My mom and dad bought my sister a horse when she was ten. Quarter horse like Sadie, but he was a black gelding. His name was Tasmanian Devil, but we just called him Taz."

"Your sister's name is Lilly?"

"Right. We both rode him every day for a while, but Lilly fell off one day and wound up with a concussion. Talked in circles for hours. We took her to the emergency room at the hospital and one of the doctors started telling my parents horror stories about people he'd treated that had been kicked by horses or thrown off horses. It freaked my dad out so much that he wound up selling the horse. He told Lilly he wouldn't be able to live with himself if she got hurt seriously or killed."

"How did she take losing the horse?"

"It broke her heart, but I think she was a little relieved, to tell you the truth. She was young, and Taz was a lot of horse."

"We'll have to go for a ride soon," Charlie said. "We can ride double. Sadie won't mind."

"Sounds like a plan. You drive."

Charlie smiled and took Jack's hand.

"I had a meeting with your father yesterday," she said. "Did he mention it to you?"

"Yesterday? Where did you meet?"

"At his office."

"He didn't say anything to me about it. What were you meeting about?"

"I found something. I probably shouldn't tell you about it, but I already know I can trust you and I just can't bear this alone. I have to make some difficult decisions and I need someone to talk to. I just ... I just ... I need *help*, Jack. Will you help me?"

"Are you in some kind of trouble?"

"I don't know. I mean, no, I'm not in trouble, but what I found could cause some trouble, I guess. I haven't done anything wrong, though. Nothing illegal or immoral or anything like that. You remember the other day when the courier came to the office? After Roscoe killed himself? There was a map in the envelope. It was a map of Roscoe's property and it led to a cave on the mountain and I followed it. I followed the map, Jack, and I found something."

Charlie studied Jack's face carefully. He was looking at her steadily. There was no sign of amusement, no sign of alarm, no sign of judgment. He was taking her seriously.

"Do you want to know what I found?" Charlie said.

"If you want me to."

Charlie held on to Jack's hand and started walking toward the trunk where she had stashed the bar of gold. She let go of his hand, bent over and opened the trunk, and pulled out the saddle blanket that contained the bar.

"Brace yourself," she said. "You're not going to believe this."

CHAPTER TWENTY-SIX

The machine filled the room, and the room wasn't small. It was a quiet monster, given to hums and clicks instead of roars and growls. It was a diagnostic, bone-scanning, imaging machine, one that would tell us whether Caroline's cancer had spread over the past three months. We were at Vanderbilt University in Nashville, engaging in the same ritual we'd been engaging in every three months for the past year, since her breast cancer had metastasized to her bones. We would avoid talking about it until a day or two before the next test. We'd talk about it briefly, express hope that the results would be good. We'd load up in the car, make the four-hour drive largely in silence.

"Don't try to interpret what you see on the screen," the heavy-set, male nurse said to me just before he disappeared into an anteroom filled with computer screens.

"I know what the lights mean," I said. "We've been through this before."

"All I'm saying is that you're not a doctor. Let the doctors worry about it."

"Right," I said, and he closed the door behind him. I watched through the large, glass panel as he sat down and started pushing buttons.

"You okay?" I said to Caroline. She was lying on her back on a long table that was attached to the machine.

"I'm good."

The table began to slide toward a large tube as a steel panel began to lower itself toward her head. Within seconds, I couldn't see her face. The bone scan would take thirty minutes. Three hours earlier, Caroline had been given a drink that was filled with radioactive isotopes. Those isotopes had attached themselves to the cancer cells inside her body, and when the machine sent electromagnetic waves through her, the isotopes lit up on a computer monitor that was mounted on the wall across from where I was sitting. Less than five minutes into the scan, I saw the first, faint glow in her skull. It was still there. The cancer was still there. Then another in her shoulder near her right clavicle. Then two more, one in each humerus. A brighter glow in her spine where the tumors had already caused three vertebrae to fracture. Two more in her legs.

"How does it look?" It was Caroline's voice from beneath the panel.

"Looks good, baby. Hasn't spread. At least I don't think it has."

"So that's a good thing."

"Yes. Yes. That's a good thing."

"But it's still there."

"It is."

"That's a bad thing."

"Could be worse. It could be a whole lot worse."

"I love you, Joe."

"I love you, too, baby."

CHAPTER TWENTY-SEVEN

More than a week had passed since Johnny and Carlo's meeting with Big Legs Mucci. Tommy Maldonado had lit up both of their cell phones looking for the weekly tribute, but they'd ignored the calls. It was 1:15 a.m. on Monday morning when they walked out of Quattro's bar on South Thirteenth Street, a place they'd been going every Sunday night for the past two months. It was a bar frequented by locals around their age, mostly blue collar types. The beer was cold, the music loud, the girls hot, and, for the most part, friendly. The Sunday crowd wasn't as big as Saturday's, but Johnny and Carlo were always busy with the drug trade on Saturday night. Sunday was the best day to party, even though the bar shut down at one. Both of them were drunk, especially Carlo, who had started a little early and had knocked back fifteen beers.

Their apartment on Passyunk was just over a mile away, so when the weather wasn't bad, they walked home, past Methodist Hospital and South Philadelphia High School. They'd just crossed West Moyamensing, less than a block from the bar, when four men stepped out onto the sidewalk from a parking lot on their right.

The night was cloudy and there was only one streetlight at the corner behind them, so Johnny didn't recognize any of the men until he got closer. Tommy Maldonado was flanked by three bruisers Johnny had never seen. He and Carlo stopped about five feet from them.

"Been trying to get ahold of you guys," Maldonado said.

"Yeah? What do you want?" Carlo spoke. Johnny could practically feel him seething.

"You forgot to pay me yesterday."

Johnny heard footsteps behind him. He turned. Four more men approached, one of them Big Legs Mucci.

"We ain't paying," Carlo said.

"That's what I heard," Maldonado said. "Yo Bobby, what else did they say? Something about soft? People don't respect us no more? What was that other thing?"

"Welfare gangsters," Mucci said as he and the three men with him fanned out around Johnny and Carlo. "They called us welfare gangsters."

Johnny looked around quickly. They could probably break through the men and run, but there was no point. The same thing would eventually happen again, maybe tomorrow, maybe next week. This was inevitable after the insults he and Carlo had hurled at Mucci. The way Johnny saw it, they could either start asking for forgiveness and pony up, or they could stand their ground and fight

"So it's like this?" Carlo said. "Eight of you against the two of us?"

"Yeah," Maldonado said, "it's like this. You need to learn to respect your elders. Some manners, you know?"

"You're about to find out how much respect I got for you."

Johnny and Carlo instinctively put their backs to the fence. They'd been in many fights, even a few involving knives and chains, but they'd never faced so many guys. And these guys were big, all of them older. He eyed them, looking for weapons, waiting for somebody to make the first move. His fingers were tingling, his vision narrowing as the adrenaline began to pump. He decided he'd go straight at the guy directly to his left, try to knock him out, and then see what happened from there. The group of men had backed up a couple of steps and formed a semi-circle with Mucci and Maldonado in the center. Johnny noticed that both of them had their right hands behind their backs. He wondered briefly whether he was about to be shot, but if they intended to shoot him and Carlo, why would they bring eight guys?

It happened quickly. Mucci and Maldonado pulled their hands from behind their backs simultaneously. Yeah, they had guns. But instead of gunshots, Johnny heard two clicks. His body exploded with pain, his muscles tightened into knots, and he felt himself falling forward onto his face. He realized he'd been tasered. Time seemed to drag from that moment forward. He was helpless on the sidewalk, became conscious of more pain, this of a different kind. He tried to move but couldn't. They were kicking him now, stomping, cursing. He felt a rib crack, saw a flash as one of them caught him flush in the temple. At some point he was able to control his body again, but by that time all he could do was draw his knees up to his chest, try to cover his head with his arms, and wait for it to be over. He could hear men close by doing the same thing to Carlo that these men were doing to him. The blows kept coming and coming and coming. There was another flash, and then, mercifully, darkness.

But the darkness didn't last. Johnny floated back into consciousness. The taste of blood was on his tongue, pain like fire stung his back, his jaw, his arms and legs. Someone was pulling his hair, lifting his face. He opened his eyes. A blurry image appeared, Maldonado's face. Johnny smelled stale beer, tobacco.

"You do business here, you pay the money." The voiced hissed like a poisonous snake. "You don't pay, you're gonna end up like your old man."

CHAPTER TWENTY-EIGHT

On Monday, Charlie put the map and the letter that had accompanied Roscoe's will in a safety deposit box at Elizabethton Federal Bank. Then she drove to Jonesborough to Joe Dillard's office, which was now also her office. Joe and Jack had set her up with a nice little desk, a personal computer and a land line phone that she doubted she would ever use.

She and Jack had talked for hours, deep into the night. Jack was torn between following his father's advice to turn the gold over to the court and smuggling it out of the cave and converting it to cash, or at least some of it. Both of them were planning on spending the morning doing research on setting up off shore businesses and bank accounts. Although she didn't believe anyone would ever find the gold, Charlie still wanted to get it out of the cave, converted to cash, and then get the cash out of the country into an off shore account. She believed she would be far better off than having the gold in a place where someone might be able to take it from her, legally or otherwise, although she just didn't see how anyone else could have a legitimate legal claim. She had Roscoe's will, it made her the sole heir to his estate, and his estate included the gold. She also had the letter and the map, both of which proved that Roscoe intended for her to have the gold. Why should she allow Zane Barnes and his lawyer to drag her through the court system for years, maybe even a decade? It wasn't fair. It just didn't make any sense to her.

Jack had agreed with her, to a point, but he'd been more cautious. He had suggested that she leave the gold right where it was. It had been there for decades, he said, it wasn't going anywhere. He had suggested that Charlie at least wait until she learned what Zane Barnes and his lawyer were going to do before she made any decisions about the gold. From what Charlie had described about where the gold was located, Jack believed she couldn't find a better hiding place. Why not just leave it there for a while? Let things calm down, see what happens with Zane, and then figure out what to do. Charlie had reluctantly agreed to wait before removing any more bars from the cave, but she had insisted on figuring out a way to cash in the bar she had already removed. It was worth more than half-a-million dollars. With that money, she could hire the best probate lawyer in the state to fight Zane Barnes and Nathaniel Mitchell, if that was what she ultimately decided to do.

There was a diner just around the corner from the office called "Granny's." Mr. Dillard had told her it was owned and operated by his sister, Sarah, and that the food was good, so Charlie decided to stop in to get some breakfast. She parked her battered Ford Ranger pick-up truck in front of the office and walked around the corner. She sat at a table near the far wall and ordered blueberry pancakes, bacon and milk from a college-age black girl who introduced herself as Rosemary. A pretty, dark-eyed brunette was collecting money at the cash register, and Charlie heard one of the other waitresses call her Sarah from across the room. Charlie got up and walked over.

"Are you Joe Dillard's sister?" Charlie said.

"Depends on what he's done to you," the woman said.

"I'm Charlie Story." Charlie offered her hand. "I'm working with him now."

"Ah, so you're the one Caroline told me about. The one that sets little Jack's heart all a flutter. She was certainly right about you being pretty."

Charlie felt herself blushing. "I don't know about—"

"It's nice to meet you," Sarah said. "Joe was in here a couple of days ago. He told me about you, too. He said nice things."

There was another person waiting behind Charlie to pay so she walked back to her table. She settled into the comfortable buzz around her and opened the *Quarter Horse Journal* that was folded in her purse. She read an article about training and ate slowly. When she was finished, Rosemary the waitress surprised her by telling her that her bill had already been paid.

"Who paid it?" Charlie asked.

"That guy at the end of the counter." Rosemary pointed, then shrugged. "He's gone. Don't know who he was. Never seen him before."

"What did he look like?"

"Creepy lookin'. Shaved head."

Charlie had been engrossed in her magazine and hadn't noticed him. She folded her magazine and was walking past her truck toward the office when she noticed a standard-sized, white envelope stuck under a wiper blade on the windshield. On the front of the envelope, handwritten in red ink, was "cHarlEston sTorY." There was no address, no return address, no postage, only her name. She picked the envelope up and opened it. There was one sheet of paper, torn from a yellow legal pad.

"dear mIss charleston Story you take my breath aWay. I have <u>admired</u> you for so long from afaR. I want to be with YOU alone and forever we will be <u>TOGEtHER</u>. just YOU and mE!!!!! this moRninG i was looking at the sun RisE and it made me Think of how you SmiLe and how <u>pretty you are in the morning and at night</u>!!! i can NOT get YOU ouT of my Head even if i trY to do IT does not work.

<u>DiE SLut!!!</u>

i did not mean that you KNOW because all i Can tHink about is you. i am fine and how are YOU???? <u>you are the prettiest girl i HAVe EvEr seen</u> there i SAID IT!!! and i am wishing we will bE ToGether so SOON it can make my <u>heAD Spin</u>! and I will MaKe you SpIN toooo ... !!! so gOOdBye for now ta ta i wiLL SEe you ... ... <u>SLuT</u> not really before you Know it!!!!"

Charlie looked around the parking lot and out to the street, scanning in every direction. She re-read the note as a feeling of terror crept through her limbs like a rising tide. She thought about going back into the diner but decided to go on to the office, which was only a short distance away. She stuffed the note in her purse and felt her hands shaking as she turned the key in the lock of the front door of the office. Joe wasn't there yet, and neither was Jack. She looked over her shoulder and scanned the lot again.

Clyde Dalton, the paranoid schizophrenic client she'd been appointed to represent, was the first person that had entered her mind as she read the note. Could it be him? She hadn't seen Clyde since she had appeared in court with him. Mr. Dillard had helped her make the arrangements for Clyde's mental evaluation, which was to have taken place the day after his court appearance at a mental hospital in Johnson City. Was he focusing on her now? Obsessed with her?

On the other hand, maybe it was a scare tactic being employed by Zane Barnes. Perhaps he was terrorizing her in the hope that she'd become so frightened she would abandon her claim to his father's property. She had no doubt that Barnes was capable of such a campaign. After observing first-hand what he'd done to his own father, she believed him capable of anything. But that would be too much of a coincidence. It had to be Dalton.

She stepped inside the office and locked the door behind her. Then she pulled her cell phone out of her purse and dialed Joe Dillard's number. She read the note to him, described the strange spacing and punctuation and capitalization.

"Go straight to the Jonesborough police department," Joe said. "Go see an investigator named Mike St. John. He's a good man. He probably won't be able to do a thing, but take the note in and show it to him. Tell him I sent you, and ask him to make a copy and start a file."

"Should I tell him about Clyde Dalton?"

"He already knows about Clyde. He's arrested him twice on stalking charges."

"Have you seen or talked to Clyde?"

"I talked to the doctor that did the evaluation. He called him a garden variety paranoid schizophrenic, whatever that means. They gave him his medication and his mother picked him up and took him home."

"Someone with a shaved head bought my breakfast at your sister's diner a few minutes ago. It has to be him. He must have followed me."

"Go see Mike, and then get your butt back to the office. I'm on my way, so I'll be there when you get back."

"Should I be afraid?"

"You should be careful, Charlie. I don't know that much about Clyde yet, but I'll make some calls. Just watch your back."

Joe was correct in his assertion that the police would be unable to help. Charlie spoke with Mike St. John, the investigator Joe had mentioned. He made a copy of the note, started a file, and expressed concern that Clyde Dalton could become violent. St. John said Dalton's disease seemed to be progressing and that he had become bolder with his latest stalking victim, a television weather woman named Veronica Simpson. Dalton had showed up at the television station twice and his notes had become progressively more threatening. They talked briefly about the legal elements of a stalking charge and agreed that the note, while frightening, didn't quite rise to the offense of stalking, even if they could prove that Clyde wrote it. Another note, perhaps, or a couple of incidents of unwelcome contact with Clyde, would probably classify as a misdemeanor.

Charlie left the police station and drove back to the office in a state of agitated paranoia. Her eyes moved constantly, her senses seemed heightened. Every person she saw was a potential enemy, every vehicle contained a potential danger. She'd never felt seriously threatened in her life, but now, in less than a week, she'd received two veiled messages of imminent harm.

"The cost ... will be higher than you can imagine."

"DiE SLut!!!"

As she parked in a space on the street in front of the office and got out of her truck, Charlie saw an old, faded-green Mercedes rolling through the parking lot in her direction. She ran to the door, ducked inside, and watched as the car approached. Her breath came in short gulps as it crawled by. The driver stared straight ahead until he was right in front of the door. The car stopped and the driver's head, a cue ball with eyes, turned toward her.

This was no scare tactic by Zane Barnes. It was Clyde Dalton, staring at her maniacally, smiling the same devious smile that Reynard the fox wore when he was eating Charlie's grapes.

CHAPTER TWENTY-NINE

The more Charlie thought about it – and she thought about it constantly – the more she leaned toward getting more of the gold out of the cave as quickly as possible. The morning after her encounter with Clyde Dalton, as soon as the sun peeked over the mountains to the east, Charlie saddled Sadie and headed for the cave. She was in awe, once again, of its size, its luster when exposed to light, its incredible mystique. It took her about two hours to retrieve four more bars of gold. She packed two in each saddlebag. A million bucks an hour, she thought as she climbed into the saddle. Not bad work if you can get it.

The morning was bright and breezy. Gauzy, white puffs of cirrus clouds floated across the blue sky above purple mountain ranges in the distance. Charlie decided to take a closer look at a couple of things. First, she rode Sadie around the west side of the mountain until she found the spot where the stream came out of the rocks. She followed it about a hundred yards where it fed into Tempest Creek. She rode back and climbed from the saddle, knelt and inspected the area where the water emerged from beneath the rock. It was moving slowly and was three, maybe four feet deep, about six feet across. She wondered how far it was beneath the rock to the lower chamber of the cave. Ten feet? Fifty? No way to tell.

She also wanted to check out the split oak. She passed the cave entrance and rode around the eastern side, found a way she could manage, and climbed. She emerged from a thicket of scrub pines into a clearing on top of the ridge near the oak. She reined Sadie in and stopped. The view was spectacular; the mountains stretched off into the distance all around her, almost glowing beneath the morning sun. She breathed in deeply, filling her lungs with the cool, clean air. She imagined herself on top of the entire world.

The wind began to carry a faint sound, one she didn't recognize but one that definitely didn't belong in this place. She listened carefully; it grew louder. Still quite a distance away, but definitely coming closer from the northeast, the direction of Roscoe's house. Charlie jumped down off of Sadie and led her back to the scrub thicket. She recognized the sound now, the unmistakable rumble of an internal combustion engine. A fourwheeler and a motorcycle were the only two vehicles that could possibly get around in this terrain, and the pitch of the engine was too low for a mountain bike.

Someone was coming toward her, toward the cave, toward her fortune.

Charlie's heart began to race. Should she run? Sit tight and hide? Bury the gold bars? Who was it? No one was supposed to be on Roscoe's land. *Her* land.

She stood still, listening.

The sound of the engine rose and fell with the terrain, louder when it topped a ridge, softer when it went into a valley. It came closer, three hundred yards away, maybe less, went silent. Suddenly, she saw it. A man sitting atop a four-wheeler, parked in a clearing on a ridge, panning the slopes and the valleys with a pair of binoculars. It was Zane Barnes. As the binoculars panned in her direction, they stopped suddenly. It looked as though Barnes was staring right at her. He stood on the running boards.

Charlie knelt instinctively. She was in the thicket, but she felt exposed, naked.

He saw me.

She didn't move for several seconds, although Sadie kept shifting her feet and switching her tail. Her stomach began to churn as anger boiled inside her. Barnes wasn't supposed to be on the land. She thought about confronting him, but she had two million dollars worth of gold in her saddlebags. She couldn't risk him discovering it, perhaps taking it as he'd done from Roscoe. If he somehow managed to overpower her and take it, what could she do? She couldn't go to the police. If she did, word about the gold would get out quickly.

The engine roared back to life. She listened closely. It was coming toward her. Charlie led Sadie out the far side of the thicket and climbed into the saddle. The north side of the slope was steeper and more treacherous than the south side where the cave was hidden, but Charlie had no intention of going anywhere near the cave. She leaned far back in the saddle as Sadie picked her way through scrub trees and loose rock. She could hear the rumble of the engine echoing off the slopes around her.

At the bottom of the slope, Charlie turned Sadie west and entered a stand of old-growth white oak. She loosened her grip on the reins, gave Sadie her head, and dug her heels into the horse's ribs. Sadie immediately broke into a gallop. Charlie could hear the gold bars clanking against each other in the saddlebags. Sadie was carrying an extra hundred pounds, but it didn't seem to matter. The horse was built for speed. Within minutes, Charlie was crossing Tempest Creek, back in familiar territory. Between the clanging of the gold, the beating of Sadie's hooves and the rush of the wind, she'd been unable to hear the ATV. She pulled back on the reins and listened. The engine sounded far off, but the sound once again started to crescendo. He was still coming.

Charlie guided Sadie up a steep slope into a stand of white pines, through a draw, up another slope, and along a ridge line covered in poplar. She could hear the ATV in the woods below her; Zane hadn't followed her up the slope. She took a circuitous route across rough terrain and finally made it home. Jasper was standing just inside the barn door when she led Sadie in to cool and groom her.

"Why's that horse in such a lather?" Jasper asked.

"I let her stretch her legs a little."

"What's in them saddlebags?"

Charlie sighed. The gold bars had stretched the saddlebags tight. They looked bloated, like the leathery stomach of a malnourished child.

"It's a surprise," Charlie said. She walked past him to the grooming area. Jasper followed.

"Why do you look like you just came face-to-face with a pointy-tailed devil carrying a pitchfork?"

Charlie stopped and faced him. "Why are you grilling me like I'm some kind of criminal?"

"Strange goings on around here, Peanut," he said. He picked up a piece of straw and let it dangle from his lips like a skinny cigarette. "First ol' Zane Barnes comes snooping around here threatening you, then you tell me you got some crazy man writing you notes and leaving them on your car. Just a little bit ago there was a man with binoculars on a four-wheeler stopped on the ridge up there looking this place over like he was planning an invasion. I ain't positive, but I think it was Barnes. Now you show up on a horse that looks like she's been sprayed with shaving cream, saddlebags that are stuffed with something you won't tell me about, and a look on your face that tells me something's bad wrong. So why don't you do your old Uncle Jasper a favor and let him in on what's going on?"

Charlie looked at her intuitive uncle with his furrowed brow above honest eyes. She knew Jasper cared deeply for her, that he would support her and do his best to protect her no matter what. She'd told Joe and Jack Dillard; she might as well tell Jasper.

"Let me take care of Sadie, Uncle," Charlie said, "and then you and I need to have a little talk."

CHAPTER THIRTY

Caroline planned the ambush. After I told her about Charlie and the gold, there was no way Jack was going to escape an interrogation by his mother, and there was no way I was going to avoid being a part of it. She told Jack that she wanted to fix his favorite dish, chicken cordon bleu, on Tuesday evening. When he asked her what the occasion was, she said she'd felt as though they hadn't been able to spend enough time together, that she'd been spending all her free time with our grandson and niece, and she wanted the three of us to have a nice meal together and catch up. I heard the conversation, and I knew exactly what she was doing, but I didn't say a word.

The dance school year, which ran from August to May, was over, and Caroline had some time on her hands. I'd become accustomed to doing most of the cooking at the house because Caroline worked in the evenings and she worked a lot on weekends, but she was an excellent cook. She spent the entire afternoon puttering around in the kitchen, and when she laid the food out on the table, it smelled fantastic.

"Wow, Mom, this looks great," Jack said as he dived into the chicken.

"You should have invited Charlie," Caroline said.

"I thought you wanted it to be just the three of us."

"I want to meet her."

"You will," Jack said.

"When?"

"I don't know. Soon."

"I understand she's come into some money."

Jack looked across the table at me. It was one of those "thanks a lot for throwing me under the bus" looks.

"I knew you'd tell her," he said.

I shrugged my shoulders. "I tell her everything."

"No, you don't. I seem to remember hearing you guys argue more than a few times about that very subject. She's always complained that you keep things to yourself, that you aren't open enough."

"I've changed," I said. "I've realized the error of my ways. I've adapted and I've overcome."

"So tell me about it," Caroline said.

"About what?" Jack said.

"About this new-found wealth that Charlie has come into."

"What do you want to hear? I'm sure Mister Recently-Converted-Master-of-Communication over there has already told you all about it."

"What does she plan to do with this gold? Your father tells me he advised her to turn it over to the court, but he doesn't think she's going to. Have you talked to her about it?"

"Not only have I talked to her about it, I've actually seen it," Jack said. "Well, I've seen one bar. She showed it to me when I went up there. We're looking into some different things, some options."

"What kind of options?" I said.

"First of all, Charlie says getting it out of this cave where she found it is going to be a logistical nightmare. There is literally a ton of gold stashed deep in a cave in the mountains. The terrain is so rugged you can't drive a truck or even a Jeep up there. She says we can get a four-wheeler to the cave, but we'll have to haul the gold out of the cave a couple of bars at a time. I've been thinking about it, and I can probably haul six or seven bars out at a time in a backpack. She could haul maybe half that much. We can haul a couple hundred pounds at a time on a four-wheeler, which means it would take us maybe ten trips up and down the mountain to get it all out. From there, we're thinking we could load it into her truck and my Jeep and take it to an armored car service. She doesn't want anyone to know where it came from, so we'll meet them somewhere and they can take it on to a gold broker. We're researching setting up offshore corporations and bank accounts. We think we'll form the corporation in the Caymans or someplace like that, then set up a bank account in maybe Switzerland, then take the gold to a broker and have them wire the money to the account. Once we do that, Charlie can have access to the money by using credit or debit cards or checks. She can withdraw cash. She can do whatever she wants."

"It isn't hers yet," I said. "She can't just start spending the money."

"Why?" Jack said. "Why can't she spend it? Roscoe gave it to her."

"Because Zane Barnes and Nathaniel Mitchell filed suit this morning in probate court to have the will declared invalid. It alleges undue influence, accuses Charlie of coercing Roscoe, of taking advantage of a mentally ill old man."

"Which is a load of crap," Jack said. "You know it and I know it."

"It might be a load of crap," I said, "but until a judge – or more likely an appellate court – rules in her favor, she can't spend it."

"Nobody knows she has it," Jack said, "except for the three people sitting at this table and maybe her uncle. I don't even know if she's told him yet. So unless you're planning on telling someone, she should be fine. And I don't think she's planning on going on a spending binge. We talked about it. She's going to keep it on the down low until she sees how things play out."

"You could wind up getting subpoenaed in this lawsuit," I said. "As a matter of fact, I'm sure you'll wind up being deposed by Nathaniel Mitchell. So will I. What are you planning to do if he starts asking you questions about it? Lie under oath?"

"You're damned right I will."

Caroline got up from the table, walked over to the refrigerator, and came back with a bottle of salad dressing. She didn't open the dressing; she didn't even have a salad. She did it just to break up the rhythm of the conversation and to let everyone calm down a bit. The tone of Jack's voice was getting sharp, and I could feel my own blood pressure rising.

"I have a bad feeling about it," Caroline said to Jack. "I don't see how she can think clearly under these circumstances, and I don't think you're thinking very clearly either. You're being seduced by two of the most powerful forces on earth – beauty and instant wealth – and I'm afraid you're going to wind up getting your heart broken. Why don't you break it off, or at least slow it down, until everything is resolved or until she comes to her senses and turns the money over to the court like your dad suggested?"

Jack pounded his fist on the table. Not too hard, but enough to make the silverware rattle.

"We're talking about a woman I may want to spend the rest of my life with," he said. "We're also talking about fifty million dollars. Fifty million! And you want me to just walk away because *you* have a *bad feeling*?"

"Watch your tone," I said. I loved Jack more than I can put into words, but nobody, *nobody*, talked to my wife in that tone in my presence. "Talk to your mother like that again and I'll kick your ass all over this property."

"Bring it on, old man," Jack said.

"Stop it! Both of you stop it right now! Joe, go to your study and ... study something. Jack, go to your room and do whatever it is you do in there. We'll talk about this some more when everyone has calmed down."

I got up and walked out of the room, feeling like a child who had been rebuked by a teacher in class. Jack did the same.

The food was wasted.

CHAPTER THIRTY-ONE

The door buzzed and clanged, and Charlie and Jack followed me into a small interview room walled by concrete blocks of gunmetal gray and floored in gray linoleum. I wondered how many times Charlie and Jack would visit jails and prisons during their lifetimes. Would they follow the path I had followed and defend men and women accused of terrible crimes? Would they have the stomach for it, or would they take an easier, saner route?

I hadn't mentioned the gold to Charlie since we'd first spoken about it at the office on Saturday and Jack and I hadn't spoken of it since the blow up the night before. It was Charlie's business and her problem, and while I was worried about how she seemed to be handling it, I figured if she wanted or needed my help, she would ask. In the meantime, I needed a little help from her.

I'd brought her along to meet Jordan Scott because I wanted Charlie to participate in the trial. I wanted her to help me with his defense, and more than that, I was entertaining the idea of letting her present the closing argument. It would be a crucial point in the trial – maybe the most important point – and I knew it would be risky, but there were several things about Charlie that I thought could benefit Jordan. First of all, she was bright and attractive and would appeal to any juror, male or female. Secondly, I thought the effect of a beautiful, young white woman arguing passionately on behalf of a young, black man accused of murder would be powerful. And finally, in spite of the things she was dealing with and my concern for her, there was an inner strength to Charlie – the kind of demeanor developed by people who have dealt with and overcome difficulties and tragedies – that became apparent as soon as she opened her mouth. I thought a jury would trust her, and if Jordan Scott was to be acquitted, he would need that kind of rapport between his lawyers and the jury.

I'd already talked to Charlie extensively about Jordan and the facts of the case. I'd also been in contact with Leon Bates, and as usual, Leon had come through for me. Leon had learned that there were a significant number of people in the Sullivan County Sheriff's Department who felt like Todd Raleigh had gotten exactly what he deserved, and a couple of them had been willing to smuggle out some important information.

Jordan stood and bowed slightly in Charlie's direction when we entered the interview room.

"Mr. Dillard," he said.

"This is Charlie Story," I said. "She just graduated from law school and she's going to be helping me out with your defense. This is my son, Jack. He's about to start his second year of law school and he's my law clerk. He'll be helping us with legal research and anything else we need."

Everyone shook hands and we sat down at the table.

"So how are you?" I said to Jordan.

"I can't complain."

I'd come to admire Jordan's well-mannered stoicism, his refusal to acknowledge, at least in my presence, that he was in a desperate situation. Jordan was a lightning rod in the community, a symbol of polarity that ignited passionate debates throughout the region and across the state. He'd shot a police officer – who also happened to be the son of a Sullivan County commissioner – in the head with a twelve-gauge shotgun and then had calmly called 9-1-1. He was an African American in a place where the black population was in the neighborhood of two percent. He didn't deny the killing. As a matter of fact, my impression was that under similar circumstances, he would do the exact same thing without hesitation.

I had already interviewed several people about Jordan and had yet to find anyone who had anything bad to say. As I had suspected, however, the district attorney's office – while silently grateful to Jordan for ridding the community of a human cancer and for stopping a brutal rape – was not impressed by the fact that Jordan had followed Todd Raleigh for days and that he carried a shotgun with him to the park that morning. They also took note that Raleigh was running away when Jordan shot him. They turned a deaf ear to my story of the rape of Jordan's girlfriend, the unsuccessful attempt to have Raleigh investigated, and Holly's suicide. Jordan's stalking of Raleigh and the fact that he was carrying a shotgun with him in a deserted park in the early morning were evidence of pre-meditation, they said. Vigilantism, no matter how righteous it may seem on the surface, could not be tolerated in a society so advanced as modern-day America nor a community so advanced as Kingsport, Tennessee. Jordan was facing a first-degree murder charge, and it was up to us to salvage his life.

We talked for a half-hour or so, going over details, before I said, "I have some good news for a change."

"Great," Jordan said, "let's hear it."

"A lot of people are upset by this entire ... situation. An employee of the sheriff's department smuggled out a copy of Raleigh's personnel file. He'd been reprimanded three times in the past two years for sexual harassment. They even suspended him for a week last year."

"But they didn't fire him."

"I've been told by more than one person that the relationship between Commissioner Raleigh and the sheriff runs pretty deep. They grew up together, went to school together, have been friends their entire lives. Commissioner Raleigh has put a lot of money into the sheriff's election campaigns, gotten him a lot of votes. That's why Todd Raleigh didn't get fired, and that's why they stonewalled you when you accused him of rape."

"So what's the plan?"

"It doesn't change a lot, but it's something we might be able to use depending on how things play out in court. If the district attorney comes into court and starts telling the jury about Raleigh's wonderful law enforcement record, which I'm sure he will, it'll give us an opening. I'm going to subpoena the sheriff. I'll confront him with the personnel file and then start on him about the accusation Holly made. I also managed to get my hands on the internal reports from the first two investigators you talked to."

"They wrote something down?"

"Police officers are part of government, Jordan. They cover their butts like any bureaucrat. And when they do, it leaves a trail. We're lucky to have someone on the inside helping us."

"Who is it?"

"That's a piece of information you don't need to know."

"I don't see how it will help much," Jordan said. "I mean, I killed him."

"I know. I wish you hadn't but you did, so we deal with it. Look, the prosecution has to prove that you pre-meditated the killing in order to convict you of first-degree murder. That means they're going to put on proof of your mental state. We'll do the same thing. We're going to show that you were enraged, frustrated and grieving after Holly's suicide. We're going to show that you went to the police for help and they turned you away. We'll do all of that when you testify. You're the key, Jordan. You're going to have to get on the witness stand and tell the jury everything you went through with Holly. You're going to have to tell them everything you've told me. The bottom line is that you're going to have to make them think that Raleigh deserved to die. On the surface, our defense will be that you killed Raleigh in defense of another person when you stopped the rape. But our real defense will be what's called the 'sumbitch needed killin' defense.' Jury nullification. We make the jury feel so sympathetic toward you and so angry toward Raleigh that they acquit you. It's a long shot, but it's been done before. We have a chance."

Jordan nodded. "I'll hope for the best, but I'm planning for the worst."

"Hang in there," I said. "This personnel file is good news. The first we've had in awhile."

I picked up my briefcase and pushed the button on the wall that would summon a guard. Jordan nodded slowly. He didn't seem to be listening; his mind was focused on something else.

"I appreciate everything you and Miss Story and Jack are doing," Jordan said. "But I want all of you to know that even if I end up going to prison for the rest of my life, I'll never regret what I did."

"I understand how much Holly meant to you," I said.

"That's not why I don't regret it. I suppose it's true that I acted out of a need for revenge, but something else came from it, something good."

"What's that?" I asked, expecting to hear that Jordan had found God inside the walls of the jail.

"Since the day I killed that man, no one else has been raped, and no one else will be."

CHAPTER THIRTY-TWO

C lyde Dalton pulled his Mercedes into a spot next to the Ford Ranger pick up. He'd followed her and the lawyer, Joe Dillard, along with a young man he didn't recognize, from the office to the jail at a discreet distance. It was the first time he'd seen her since he paid for her breakfast and left the note on her car. The same police officer who arrested him for stalking had showed up on his doorstep and threatened to arrest him again, and his mother had been preaching at him like an evangelist. He must stay away from Charleston Story, they said. He must *leave her alone.* But Clyde had once again stopped taking the medication that gave him headaches and made him feel like a zombie and now all he could think about was Charleston.

Clyde suspected that the Central Intelligence Agency was using satellite and microwaves to read his thoughts. They'd put out the word that he was crazy, and he couldn't get a job. If he couldn't get a job, how did they expect him to live? He was living in a vicious cycle caused by a conspiracy, a conspiracy to keep him from revealing the truth about the CIA's lies and illegal spying, and now they were trying to turn Charleston, his young lovely, against him.

She was like a star, a brilliant light in an otherwise dark universe. When she walked, she seemed to float like a swan on a moonlit pond. Her eyes were sapphires, her hair fine silk. Her voice was as soothing as a whippoorwill on a summer's evening. And her name, Charleston, ah, even the name was symphonic. He would talk to her this time instead of writing. He would profess his love face-to-face, make her understand that all the things the CIA and everyone else were saying about him were lies, that he meant her no harm, that he *loved* her.

Clyde scanned the outside of the jail, an ominous brick box with narrow, slit windows. It was after lunchtime, warm and humid. It was getting hot inside the car. He cracked a window.

"You need to kill the bitch," said a tinny voice, a voice identical to the voice of a bully named Bodie Scaggs who had tormented Clyde in high school.

"Shut up, Bodie," Clyde replied aloud inside the car.

The voice had been bothering him for years. It started around the time he graduated from high school, he wasn't exactly sure. At first, he heard it only once every five or six months. It would make suggestions, suggestions which Clyde was free to follow or ignore. But as time had gone on, as he grew older and got married and lived the life of a young insurance agent, the voice became more assertive. It was Bodie's voice that constantly suggested he drink vodka or ingest cocaine or take pills. It was Bodie's voice that ruined his marriage by telling him to do perverted and violent things to his wife. It was Bodie who first told him about the CIA and the plot, Bodie who told him to buy a gun and start practicing at the indoor range and shave his head.

Bodie spoke to him constantly now. It was a battle of wills, a battle which, at some level, Clyde knew he was losing. Clyde sometimes clawed at his ears in an effort to reach inside his brain and tear Bodie out by the roots, but Bodie was clever and elusive. The medication they'd given Clyde in the hospital had silenced Bodie for a few days, but the medication made him feel thick and lethargic, so he stopped taking it. As soon as he stopped taking it, Bodie returned.

"She's going to betray you," Bodie said. "You're going to wind up back in jail."

"No. They're using her as a patsy. They're filling her head full of lies."

"She knows the truth about you. She knows you're insane. You need to kill her before she tells everyone else."

"Shut up! Shut your mouth, Bodie!"

"She won't stop until you're in prison, or even worse, locked up on a mental ward with a bunch of droolers. She's in on it now. She's out to get you."

"I said shut up!"

"She needs to die! Be a man and kill her!"

Clyde covered his ears with his palms and shook his head violently. "I'm not listening to you," he said in a high-pitched whine. "I'm not listening to you. I'm not listening to you. You're not real. You're not real. You're not real."

"You're such a pussy," Bodie said. "Do you really believe a girl like that would have anything to do with you? She's beautiful. You look like Uncle Fester. She's smart. You have the brains of a flat rock. She's sane. You're—"

Clyde could take no more. He pushed the door open with his shoulder and got out, began pacing around the car with his head in his hands, muttering to himself and cursing Bodie. On the second trip around the car he noticed someone out of the corner of his eye. It was her, Charleston, standing dead still, no more than twenty feet away, staring at him. Joe and the other man were another fifty feet back, just coming out the door.

"Uh, uh, M-miss Story," Clyde stammered. "Charleston. I was waiting for you so I could tell you that you don't have to be afraid of me and that I would never hurt you and I think you're beautiful and we could be friends you know. I ... I ... I didn't scare you I don't think but I'm not a bad person really I'm not I'm good ..."

She was backing away, so gorgeous in the dark skirt and pink blouse. She'd dropped her briefcase and was reaching into her purse and screaming. He heard Joe yell something, paid no attention.

"Wait, wait, don't, I mean, you don't have to, don't be scared, you know?"

"What do you want from me? Why are you following me? Leave me alone or I'll have you arrested!"

"She *spoke* to him. She actually spoke to him!"

"She hates you!" It was Bodie, back in his head. "Look at her. The look on her face. She's terrified."

Charleston was holding something in her hand.

"I have pepper spray. Don't come any closer!"

"Wait, please, I just want to talk to you."

Clyde took another step toward her. Something wet hit him in the forehead; a tiny drop went into his right eye. It burned like acid. Clyde rubbed his eye with the heel of his hand, howled, and jumped up and down. Bodie was screaming at him to get the gun. Where was it? *It's in the glove compartment!* Charleston was backing toward the entrance to the jail. Joe and the other man had come up beside her and had taken her arm. A cop car was pulling into the parking lot, coming toward them. Clyde turned and hurried back to his car. He started it and drove away from her, away from the police car, away from the jail.

"Idiot!" Bodie was railing at him now. "Moron! She was five steps away and you blew it! Did you see how she was mocking you? She made a fool of you again! She pepper-sprayed you!"

Clyde nodded his head as he pulled onto the highway. "I know, I know."

"You need to kill her!"

"Next time." Clyde said. "I'll do it next time."

CHAPTER THIRTY-THREE

Sullivan County Sheriff Raymond Peale leaned back in his swivel chair and rested his black cowboy boots on top of his desk. The walls surrounding Peale were covered in law enforcement and political memorabilia: plaques, certificates, photographs. Peale, a dark-haired, dark-eyed man, weighed a muscular hundred and eighty pounds and was fond of western shirts, blue jeans and oversized belt buckles. He twisted the end of his handlebar mustache with his right hand and pushed his cowboy hat back on his large head with the other.

"I reckon we got ourselves a mole," Peale said.

Sitting on the desk near Peale's boots was a laptop computer. The computer was equipped with a receiver that captured the signal from a tiny microphone and transmitter Peale had placed in the ceiling of the attorney/prisoner interview room before Joe Dillard arrived to talk with Jordan Scott.

"How could you let this happen?"

Peale looked across the desk at Howard Raleigh, a slim, blue-eyed man with the personality and demeanor of a southern Baptist evangelist and a hairdo to match. He was a leader in the community, a county commissioner and father of Todd Raleigh, the deputy Jordan Scott had killed. Raleigh's money and influence were the primary reasons Peale remained in office. He served at Raleigh's pleasure and protected Raleigh's passion, a cockfighting ring that hosted fights every other week from June to November and from which Raleigh had earned millions.

"What do you mean, Howie?" Peale pulled his boots off the desk and leaned forward. "I didn't *let* it happen. I've got a lot of people working for me. I can't keep an eye on every one of them all the time."

"They're planning to put my boy on trial. Did you hear that? The 'sumbitch needed killin'' defense? Needed killing? Todd was murdered, Raymond, and you know it. He never raped anybody. That black boy and that trashy white girl cooked up a story because Todd caught them in the bushes together."

Peale looked down at the laptop, disgusted. Raleigh had repeated this ridiculous accusation so many times that he'd convinced himself it was true. But Peale knew better. He'd been to the crime scene, interviewed the girl. He'd seen the ski mask that covered what was left of Todd Raleigh's head. He'd destroyed the samples of blood and tissue that the medical examiner had gathered and preserved so that Jordan Scott's defense team couldn't subpoena the samples for DNA testing, and he'd urged Howard to have his son cremated so the body couldn't be exhumed. He'd also seen Todd Raleigh in action for the past several years after he'd given Todd a job, and he had fielded the complaints about sexual harassment. He'd counseled Todd, threatened him, but nothing worked. Todd was a sociopath and a rapist and Peale was glad he was dead.

"Jury will see right through it," Peale said. "They'll convict him and they'll give him the death penalty."

"Death penalty my ass. The district attorney hasn't even filed a death penalty notice yet, and I don't think he's going to. Besides, this state doesn't execute people anymore. There are men sitting on death row that have been there for more than thirty years. We're gonna wind up supporting him, feeding him, clothing him, bathing him, putting a roof over his head for fifty years."

Peale shrugged his shoulders. "Nothing we can do about that."

Raleigh stood and walked over to the wall, looked at all the photos.

"You've had a pretty good run, haven't you, Raymond?"

Peale didn't respond.

"Make a good salary, plus what I pay you and what you skim here and there. Got a nice house, nice cars, nice wife, nice kids. Be a shame if you got beat in the next election. How in the world would you pay for everything?"

"I'm not planning on losing the next election. Haven't even heard of anyone that wants to run against me."

"That could change in a hurry. Right man with the right support behind him, you could lose it all."

Raleigh's fangs were coming out, something Peale had seen many times during his life

"This black boy," Raleigh said, "something's got to be done about him. I'm not going to let them drag my son through the mud again. The newspapers have already spread enough lies."

"What do you want me to do, Howie? Go up to his cell and kill him?"

"Not exactly." Raleigh turned away from the photos and walked toward Peale. He leaned over and put his fists on top of the desk. "I want you to let him out."

"Let him out?"

"Where do you think he'd go if he escaped?"

"Most of them head straight for family or friends. I don't think he'd go far."

"Good. Let him escape. Make it look good. Then hunt him down and kill him."

CHAPTER THIRTY-FOUR

The story of Russo's gold, beneath the headline of "Could There be Gold in Them Thar Hills?" and beneath the byline of Ted Sams, was published in both the print and online editions of *The Carter County Comet* on Thursday morning. It was picked up by the Associated Press in the afternoon and circulated nationwide.

By Friday morning, the online version had made its way before the eyes of Isabella Greatti, formerly Isabella Russo, in Atlanta. She immediately called her mother in Philadelphia, who found the story online and immediately called her son, Johnny. By the time Johnny Russo finished reading the story, his mouth had dropped open and limitless possibilities were running through his mind. He called Carlo Lanzetti.

"Who's that guy with Donnie Blue's crew?" Johnny said.

"What guy?" Carlo said.

"That guy! The hacker. The geek. The one they say can find out anything about anybody."

"You talking about Reno?"

"Yeah, yeah, Reno. That's him. We need to get with him today. Right now."

"Reno's a tool. I don't want to have nothing to do with him."

"I don't care if he's a tool, Carlo. We need him. You're tight with Donnie Blue, right?"

"Need him for what? He's a dick with ears, that guy. Thinks he's smarter than everybody—"

"Shut up and listen. My ma called me a little while ago. She read this story on the internet. It's out of a little county in Tennessee about some gold. Ma thinks it might be the gold my great-great-great grandfather Carmine left with a hick bootlegger back in the day."

"What are you talking about?" Carlo said. "You high or something?"

"I need to find out everything I can about these people down in Tennessee. This guy named Barnes and this girl named Story. I need to know everything there is to know about them, and Reno can do that for me. I want you to make the contact through Donnie Blue and set up a meet."

"I still got no clue what the hell you're talking about."

"I'm talking about gold, Carlo!" Johnny could feel his face reddening. He was screaming into the phone. "Maybe fifty million dollars in gold that rightfully belongs to my family! Are you gonna help me get it or are you gonna jerk me around?"

"Damn, man, take it easy. You don't gotta yell at me like that."

"Listen close, Carlo," Johnny said. "I'm gonna talk slow so maybe you can understand me. There might be fifty million in gold hidden in Tennessee. If it's really there, me and you are going to go get it, but before we go,

I need to know as much as I can about the people I'll be dealing with. *Capisci*?"

"What do you need to know anything about anybody for? If the gold belongs to you, we just go take it, right? We kill anybody who tries to stop us."

"Carlo, if you don't set up a meet with Reno in the next five minutes, I swear on my mother I'm going to find you and shoot you in the head."

"Listen to you threatening me," Carlo said. "Ain't you the one that's always telling me I shouldn't be so quick to violence?"

"Get it done," Johnny hissed, "and call me back as soon as you have it set up."

CHAPTER THIRTY-FIVE

I went with Charlie while she reported the second incident with Clyde Dalton to the same police officer, Mike St. John. His question to her was whether she felt legitimately threatened by Clyde during the encounter, to which she replied honestly, "I was terrified. He looked so ... so ... deranged."

"Okay, we'll arrest him," St. John had said.

The next morning, Charlie, Jack and I were all in the office preparing for Jordan Scott's trial. Jack and Charlie were researching legal issues and I was going over written summaries of interviews with potential witnesses I'd already conducted. Each of us were in our separate offices when I heard the tone that told me someone was walking through the front door. Thinking back on it, I suppose leaving the door unlocked had been stupid because I hadn't heard anything from Mike St. John about Clyde Dalton being arrested, which meant he was still on the street.

As soon as I heard the beep tone, I got up and walked toward the door that separated my office from the foyer. Before I got to the door, I heard three gunshots.

Pop! Pop!

Pop!

I pulled the door open and burst through, not thinking about myself. Charlie was in danger. My *son* was in danger. I saw Clyde Dalton as soon as I cleared the door, his face expressionless, his eyes as dull as sandstone. He raised his right arm and there was a deafening explosion. I saw the flash, felt the shock wave of a bullet passing by my left ear. I picked up one of the two small chairs in the foyer, heard myself curse, and threw the chair at him as another gunshot rocked the short hallway. I rushed him and got my right shoulder into him. He bounced off the wall as I slipped on the carpet and fell to my knees.

Then I heard Jack's voice, pained, almost pitiful: "I'm shot. Oh God, I'm shot."

Time suspended. Endless seconds. I scrambled into Jack's office. He was sitting in his chair, his face white, his left hand covering his upper chest and neck. I forgot all about Clyde as I knelt beside Jack.

"It went through," he said. "I think it went right through me."

I sensed someone behind me and turned, ready to throw myself at Clyde Dalton again. It was Charlie, her face contorted by fear.

"He went out the back door," she said.

"Call nine-one-one," I said, and I turned back to Jack. Dark, red blood was oozing from Jack's white shirt near his collarbone. I reached out and gently lifted Jack's hand, pulled his shirt away from the wound. The hole was small and almost black with red blood oozing from it.

"I'm going to raise your shoulder a little," I said. "I need to look at the back."

Jack groaned as I lifted his shoulder. I saw nothing, so I lifted his right arm. There was a pink hole the size of a silver dollar. I could hear Charlie's frantic voice over my shoulder: "There's been a shooting ... Yes ... Charleston Story ... Joe Dillard's office ... *Calm!* What are you talking about? Get somebody down here! No, no, he's gone! He walked out the back door! Jack's been shot! He's bleeding! Please hurry!"

"It came out under your arm," I said to Jack as calmly as I could. "We need to get you onto the floor and get your feet up. I don't want you to go into shock."

I helped Jack out of the chair and onto his back on the floor.

"Charlie, there's a first aid kit under the sink in the bathroom. Bring it to me. And grab my jacket. It's on the chair in front of my desk."

"Talk to me, Jack," I said. "Does anything else hurt? Are you hit anywhere else?"

"I don't think so. I'm sorry, dad, I didn't ... it just happened so—"

"You don't have anything to be sorry about," I said. "Just lie still now. You're going to be fine. Hear the sirens? The EMTs are almost here."

Charlie brought me the first-aid kit and the jacket. I rolled the jacket up and placed it beneath Jack's ankles, and I pressed gauze into the wounds, applying pressure to slow the bleeding. Then the door burst open and the placed filled with commotion. Police officers with guns drawn barked at us and at each other while the EMTs took me by the arm and helped me up so they could attend to Jack. Charlie was crying, mumbling something about it being her fault. Mike St. John appeared at my elbow.

"Did you see who it was?" he asked.

"It was him."

"Him? You mean Dalton?"

"Yes."

"Are you sure?"

"I'm positive. He tried to kill me."

"We'll get him."

"You better. He shot my son. If you don't get him, I will."

"Don't talk like that, Joe. We'll take care of it."

"He shot my son," I said. "The crazy son of a bitch shot my son."

CHAPTER THIRTY-SIX

L ater that evening, after we'd spent the day at the hospital and were sure Jack would be all right, I offered Charlie a ride home. The doctor who worked on Jack said the bullet had bounced off of his collar bone, fracturing it in the process, and had traveled straight down and out beneath his arm. It had done some damage to tissue, but the doctor said Jack should be "as good as new" in a couple of months. I spent the day alternating between beating myself up for leaving the office door unlocked and thinking of the terrible things I wanted to do to Clyde Dalton. I tried to keep the anger bottled up and focus on Jack and the rest of my family, but Caroline had mentioned more than once during the day that she was more worried about me and what I might do than she was about Jack.

Leon Bates had come to the hospital late in the afternoon to check on Jack, but he had stayed so long that I suspected he was also there to keep an eye on me. When Charlie accepted my offer of a ride home, Leon had volunteered to follow us in her truck and ride back with me. I was trying to keep the conversation light with Charlie. She, too, had been through a terrifying experience. Two of the bullets Clyde Dalton fired had narrowly missed her and had lodged themselves in the wall behind her desk. I'd heard her tell the police that she had crawled beneath her desk and was waiting for Clyde to walk in and kill her when I walked out of my office and distracted him.

"So tell me more about this uncle I've heard you talk about," I said.

"He's different," Charlie said. "Eccentric is probably a good word."

"Eccentric how?"

"Do you know anything about Irish wolfhounds?"

"Just that they're huge."

"Jasper loves Irish wolfhounds. He's had four of them that I can remember. They don't live long, anywhere from five to seven years. He names them all Biscuit. The dog he has rides in his truck with him all the time and hangs his head out the passenger window. It's a sight to see. He's also a master taxidermist. He looks at what he does as a kind of post-mortem fountain of youth. He says he preserves beauty. He takes a lot of pride in it."

"How does he do it?" I asked. "I've never been around a taxidermist. I have no idea how they do what they do."

"Jasper is secretive about it, won't let anybody set foot in his shop. But from what I've heard him say, the most important part is skinning the animal perfectly and preserving the hide perfectly. He tans the hides different ways – salt baths and chemicals he's developed over the years. He incinerates the bones and the internal organs, and then takes the hides and mounts them on mannequins."

"Mannequins? They have deer mannequins?"

"Yeah, and bear and squirrel and fish and everything else. They make eyes and jaws and teeth and noses, even tongues. I've actually heard him ordering tongues over the telephone. I think he basically skins the animal and then reconstructs it using all these artificial parts. I've seen some of his finished work. He's an artist, really. I heard him threaten to skin a man and mount him on a mannequin not too long ago. I'll bet he could do it, too, and make whoever he mounted look as good, or even better, than they did when they were alive."

"That's a little creepy, Charlie."

"I'm not saying he would, but he could."

Joe dropped Charlie off just before dark. The last thing he said before she got out of his truck was not to worry, that the police would have Clyde Dalton in custody before morning. Jasper was walking out of his shop when they pulled in. He walked over to Charlie as she stood next to her truck and watched Dillard drive away.

"Who was that, Peanut?"

"My boss."

"Everything all right? You look a little washed out."

"Let's go inside."

While Charlie heated some leftover lasagna and Jasper made a salad, she told him about the day's events. He received the bizarre news quietly, asking few questions and making no comments. When they sat down to eat, Charlie said, "Joe told me at the hospital that he thinks maybe I should leave until they catch Clyde Dalton."

Jasper considered this briefly. He nodded.

"Fine idea," he said. "Get you out of harm's way until somebody can deal with this crazy man. You reckon he might show up here?"

"I don't know. After what happened today, it wouldn't surprise me."

"Wouldn't be healthy for him."

"Do you really think I should go away? I hate the thought of letting anybody chase me out of my own life."

"It'll just be temporary, Peanut. Better safe than sorry, right?"

"Why don't you come with me?"

Jasper shook his head. "You know better than that. Besides, who would take care of your horse and Biscuit?"

"We could board them."

"Thanks, but I reckon I'll just stay right here. What are you gonna do about the rest of that gold up on the mountain?"

When Charlie told Jasper about the gold, she had drawn the map Roscoe gave her from memory. Jasper had hunted on Roscoe's land for decades. He said he knew exactly where the hourglass rock was, but he'd never noticed the cave. Charlie had described it to him, the vast chambers, the stream at the bottom, the still. She'd offered to show him, but he declined.

"I don't know, uncle," she said. "I still have five bars in the barn, but I'm not sure what to do with it. I really don't know what I'm going to do."

"I been thinking about it a lot. It's blood money, Peanut. Bad juju."

"You aren't the first person to say that."

Jasper stuffed a fork full of lasagna into his mouth. "Zane Barnes is still looking for it, you can bet on that."

"Doesn't matter. He won't find it."

"You oughta just let him have it. If it's cursed, let the curse fall on him."

"Not going to happen, uncle. Roscoe didn't want him to have a bit of it."

"Then hire somebody to blow the mouth of the cave shut. Seal it off and be done with it once and for all."

Charlie wasn't really surprised by Jasper's indifference to the gold. He'd never cared about wealth. He was satisfied with himself and the way he lived.

"Do you ever think about leaving here?" Charlie asked.

"Leaving? You mean for good?"

"Yeah, moving away somewhere and starting fresh."

"Ain't no such thing as starting fresh," Jasper said. "You've already made your mark in this life. What's past is past, but that don't mean it's gone. You can't just wipe the board clean."

"Maybe not, but—"

"Where would you go?" Jasper asked.

"I'm not sure. Someplace where the horizon is bigger. The mountains make me feel cut off sometimes, kind of closed in."

"I love the mountains. They ain't for everybody, but I love 'em."

"I know you do."

"Wouldn't leave 'em for nothing. Speaking of leaving, where you gonna go on this little vacation of yours?"

"I'm not sure I'm going on vacation."

"Go, Peanut. Tomorrow morning. Get in your truck or get on a plane or a train and go. Don't even think about this place for a while."

Charlie thought for a minute and smiled.

"If you aren't going anywhere, then neither am I," she said. "I'm not letting anybody run me off."

Jasper washed the last bite of his lasagna down with a swig of sweet tea.

"Figured as much," he said. "Reckon we'll just stay here and if it comes to it, we'll make our stand together."

CHAPTER THIRTY-SEVEN

Jordan Scott heard heavy footsteps coming down the hallway, a key turning the lock on his cell door. He threw his feet over the side of his bunk and sat up. He didn't know exactly what time it was, but it was late. Supper had been slid through the slot in the door hours ago. There was no good reason for a guard to be entering his cell.

Jordan was being held in a segregation unit "for his own protection," according to the guards. The cell was forty-eight square feet with a stainless steel bunk, toilet and sink. He was not allowed to have a television or a radio. He was not allowed to purchase items from the commissary. Had it not been for his mother going to the newspaper and complaining, he wouldn't even have the books she sent him. He wasn't let out for exercise, so he did push-ups and sit-ups and ran in place in his cell. He wasn't allowed to use the phone. His parents visited once a week for fifteen minutes. He talked to them through Plexiglas. He met with his lawyers when they came to the jail. He was served two meals a day, always cold and tasteless. He showered once a week. He'd lived this way since his arrest.

"Get your clothes on," the guard said.

The hallway was dimly lit and the cell was dark. Jordan didn't recognize the guard's voice or his shadowy form.

"What's going on?"

"I said get your clothes on!"

Jordan's striped jumpsuit was folded on the floor. He stood and put it on slowly.

"Turn around. Hands back."

Jordan felt the cold steel of the handcuffs wrap around his wrists. He'd expected to be killed by a guard or an inmate since the day he was arrested. It looked like the time had come. The guard jerked his elbow, turned him toward the door, and stuck a nightstick into the small of his back.

"Walk."

The cell block was silent except for the usual clinks and bangs in the old building. The regular guard wasn't sitting behind the desk in the corridor. The man holding Jordan's arm smelled of tobacco and cheap cologne. He guided Jordan out of the block, through a labyrinth of hallways and down three flights of steps into a dark room. He flipped on a flashlight and Jordan walked past a humming boiler. He climbed a short set of steps and was pushed through another door. Jordan felt the cool night air. The guard unlocked the handcuffs, stepped back.

"They're planning to kill you," the guard said. "I can't let that happen."

"I don't understand."

"Take this." He held out a small cell phone. "It's pre-paid. Nobody can trace it. It's already turned on. Get out of here. Hide in the woods back there and call somebody to come pick you up. Don't let them find you."

Jordan looked down at the phone, back up at the guard. He couldn't see him very well in the darkness, but he could tell he was maybe thirty, average size, wearing the black uniform that all the guards wore, a black ball cap pulled down low on his forehead.

"No," Jordan said, "take me back inside."

"Didn't you hear what I said? They're planning to kill you before daylight. If you stay in this jail, you're going to die."

"How do I know you won't shoot me if I run?"

"I'm not going to shoot you. How the hell would I explain you being out here in the first place? I'm trying to help you. If you want to live, run."

The guard turned and walked back through the door, closing it behind him. Jordan reached for the doorknob. It was locked. He looked around frantically. There was no moon, no wind. It was absolutely still. He put his back against the door, felt the coolness of the metal through his jumpsuit. His eyes began to adjust to the darkness. He could make out a tree line, black and ominous against the night sky.

Hide in the woods back there and call somebody ...

He was unshackled, no handcuffs, but he felt as though there was a bulls eye on his back. He ran for the trees, made it, and knelt next to an oak. He punched numbers into the cell phone with trembling fingers. His father's sleepy voice came on the line.

"Pops, it's me."

"Jordan?"

"I'm out."

"What do you mean, out?"

"A guard let me out. He said they were going to kill me tonight. Told me to run. I don't know what's going on, but please come get me, Pops. I'm scared."

CHAPTER THIRTY-EIGHT

Jasper turned out the light in his shop and stepped outside. The mountain air was cool and fresh, the stars sparkling above. The moon was full, a pale, white, small globe high in the sky. It was well after midnight. He didn't usually work so late, but he'd been unable to sleep after hearing about Peanut's scare earlier in the day. He'd waited until he had heard her steady breathing in her bedroom and had gone out to his shop. He'd spent the last few hours working on placing the antlers on a bull elk mount that he was doing for a rich horse rancher from Lexington, Kentucky. The rancher had shot the animal in Colorado, and as soon as he got it out of the field he had it frozen and shipped to Jasper. Jasper had been working on it for months. The rancher wanted the entire thing mounted, not just the head, and he wanted it mounted in a "natural" setting. It was a challenge, but Jasper was pleased with the way it was turning out. He'd have it finished in a few weeks.

He secured the padlock on the shop door and started walking toward the barn to check on Sadie before he turned in. Biscuit had spent the evening in the shop with him. The dog was a few steps ahead of Jasper, also headed toward the barn where he would bed down outside the stall near Sadie. Jasper had taken about ten steps when the dog froze. He lifted his nose to the breeze, his tail stiffened, and he started a quiet, threatening growl that Jasper didn't hear often. Someone was nearby.

"Biscuit! No!" Jasper whispered the command sharply. He grabbed the nylon harness that he kept on the dog so he could control him when he needed to and started pulling him back toward the shop.

"No! Come!"

The dog was strong, but he was also obedient. He allowed himself to be pulled toward the shop, growling every step of the way. Jasper was certain someone was in the tree line near the back porch a couple of hundred feet away, and he believed it was Clyde Dalton. He'd kept his radio on during the evening, something he rarely did, and he knew Dalton hadn't been arrested. He didn't know exactly what Dalton looked like, all Peanut had told him was that the man was bald. He did know something about obsessive behavior, however, and he didn't believe that Dalton would be able to stay away from Peanut.

Jasper pulled Biscuit into the shop and closed the door behind him. He had dozens of knives in there, nearly all of them sharp enough to shave hair from a wet frog, but the weapon he wanted was an old-fashioned, re-curve bow that he'd had since he was a boy. He had gone through spells of collecting bows – there were several of them in his bedroom – but the one he liked the best was the old re-curve. It was hanging on a rack above his work bench.

Jasper had been hunting all his life. He could hit a bullseye with an arrow from sixty yards. It was pitch black inside the shop, but Jasper knew it so well he didn't need light. He took the bow down from its rack on the wall along with a quiver full of razor-sharp, broad head arrows. He slipped his arms through the quiver straps and walked to the back door of the shop. He unlocked two deadbolts and had to squeeze through the door to keep the dog from following. Clyde Dalton had used a gun when he tried to kill Peanut and had shot Joe Dillard's son. Jasper wasn't about to let the fool shoot his dog.

Jasper slipped into the trees and knelt beneath a laurel bush. All he knew about Clyde Dalton was what he had heard from Peanut, and based on what she'd told him, he was dealing with a crazy man, probably schizophrenic, definitely psychotically obsessed and extremely unstable. Jasper moved a little deeper into the trees and began to circle silently toward the house, stopping every few steps to watch and listen. There was a mild breeze, just enough to rustle the canopy above, and there was enough light from the moon and stars to enable him to make out shapes on the open ground. He was far enough away from the shop now that he could just barely make out Biscuit's muffled whines. He sat down, leaned his back against a tree, and settled in to wait. A thought stuck him: *"I'm stalking the stalker."*

A few minutes later, a dark shape came out of the tree line near the back porch, right where the dog had indicated earlier. Jasper felt his heart quicken as he watched the figure move slowly around the front of the house and disappear. Jasper moved to his right around the other side of the house, staying tight to the trees. If the man circled the house, Jasper would then be in front of him. He broke from the trees and jogged to Charlie's old truck, which was sitting in the driveway about twenty feet from the northeast corner of the back porch. He leaned against the truck and raised the bow.

Only the kitchen light was on inside the house. It wasn't much, but combined with the stars and moon, there was enough light so that Jasper could clearly make out the figure of a man wearing dark clothing and a floppy hat, crouched down, moving carefully along the side of the house. The man came out of the crouch and craned his neck to look in the kitchen window. Jasper could make out the features on his face; they were unfamiliar. He pulled the bowstring back to the corner of his mouth, aimed for the man's chest. He thought fleetingly of saying something, giving the man some command to stop, but when he saw a glint of light reflect off of a gun barrel and remembered the strain in Peanut's voice when she was telling him about the bullets whizzing past her, he let the arrow fly without saying a word. The man grunted and staggered back a couple of steps, the pistol fell from his hand, and he dropped to his knees as Jasper pulled another arrow from the quiver and raised the bow again. The man fell forward on his face. Jasper moved around the pickup and kicked the gun away. He rolled the man over with his right foot. He was still alive, but had that far off look in his eye that told Jasper he would be dead soon. Jasper knelt next to him.

"You Dalton?"

There was no response. Blood was beginning to trickle from the man's mouth. Jasper patted him, looking for some kind of identification. There was none. He pulled the floppy hat from the man's head. He was completely bald. It was Dalton.

"I told Peanut it'd be unhealthy for you to show up here."

Jasper stood, slung his bow across his back, reached down, grabbed Dalton by his feet, and starting dragging him toward the taxidermy shop.

The bull elk would have to wait. Jasper had more important work to do.

CHAPTER THIRTY-NINE

'd taken a frantic telephone call at 3:22 a.m. from Duane Scott, Jordan Scott's father. Jordan had been let out through a back door of the jail, told he was about to be killed, given a cell phone, and instructed to run. Jordan was making his way through a wooded ravine and Duane was on his way to pick him up near the Sullivan County fairgrounds on the outskirts of Blountville. What should they do? Where should they go?

"Bring him here, to my house," I said. "Tell him to get rid of the cell phone and then call me back as soon as he's in the car. I'll give you directions."

Caroline was at the hospital with Jack. I'd come home at midnight, fed the dogs, and had planned to catch a few hours of sleep and go back to the hospital at 4:00 a.m. to relieve Caroline. We lived on a large plot of land on a bluff overlooking Boone Lake in Washington County. Land owned by the Tennessee Valley Authority bordered my property on one side, the lake bordered another. My nearest neighbor owned the rest of the land that surrounded my property, and he lived more than half-a-mile away.

I dressed, made a pot of coffee, and turned on the small television that Caroline kept on the kitchen counter. Duane Scott called again and I gave him more specific directions to the house. A couple of minutes later, a young, stiff-haired talking head appeared on the television screen.

"We interrupt this program for a special news bulletin," the young man said as an image of Jordan Scott's booking photo appeared on the screen. "The Sullivan County Sheriff's Department is reporting that accused cop-killer Jordan Scott has escaped from the Sullivan County Jail. Sheriff Raymond Peale tells News Channel Nine that Scott faked a medical condition less than an hour ago, overpowered a guard and took his keys. He locked the guard in his cell, used the keys to steal a service revolver and a cell phone from a desk on the cell block, and then escaped through a service entrance. Peale warns that Scott should be considered armed and extremely dangerous. He urges residents in the Blountville area to lock their doors and keep a sharp lookout for what the sheriff is calling a desperate, dangerous criminal."

I knew from talking to Leon Bates about the association between Raymond Peale and Howard Raleigh, about the corruption within the Sullivan County Sheriff's Department, and I knew I'd put myself in the middle of a dangerous situation. I called Leon and told him to come to my house and to bring the cavalry with him. Leon was groggy and it took him a few seconds to understand what I was saying, but he finally got the message. He said he'd be there as soon as he could. I just hoped it wouldn't be too late. I shut the dogs in our bedroom and walked outside just as Duane Scott's car pulled into the driveway.

"Come on," I said. "Hurry."

Jordan was wide-eyed, obviously terrified, and looked haggard. His father, a tall, solidly-built, proud man, looked even worse.

"Did you see anyone following you?" I said as we hurried toward the front door.

"I don't think so," Duane Scott said. "Have you heard what they're saying on the news? The radio ... they said Jordan overpowered a guard."

I nodded and put my hand on Duane's arm. "I've been watching. It isn't good, but try not to worry."

The news bulletin was blaring again as I led Duane and Jordan through the kitchen.

"These steps lead up to my daughter's old room," I said. "I want you to go up there, lock yourselves in the bathroom, and wait until I come for you."

"What's going on, Mr. Dillard?" Jordan asked. "What's happening?"

"I'm not sure, Jordan. But I promise you that Raymond Peale will have to kill me to get into this house."

I watched them walk up the stairs and then went to our bedroom. I pushed the dogs back, pulled a pistol from the drawer in the nightstand next to my bed and then went back to the kitchen and turned off the television and all of the lights. I walked to the front door and turned on the outdoor security lights, stepped through onto the front porch, closed and locked the door behind me, and pulled a wooden rocking chair over. I slid the pistol into my belt beneath the light jacket I was wearing, sat down, folded my arms across my chest, and started rocking.

Almost immediately, I heard the roar of the engines. Four police cruisers pulled into my front yard, blue and red lights flashing. I felt my heart begin to race, but I didn't budge. I watched as car doors opened and men took cover behind the cruisers, pointing rifles, shotguns and pistols at me. High-powered spotlights blazed on, blinding me. No one said a word for thirty seconds; the night was still and cool and filled with tension. I heard another engine and a gaudy, black Crown Victoria with gold lettering that read "High Sheriff of Sullivan County" pulled up next to Duane Scott's car. A man I assumed must be Raymond Peale climbed out. I could see the gleam off of his belt buckle and the outline of his cowboy hat. As he came closer, I saw a shotgun in his hands. Peale walked up onto the porch and stood less than five feet from me.

"You're in the wrong county, sheriff," I said. "My name is Dillard, Joe Dillard, and this is my property. I'm asking you to leave."

"I know who you are," Peale said. "I also know you're harboring an escaped murderer and a dangerous fugitive."

"What makes you think that?"

"Don't play games with me, counselor. I know he's here."

"And how would you know that? Do you have some kind of tracking device on his father's car or did you bug his father's cell phone? Either of those things would be illegal unless you got a warrant. Did you get a warrant, sheriff?"

"Move aside," Peale said. "We're going in."

"You would also need a warrant to go into my house. Can I see it?"

"I don't need no warrant and you damned well know it! Now move aside!"

I thought about drawing the pistol but decided against it, at least for the moment. I stood.

"This is my home," I said, raising my voice so all of the deputies could hear clearly. "This is *my home*, and I won't let you invade it. If my client is inside, he's there because he fears for his life. This is not what you men think it is. Your boss, your sheriff, wants to turn you into assassins. He wants you to kill Jordan Scott, most likely because his friend Howard Raleigh wants you to kill Jordan Scott."

"Shut your mouth and get out of the way," Peale hissed. He leveled the shotgun at my chest.

"Jordan Scott will turn himself in," I said, "but not to you."

That was when I heard Leon Bates and his men, sirens screaming, coming across the hill. I felt a tremendous surge of relief.

"Looks like we've got ourselves a real party now," I said to Peale.

Within a minute, Leon, flanked by three of his own deputies, walked up the sidewalk. He stopped a few feet from Peale, who was still pointing the gun at me.

"What in the dickens is going on here?" Leon said. I noticed that Leon's right hand was resting on the butt of the nine-millimeter pistol holstered at his side.

"He's harboring an escaped convict. We're here to take him back into custody," Peale said.

"Without so much as a courtesy call to my department? Lower that weapon and tell your men to stand down."

Peale turned toward Leon. I don't think I'd ever seen such a look of unadulterated contempt.

"No," Peale said. "He's in there, and he's going back with me."

"Sheriff Peale," Leon barked, "if you think I'm going to let you come into my county and act like a Nazi, you're a fool. In ten seconds I'm going to draw my weapon, and if that shotgun isn't stowed and your men aren't packing up, I swear on the blood of my beloved lord and savior Jesus Christ I'll shoot you where you stand."

Leon's deputies, as though on command, fanned out, put their hands on their weapons, and faced Peale's deputies. My throat tightened and my stomach cramped ever so slightly. If this turned into a shootout, Leon and his men would be slaughtered. I looked at Peale, at the barrel of the shotgun. It was shaking.

"Ten," Leon said, "nine, eight, seven..." I watched as Leon's fingers wrapped around the pistol grip. "... six, five, four—"

Peale lowered the shotgun.

"Leon, this is crazy," he said. "You don't want to shoot me and I don't want to shoot you."

"Tell your men to stand down," Leon said. "Right now. Tell them to get in their cars and leave."

"I want that boy, Leon. He's my prisoner and I want him."

Leon stepped to within a foot of Peale and said, "Hell will freeze over before you take him."

"But he murdered one of my deputies! He escaped from my jail!"

Leon removed his pistol from the holster, but kept it pointed toward the ground.

"Go back to Sullivan County where you belong, sheriff. Right now."

Peale's shoulders slumped. He muttered something under his breath and started walking away. The spot-lights were turned off, the deputies got into their cruisers and quietly backed out onto the road. When the sounds of the engines faded, I looked at Leon's deputies. All three of them were young, mid-to-late twenties. Their faces revealed neither fear nor relief. The air suddenly seemed fresh, cool and glorious. I turned my attention to Leon, who had holstered the pistol and was now stand-ing with his hands on his hips, staring in the direction of the disappearing cruisers.

"You, my friend, have *cojones* the size of church bells," I said.

"And you, my friend, have an accused murderer and escapee in your house."

I nodded and smiled. "Yes, yes I do."

"What are we going to do about that?"

I sighed, sat down in the rocker, and rocked a few times.

"I don't know," I said. "Why don't we go inside? I'll introduce you to the crazed murderer and his father."

"You know I can't guarantee you I'll be able to keep him," Leon said. "As soon as he's arraigned on the escape charge, they might send him back to Sullivan County."

"Let me worry about that. Listen, are you and your guys hungry? I have some fresh sausage and some beautiful brown eggs one of my neighbors gave me. I make a mean pancake. I'd consider it an honor to fix you breakfast."

Leon took his hat off, turned to his deputies.

"I don't know about you boys, but after all this, I'm starved."

"So am I," I said as I got up from the chair. "Nothing like a near massacre to fuel a man's appetite."

CHAPTER FORTY

J asper was whistling "Skillet Good and Greasy" as he pulled the skin out of the tanning solution. It was about the size of a hand towel, and was all that was left of Clyde Dalton. The rest of Clyde, along with his clothing and shoes, had gone into the incinerator. A ring he was wearing and his gun had been tossed into Watauga Lake off the Butler Bridge the night after Clyde died. Jasper had hosed down the spot where Clyde had fallen and the blood trail he'd left when Jasper dragged him to the shop. Whatever blood Jasper had missed, Biscuit had taken care of, and Peanut didn't suspect a thing. Jasper smiled to himself as he looked at the soft, pliable skin. What he was planning would make a heck of a gift to Peanut, though he knew he'd probably never find the nerve to give it to her.

Fifty-six hours had passed since Clyde Dalton's death. It was 8:20 a.m. A summer rain had started falling a few hours earlier and was cleansing the mountain. Jasper enjoyed the steady percussion of the rain dropping on the roof. He liked the smell of the forest after a shower. He thought about Peanut's question about him leaving the mountains. He truly did love it here. He'd never leave.

Biscuit started barking outside and Jasper heard the hum of an engine and gravel crunching beneath tires. He removed his rubber gloves and walked outside. There was virtually no breeze. The rain was heavy but quiet, the drops falling straight down from the clouds. The car was a white Ford Crown Victoria. Behind it was a cruiser from the Carter County Sheriff's Department. Jasper spoke to the dog and he went silent. A man got out of the Crown Vic, popped open a black umbrella, and started walking toward Jasper. He was shorter than Jasper, barrel-chested, with short, black hair. He was wearing a short-sleeved, white shirt, open at the collar, and gray dress slacks. There was a gun in a shoulder holster beneath his left arm and a badge attached to his belt.

"Morning," he said as he approached.

"Morning." Jasper took the hand he offered.

"Name's David Delaney," he said. "I'm an investigator with the Carter County Sheriff's Department. You must be Jasper Story."

"I am. What can I do for you?"

"Is Charleston ... is Miss Story around?"

"No sir, she ain't here," Jasper said. Charlie had gotten on her horse early in the morning and headed off up the mountain with Jack Dillard. "She went on a little vacation."

"Is that right? Where'd she go?"

"I don't believe she wants anybody to know."

"That her Jeep over there?"

"Belongs to a friend of hers. He went on vacation with her."

Delaney nodded. "That's probably a good idea."

"Have y'all had any luck finding the feller that tried to kill her?"

"That's why I'm here. We found his car a little while ago."

"Is that a fact?"

"It's less than a half-mile down the road, parked in some trees. Your neighbor ran across it and called it in."

"So you think he's around somewhere?"

"It looks that way. We have dogs coming, but with all this rain I don't know if it'll do any good. We have men in the woods already."

"Y'all want some help? I know these woods better than anybody."

"I appreciate that, but we can handle it. Our guys are well-trained."

"You reckon I should arm myself?"

"That might not be a bad idea, Mr. Story. And it would probably be best if you stay in the house until we find him. I'd hate to see anybody else get hurt."

Jasper shook his head. Droplets of water fell from the bill of his Atlanta Braves cap.

"No, sir," he said. "We don't want nobody getting hurt. We don't want that at all."

CHAPTER FORTY-ONE

Jack Dillard's left arm was wrapped around Charlie's waist while the sling held his right arm close to his body. He squeezed Sadie's hindquarters tightly between his thighs as she climbed yet another steep ridge. The pills he'd been given had reduced the sharp pain in his collarbone and shoulder to a dull ache, but he was struggling to stay on the back of the horse.

"You all right?" Charlie asked over her shoulder as Sadie finally topped the ridge and started down the other side.

"I'm great," Jack said.

"You sure? I thought I heard you groan a second ago."

"Must have been the saddle creaking. I'm fine."

They'd been on the horse for nearly an hour. The doctors had kept Jack at the hospital until late yesterday afternoon, and Charlie had spent the entire day with him. When he had finally been discharged, she'd pulled him into the hallway and asked him to come up to her place early the next morning. She wanted to take him riding, to show him the cave. She'd asked whether he felt up to it and he'd enthusiastically said yes. Of course he was up to it. He was Jack Dillard, destroyer of baseballs, tougher than a pine knot. He had failed to mention to his parents that he was going for a ride through rough terrain on a horse. He'd simply told them he was going to visit Charlie, and neither of them had voiced any opposition.

The hospital stay had been like a reunion. Once word of the shooting got out, a steady stream of family and old friends had descended upon his small room. His sister, Lilly, had been among them and had spent a couple of hours there early on the second morning. Joe and Caroline had gone home for a little while, and they'd been alone in the room. Lilly had asked him about Charlie, and he'd talked for fifteen minutes straight before he realized that Lilly was grinning widely at him.

"You're in love," she'd said.

"Maybe. I think it's a little early for that word."

"You're in love," she said again. "I can tell by the tone of your voice, the look on your face when you talk about her."

"You sound like Mom."

"Of course I sound like Mom. I'm her daughter, practically her clone. I'm also a woman who knows what it's like to be in love, and you, young man, are in love. I'm happy for you."

"Does being in love mean that your skin tingles and your stomach tightens every time you see someone? That you can't stop thinking about them? That you lose your appetite when they're not around?"

"All of those things," Lilly said, "and much more."

"I don't know what I'll do when the time comes for me to go back to school in Nashville," Jack said. "I'll starve to death."

"What do you like best about her?"

"Everything."

"Come on, give me one thing."

"Her smile. No, her wit, maybe. She's really sharp. I also like her eyes, the way they change color in different light and the way they sparkle. Her hair is beautiful, her skin is clear and smooth, and the way she carries herself is—"

"I said one thing, Jack. Have you slept with her?"

"That's none of your business. But no, I haven't slept with her."

"Why not? Aren't you attracted to her?"

"I'm a gentleman. You should know that as well as anyone."

"But you'd like to rip her clothes off and ravage her, wouldn't you?"

"Absolutely. Damn, Lilly, what *am* I going to do when I have to go back to law school? I'll go completely bonkers."

"You'll be fine. Maybe Charlie can find a job down there after she passes the bar. When does she take it?"

"In a month. She'll get the results in October."

"It'll work out," Lilly said. "If it's really love, and it sounds to me like it is, everything will work out fine."

Charlie pulled back on the reins, slipped her leg over the saddle horn, and slid to the ground.

"This is it," she said. "We're here."

She reached up, took Jack's left hand in hers, and helped him slide out of the saddle. Jack watched and listened as she spoke in a soothing tone to Sadie and led her to a laurel bush near a creek a few yards away. She wrapped the reins around a branch, retrieved something from a saddlebag, and walked back to where Jack stood.

"It's there," she said, pointing to a large rock. "Across the creek and behind that rock, the one shaped like an hour glass. Come on."

They waded across the shallow creek and climbed a slope. Charlie was carrying a spotlight in one hand and a flashlight in the other.

"Look. Right there," Charlie said.

It took a minute, but Jack eventually made out the narrow, vine-covered opening. Charlie handed him the flashlight and said, "Come on, just follow me."

Charlie had instructed Jack to wear boots, warm clothing and to bring gloves. He donned the gloves, wrapped his covered fingers around the flashlight and started walking. As soon as he breached the entrance, he stopped. His legs suddenly felt like tree limbs, as though he had no joints, no knees or ankles. His heart was racing, his breathing labored, and despite the sudden drop in temperature, a sheen of perspiration had formed on his forehead.

"Charlie?" he said.

She'd moved a few feet in front of him. She turned. "What's wrong?"

"I'm not sure. Something is telling me not to go in there."

"Are you afraid?"

"I don't know. I don't remember being afraid of anything in my entire life. I'm not shaking, but I'm sweating and my heart is beating like I've been running all morning. I'm sweating and I don't think I can move my legs."

"Maybe it's just claustrophobia," Charlie said. "Let's go back out for a minute and talk, see how you feel."

"Right now I'm starting to feel like a coward."

"It's probably the medication you're on," Charlie said, "or maybe there's some kind of infection starting up in your wound. This was a bad idea, Jack. I'm sorry. Let's go back out."

They turned and walked back out of the cave. Jack looked up at the gray clouds boiling on the horizon. A brisk wind was blowing and the sky seemed angry.

"Feel better?" Charlie said. She moved close to Jack, removed the glove from her right hand, and caressed his cheek.

He looked into her eyes, the clearest, most beautiful blue he had ever seen.

"I'm not sure how I feel," Jack said, "but there's something about this place that is bothering me. I've always had this sort of knack for sensing when something isn't right, almost a sixth sense sometimes. I think I get it from my mother. She can smell danger a mile away. But this is ... this is ... more intense than anything I've ever felt."

"What do you think is causing it?"

"It has to be the gold. I've thought about it a lot since you showed me the bar. My dad and I have talked about it some. That gold ... it came from a man who was probably evil. He had to be. I mean, who knows how many people he killed to climb to the top of the world he ruled and stay there? People glorify them, Hollywood loves them, but those men were ruthless and cruel. They were thieves and killers and extortionists. And sitting at the bottom of this cave is the fruit of their labors."

"I know," Charlie said. "I've been thinking about it, too. But what do I do? Just leave it there? It was a gift, a gift that can change my life. Surely I can take it and do some good with it."

"I think you should leave it alone. It's like an evil spirit that has been sealed up in a tomb for centuries and then someone accidentally stumbles across it and sets it free to wreak havoc on an unsuspecting world. I could be entirely wrong, or maybe I'm just being overly dramatic, or maybe you're right and it's just the medication, but I think what I'm feeling is the presence of real evil. I don't want any part of it, and I don't want you to wind up being hurt by it."

"Maybe we should just ride back down the mountain," Charlie said, "and deal with it when you're feeling better."

Jack shrugged his shoulders. He knew he would never willingly set foot on this particular piece of the earth again, and he desperately hoped that the gold hidden in the cave would not become a wedge that would drive itself between him and Charlie.

"Another day," Jack said, nodding his head, "when I'm feeling better. Let's get out of here."

CHAPTER FORTY-TWO

I t had taken Johnny Russo about two minutes to convince Carlo Lanzetti that they should do this. "It'll be the biggest score ever," Johnny had said to Carlo. "Bigger than Lufthansa. We pull this off, we come back here, and we rule this town. We rule the *world*."

The story of his great-great-great-grandfather Russo's gold had been a popular topic of conversation around the Russo family dinner table on Sunday when Johnny was young. His father had spoken of it many times, especially after he'd had a little too much wine, dreaming aloud about what he would do if he got his hands on it. His dreams stayed within the borders of the Delaware and Schuylkill Rivers; they involved buying and restoring Carmine's old place in Bella Vista, sending the children to expensive, private schools, owning luxury automobiles, getting the best tables at the best Italian restaurants in South Philly. As he grew older, Johnny suspected his father's dreams involved a few other things, too, things like usurping Sal Pistone and taking over all of the rackets in Philadelphia and Jersey and restoring the Russo family to the position of power and prestige it deserved.

Johnny's meeting with the computer geek named Reno had provided basic information. He learned the full names and addresses of Zane Barnes and Charleston Story and their birthdates. He learned that Barnes was divorced and that Charleston Story had just graduated from law school. He learned that neither of them had a criminal history – although Charleston Story's father was in prison in Beckley, West Virginia – and he knew their credit scores, which was of absolutely no use. He learned what kind of vehicles Barnes and Story owned. He had learned the address of the old man, Roscoe Barnes, who had jumped from a clock tower at a courthouse and splattered himself all over the steps. The newspaper story said the gold was probably hidden somewhere on the old man's property. Reno had also managed to come up with electronic images of both Zane Barnes and Charleston Story, which he'd printed out and given to Johnny.

They'd left Philadelphia without telling anyone where they were going. They'd put their street business in the hands of a guy named Vincenzo Matta, telling him only that they were going out of town for a few days, maybe a week. Both Johnny and Carlo had known Vinny for years and he'd never given them a reason to distrust him. But they still threatened to behead him and stuff him in a meat grinder if he stole so much as a dime while they were gone. It was actually a good time to leave town. Their wounds from the beating were healing. Big Legs Mucci and Tommy Maldonado had taken all the money in their wallets that night – almost two thousand dollars – so they figured they were good on the tribute for a few weeks, but they'd talked it over and they still weren't going to pay. That meant, at some point, there would be blood running in the Philly streets. And if Johnny could make this thing in Tennessee happen, if he and Carlo could walk away with millions, they could go back to Philly, hire whatever muscle they needed to hire, and take down Mucci, Maldonado, Pistone, all of them. Johnny would be boss, Carlo would be underboss. Pistone would be dead along with Mucci and Maldonado. The rest of his crew would either fall in line or die.

It had taken them eight hours to drive from South Philly to Northeast Tennessee. They'd rented a room in a flea bag motel off Highway 19E near Roan Mountain and had spent three days doing surveillance. They used the GPS on their cell phones to find the various places they needed to find and had spent a good deal of time hiking through the rugged terrain, trying to find good vantage points from which they could stalk their prey.

Johnny had decided to concentrate on Zane Barnes first. He reasoned that since Barnes was the old man's son, and since he seemed to be living in the old man's house, he would be the most likely candidate to be able to tell them where the gold was. They had seen Barnes walk out of the house to the barn and emerge on a four-wheeler several times. He would disappear into the woods behind the house and they could hear him heading up the mountain. He would stay gone for an hour or two and then return, but as yet, they hadn't seen any gold. They'd broken into the house while Barnes was gone and had searched it. They'd also searched the barn and the two other outbuildings on the property, but so far, nothing.

On their third night in Tennessee, both Johnny and Carlo were growing impatient. They had a discussion and decided their best course of action was to get their hands on Barnes and extract some information from him. Carlo was the one who suggested the vise. He'd seen one in an outbuilding and had mentioned a scene from a movie, *Goodfellas* or *The Godfather* or *Casino*, he couldn't remember which, where some gangsters got some information out of a guy by putting his head in a vise and slowly tightening it. Carlo thought it would be an effective means of torture, and Johnny agreed.

The light in the old man's house went out at eleven, and at midnight, Johnny and Carlo walked into the outbuilding. They rummaged around, found some hardware, and anchored the bench vise to an old picnic table. Once they were satisfied their torture device would work, they walked into the house and found Zane Barnes sound asleep in a bedroom.

"Get up," Johnny said, pointing a pistol at Barnes's forehead.

They forced him to the outbuilding in his pajamas at gunpoint, made him lie on his back on the table, and tied him down. Carlo positioned himself so he could operate the vise while Johnny stood over the wide-eyed, sniveling man. Carlo turned the handle on the vise and the jaws tightened snugly on Barnes's ears.

"Name's Russo," Johnny said. "That mean anything to you?"

"What? Who?"

"Russo! As in Russo's gold! Ring a bell?"

"I don't ... I don't understand—"

"Shut up. I'm going to ask you some questions, and every time I don't like the answer, my friend here is going tighten this vise. If you give me the wrong answer too many times, your head is going to explode. Got it? Good. So, first things first. Where is the gold?"

"I don't have it," Barnes said.

"Turn it," Johnny said to Carlo. Carlo turned the handle a quarter turn and the vise tightened. Barnes shrieked.

"Don't feel so good, does it?" Johnny said. "You didn't answer my question, see? I didn't ask you if you have the gold, I asked you where it is. So I'm going to ask you again, okay? Where is the gold?"

"I don't know," Barnes said. "I swear it."

"Turn it again."

Carlo tightened the vise a little more as Barnes howled in pain.

"This is gonna get real bad real quick, Zane," Johnny said. "Don't mind if I call you Zane, right? I mean, that's your name, right? You are Zane Barnes, aren't you? Say yes or no. Are you Zane Barnes?"

"Yes."

"That's good. You see? Carlo didn't tighten the vise. Three or four more turns on that thing and your skull is gonna start cracking. Now me and Carlo here, we came all the way down here from Philadelphia to get what is rightfully ours. My grandfather, my great-great-great grandfather, brought that gold down here. I guess maybe he brought it to your great-great-great grandfather, right? Or maybe he was your great-great grandfather. I'm not so good at that generation stuff. And your grandfather was supposed to give it back to my grandfather, but he acted like a mope and didn't do it, so he wound up getting himself whacked. But from everything I've been hearing, the gold is still here, and since *you're* here, I figure you know where it is. So again, where is it?"

"Please," Barnes said pitifully. "Please, don't do this. It's here ... you're right ... it's here ... somewhere. But I don't know where. It's hidden somewhere on the mountain I think. I've been trying to find it. I can help you find it."

"How do you know it's hidden? How do you know?"

"My father. Before he killed himself he showed me one bar. One bar. He said there was more but he wouldn't tell me where it was."

"How much is there? How much is it worth?"

"I don't know ... He said there's a lot. Worth millions, but I can't find it. I think she took it. I've seen her on the mountain riding her horse. I think maybe she has it."

"She? Who is she?"

"The Story girl. Her name is Charleston. My father left everything to her in his will. I think she already took it."

"I already know about her. Why would your father leave everything to her and nothing to his son? And if he left everything to her, what are you doing living in this house? I think you're lying to me. Turn it again, Carlo."

"No!" Foam was bubbling from the corners of Barnes' mouth and tears were streaming from his eyes.

"Do it," Johnny said.

Carlo turned the handle on the vise. Barnes screamed and his face contorted.

"Last chance," Johnny said. "I'm getting bored with this. If you don't tell me what I want to know in the next thirty seconds, Carlo is going to squash your head like a grape."

"You need me to find it!" Barnes said. "You need me! There are a hundred gold bars worth fifty million dollars. I think the girl knows where it is. She's the one whose head should be in a vise. I know her. I can help you get to her."

"That's better," Johnny said. He winked at Carlo, who backed the pressure off just a bit. "How can you help us get to her?"

"I know what she cares about, what she wouldn't want to lose."

"Like what?"

"Her father, her uncle, her horse. That's how you get to her. I can tell you all about her. I know this land like the back of my hand. I can help you get the gold. We can be partners."

"Partners? Really? You want to be partners with me and Carlo? What kind of split are we talking?"

"I'll give you eighty bars," Barnes said. "I'll take what's left."

Johnny heard Carlo laugh. "That's rich," Carlo said. "He'll give us eighty bars and keep what's left. That's funny."

"Finish this piece of garbage," Johnny said. "He ain't gonna do nothing for us."

Carlo turned the handle. Barnes screamed again. Carlo kept turning. Barnes' head began to elongate as the jaws of the vise closed. Johnny walked away, but Carlo was fascinated. Barnes' eyes became larger and larger. They looked like red yolks on a fried egg. The tops and bottoms of Barnes' ears began to curl around the jaws.

Carlo heard the skull begin to crack, a sound like wadding up dry paper. Carlo gave the handle another, vicious twist and the skin across the forehead stretched like hot plastic, the wrinkles disappeared. There was a *pop* and the crown of the skull separated. Pink pudding oozed as a hiss of air escaped from the mouth. Barnes went limp.

"That's it," Carlo said. "He's gone."

They wrapped Barnes in a plastic drop cloth and loaded him in the trunk of the Mercedes. Then they drove in separate cars to the hotel, took naps and showers, hung out and watched television for a couple of hours. At four in the morning Carlo drove the Mercedes to Elizabethton with Johnny behind him. They had learned that one of the town's prized attractions was an old covered bridge that spanned the Doe River. It was maybe a hundred feet long, at the northeast edge of the town, close to the jail. There was a park on the north side of the river. On the other side was downtown, which was as still as a cemetery. They pulled down South Riverside Drive and parked about fifty feet from the bridge. Carlo carried the body onto the bridge while Johnny followed with the same length of rope they had used to secure Barnes to the picnic table. They strung Barnes up in the middle of the bridge, plastic wrapping and all, and left him swinging.

"That was fun," Carlo said as they walked back to their car. "We gotta do the same thing to Mucci and Maldonado as soon as we get back to Philly."

"Yeah, it'll send a nice little message to the hillbillies when they wake up," Johnny said. "But now it's time to start sending messages to the girl."

CHAPTER FORTY-THREE

Luke Story's life was one of drudgery and routines. Things were a little easier and a little less dangerous these days, now that they'd finally moved him to a minimum security camp, but they weren't any less boring. He was up at six every morning during the week. He dressed in his drab, khaki uniform and made his bed in the required, hospital corner fashion, swept his room, used the bathroom, and washed his face and hands. He went to breakfast at seven. At seven-thirty, he went to his job cleaning the prison's administrative offices. Lunch was at eleven, then back to work until three-thirty. Supper at four. From four-thirty to ten o'clock, he had free time, which he thought was ironic. Free time? He couldn't even leave the place. How could the time be free? He killed the time in the evening walking on the track over the hill from the dormitory-style housing units, playing cards or chess with other inmates, reading and watching television. He was even taking a cooking class now. Charlie had arranged a job for him at Buddy's Diner when he got out. It was the same place she'd worked as a waitress in high school and college.

There were no walls at the camp, not even a fence. There were usually no more than two guards on duty,

SCOTT PRATT

and they were unarmed. It was far different from what he'd become accustomed to during the first twenty years of his incarceration. He'd spent the first five years in Atlanta, classified as a close security inmate because his sentence was so long. He quickly learned the most important rules, the unwritten rules, of prison survival: trust no one, don't show emotion, don't show weakness, say as little as possible, don't be friendly with the guards, don't be too friendly with members of other races, stay away from gangs, drugs and homosexuals, don't stare, don't reach across people's plates in the chow hall, be careful what you say on the phone. He'd been forced to fight a few times during the early years – everybody is forced to fight eventually – but even with only one functional arm, he'd never been seriously injured. They moved him to the medium-security prison at Beckley when Charlie was ten. He spent ten years there, surviving the same way he had in Atlanta. Five years ago, they'd finally moved him to the camp.

Luke tried not to think about getting out, because he'd discovered that thinking about anything other than what was going on around him every day was both dangerous and futile. He looked forward to the visits from Charlie, as he had to visits from his parents when they were alive, but as soon as they walked out the door it was back to survival mode. He hadn't felt joy or pain or compassion in so long that he sometimes wondered whether he'd be able to feel anything ever again. He hoped he would, though. He wanted to feel alive again before he died.

It was getting dark as he started the thirteenth lap around the quarter-mile track. Four miles was his routine these days, sixteen laps. Charlie had told him about finding her fortune during her last visit. He'd been astounded at first, but then he'd given her his best advice: keep your mouth shut, don't trust anybody. There was really nothing he could do to help. He was stuck, just as he'd been stuck for more than two decades. Maybe the money would make their lives easier when he got out, maybe it would make things harder. He knew he was ill-equipped to deal with something so complicated. His main concern was whether he'd be able to adapt to life without someone telling him what he could and couldn't do every second of the day.

A large man walked out of the thick forest near the end of the straightaway to Luke's right. He wasn't wearing the khaki of a prisoner or the blue uniform worn by the guards. A cap was pulled down tightly over his head, a dark jacket draped over his torso. Luke kept walking, more curious than anything else.

The man approached. Luke slowed as he drew closer, beginning to grow uneasy. The man was smiling.

"You're Luke Story, right?" His tone was friendly, casual.

The man was less than five feet away. "Yeah, who are you?"

Luke saw his hand go to his waist. A gun appeared.

The last thing Luke saw was a flash.

CHAPTER FORTY-FOUR

The news of Zane Barnes's grisly death had shocked Charlie, but the news of her father's murder the following day had buckled her knees. She was fixing breakfast for herself and Jasper at six o'clock in the morning when she received a phone call from the warden of the prison. Jasper had helped her into a chair in the den where she'd cried for an hour. Then they moved into the kitchen and Charlie had tried to talk about it, to make some sense of it, but she'd lost control of herself again and cried for another hour. She'd finally gone to her bedroom and was lying face down across the bed, still clothed and still weeping, when she heard Jasper step inside.

"I want to show you something," he said. "I'm thinking it might make you feel a little better."

Charlie sat up and Jasper took her arm. He led her out the back door and up the path to his shop.

"We're going in there?" Charlie asked as he unlocked the padlock.

"Yes, ma'am."

"I haven't been in there since you kicked me out when I was a little girl."

"I know, and don't think you can come sniffing around here any time you want just because I'm letting you in now."

Jasper turned on a couple of lights. The room was large, maybe twenty feet by thirty feet. The floor was concrete with a drain in the middle. There was a long work bench along the far wall, a refrigerator and a freezer next to another, a chain lift in the corner, and an incinerator along the wall to her left. There was a work table to Charlie's right, next to it was a huge elk with no eyes, no nose, and no mouth. The plank walls were covered in animal heads, animal hides, knives and saws. There was a shelf full of chemicals, a couple of tool chests, and a large, metal vat. The room had a faint chemical smell, a mixture of paint, glue and solvent.

Jasper walked to a door between the refrigerator and the freezer and unlocked another padlock. Charlie followed.

"This is what I want you to see," he said. "Just hold up one second."

Jasper walked through the door and pulled it closed behind him. Charlie saw another light come on and he stepped back out.

"Okay now, Peanut, this is probably gonna shock you a little at first, but you have to promise me you won't scream or faint or nothing like that."

"Maybe I shouldn't go in," Charlie said. "I think I've had enough shock for one day."

"I want you to see it. Like I said, I think it'll make you feel better, as long as you can keep an open mind."

Charlie nodded and took a deep breath. Jasper pulled the door open slowly and led her in. He stepped to the side, revealing one of the most bizarre scenes Charlie had ever witnessed.

"Is that ... ? Is that ... ? Is that what I think it is?"

She turned her head to Jasper, who was nodding slowly, then back to the display. There were three small spotlights above, each one illuminating a different ... *person*. All of them were on a raised platform about a foot off the floor. On the right was Grandpa Story. He was wearing the old hat he always wore, a green hunting jacket over a blue, denim shirt, a pair of green pants and hiking boots. There was a shotgun laid across his shoulders behind his head. His left hand was wrapped around the stock and his right was draped over the barrel. He was looking upward, into the spotlight, and he was smiling. He looked happy. He looked *alive.*

In the middle, sitting in a rocking chair, wearing a long, purple dress, was Charlie's grandmother. Her silver hair was pulled back into a bun and her glasses were resting on the end of her nose. She was holding a knitting needle in each hand and appeared to be halfway through a red sweater. She, too, was smiling, though it wasn't a grin like the one on Grandpa's face. Her smile was almost coy; it reminded Charlie of the Mona Lisa.

The person, figure, whatever it was, on the other end was a young woman, beautiful with long, reddish hair and blue eyes, wearing a pink, summer dress and holding an artificial red rose. Charlie recognized her from photos she'd seen. It was Rachel, Jasper's wife. She appeared to be sniffing the flower, and the expression on her face was one of contentment and joy. Charlie looked at her, then back at the others, with a sense of wonder. They looked so ... so real. How did he do this? How could he possibly—?

"I keep them here with me," Jasper said quietly. "They're a comfort."

"I don't understand," Charlie said. "How?"

"I know you're gonna think I'm crazy. Most people already think I'm crazy, and maybe I am. But the way I looked at it was they could just rot in the ground, or I could bring 'em home with me and make 'em beautiful and keep 'em close. I think they like it better this way."

"So it's actually *them*? Their *bodies*?"

"No, Peanut, it ain't them. Well, sorta. I did the same for them that I do for the animals that come in here. I preserved them. I tried to make them look like they did when they were alive."

"But how did you get them? I mean, I saw Grandma and Grandpa go into the ground."

"I dug 'em up, simple as that. Same night they was buried. I just took the bodies and put the caskets back in the ground. I know it's against the law, but nobody knows. No harm done. I bought mannequins and I added a little putty here, shaved a little there, matched up the eyes and the hair, got the skin color just the way I wanted. I freshen 'em up every now and then. Don't you think they look good?"

Charlie nodded. She felt as though she were dreaming. "This is weird, uncle. I'm not sure how I feel about this."

"To each his own," Jasper said. "I just wanted you to know that I can do the same for Luke if you'd like, if it would ease your mind. You could come in and visit from time to time."

"I don't know. No, I don't think so. I wouldn't get the same ... no, thank you, but I don't think so."

"Suit yourself."

Charlie thought about asking how long he planned to keep them, but the answer was obvious. He'd keep them until he died. She supposed if she outlived him, she'd have an unusual and difficult decision to make.

"There's one more thing I want to show you," he said.

"I don't know how you could top this."

Jasper turned forty-five degrees and walked to the corner of the room. A black curtain that Charlie hadn't noticed was hanging at an angle across the corner from the ceiling to the floor. Jasper pulled the curtain to the side. His body blocked Charlie's view; she couldn't see what was in front of him.

"He came for you the night he shot that Dillard boy."

Charlie walked slowly toward her uncle's back.

"I had to do it, Peanut. Didn't see no other way. But you can rest easy now. He won't be bothering you again."

Charlie moved up beside Jasper and gasped.

On a small table in the corner, resting on a silver platter, was Clyde Dalton's bald head.

CHAPTER FORTY-FIVE

Luke's graveside service was held on a bright morning in the same cemetery where Roscoe Barnes was buried. Charlie was surprised at the number of people who showed up: high school and college classmates of hers that she hadn't seen in years, old friends of her father's, friends of Jasper's. Joe Dillard, along with his wife and Jack, were there. Jack's arm was still in a sling from the fractured collarbone. Charlie felt her spirit lift when she saw Jack, but there was a distance between them now that hadn't been there before she took him up to the cave. He would respond to a text message if she sent him one and was always polite in her presence, but he had stopped initiating communication and seemed to be somewhat distracted.

Charlie found herself thinking strange thoughts as she and Jasper sat beneath the small canopy that had been erected over the grave and the preacher went through the motions of praising a man he'd never met. She wondered what all these people would think if they knew the two graves next to Luke were empty. What if she had allowed Jasper to "preserve" Luke and they'd held the ceremony in Jasper's macabre little theater and unveiled Luke like a statue or sculpture?

Charlie spent almost an hour after the ceremony talking to the people who'd come, accepting their condolences with a sense of gratitude. When everyone had left, she got into the passenger's side of Jasper's truck and they headed for home.

"You promise you'll leave him there?" she asked. "I want him to just rest in peace."

"Already told you I would."

"You promise, though? Do you swear?"

"No need for that."

They rode in silence for a few minutes along the mountain road, Jasper moving slowly through the switchbacks and up and down the slopes. Charlie's grief had ebbed and flowed over the past few days. She'd long envisioned the day she would pick her father up at the prison, take him by the hand, and lead him back to the world. Twenty years. Twenty years of missed birthdays and holidays and proms and graduations. Twenty years of people asking about her father along with twenty years of embarrassed, untruthful responses. She felt cheated out of her past and cheated out of her future. She'd spent hours at night asking herself questions, terrified of what the answers might be.

"So who do you think killed him?" she asked Jasper.

The phone calls Charlie had made to the warden were frustrating. At first, all he would say was that the Bureau of Prisons had their "best investigators" on the case and that Luke had been shot, but after Charlie told him she was a lawyer and threatened to sue, he became a little more cooperative.

"Could an inmate smuggle a gun in?" Charlie had asked.

"Not likely, but there are no walls."

"So people can just wander on and off the property? Anybody can get in?"

"It's unusual that someone would want to get *into* a prison, even a minimum security facility like this. And the inmates here are all short-timers. None of them want to go back to medium or high security. I can assure you that nothing like this has ever happened."

"Where was he when he was shot?"

"He was walking on the track. He walked every evening at the same time from what I understand."

"Nobody else was there?"

"No."

"Nobody saw anything unusual? Nobody heard anything?"

"The investigators are talking to every inmate, every staff member. So far, nobody's been able to provide anything useful."

"Any physical evidence?"

"Just the bullet that was removed from his ... from the body. It was a .22-caliber long rifle. The investigators think whoever shot him used a silencer. It looks like it was done by a professional."

There was a faded blue Camaro that Charlie didn't recognize sitting in the driveway when she and Jasper pulled up to the house. Charlie looked at the tags: West Virginia.

"Didn't think she'd have the nerve," Jasper said.

"Who? What do you mean?"

"It's your momma. I seen her at the funeral."

Charlie sat in stupefied silence as Jasper parked the truck. She looked closely at the car; there didn't appear to be anyone inside. She turned and looked at Jasper.

"Turn around," she said, almost whispering. "Drive away."

Jasper shook his head. "That ain't the way to do this. Might as well let her say what she's got to say."

"I don't want to talk to her."

"You don't have to talk."

"But I don't ... I don't—"

"C'mon." Jasper was opening his door and climbing out. "I got a thing or two to say to her."

Charlie had to concentrate on putting one foot in front of the other as they walked up the steps to the back porch, past the lounging Biscuit. When they walked through the back door, Charlie saw her sitting at the kitchen table, smoking a cigarette. Her hair was long and auburn, lighter than Charlie's with streaks of gray, her eyes large and turquoise. She was slim and still attractive, but had a hard look about her, a look of poverty and struggle, much like the people who congregated on the courthouse steps when court was in session. She was wearing a short-sleeved, black dress with a high neckline. She looked at Jasper first, then at Charlie. Her eyes seemed to soften.

"What are you doing here, Ruth Ann?" Jasper said.

She was still looking at Charlie as though she were measuring her up before a fistfight.

"Came to pay my respects to you and my daughter," she said.

Charlie had stopped in the middle of the kitchen. She met her mother's gaze and held it steadily. There was no sense of familiarity, no instinctive twinge of recognition or maternal longing. It had been so long since Charlie had heard her mother's voice. And now that she was hearing it, it was the voice of a stranger.

"Consider 'em paid," Jasper said.

"You grew up fine." Ruth Ann's eyes hadn't left Charlie's. "Pretty and fine."

"You just get on outta here," Jasper said. "Who do you think you are to come waltzing in here like you own the place? Go on back to West Virginia, back to your people."

"Why did you abandon me?"

The question Charlie had asked in her mind a million times, a question to which she desperately needed an answer, had come out spontaneously, almost involuntarily. It was as though someone else's voice had come out of her body, as though she'd exited herself and was hovering near the ceiling, watching the scene unfold beneath her.

Ruth Ann took a long drag from her cigarette and blew the smoke out slowly.

"I couldn't take care of you," she said. "Couldn't take care of myself at the time, let alone a child. Your daddy was in jail, the government took everything we had. I started drinking a lot, taking pills. I wasn't in my right mind."

Charlie took a couple of steps toward the table, pulled out a chair, sat down.

"But all these years, not a word. Why?"

"I was ashamed. I'm still ashamed."

"You ought to be." Jasper's voice was sharp with anger. "Run off and leave a little girl, your own flesh and blood, without so much as a fare thee well. Leave Momma and Daddy to raise her, both of them already sick about what happened to Luke. You can say what you want about liquor or pills or whatever, but the plain truth is that you just didn't want to face up to it. You ain't nothing but a coward, plain and simple. Ain't no other word for it."

Ruth Ann dropped her cigarette into a Styrofoam cup that was sitting in front of her and stood up.

"I guess you've been waiting a long time to say that to me," she said.

She picked up the cup and started around the table. She paused and put her hand on Charlie's shoulder.

"I'm sorry about your daddy, and I'm sorry for what I did to you. I live in Mount Hope, West Virginia, just north of the prison where they were keeping Luke. You'd be welcome there any time."

Charlie sat motionless. She listened to Ruth Ann's heels clicking on the back porch, listened to her car start up, listened to the gravel crackling as she drove away.

"Goodbye," she whispered.

CHAPTER FORTY-SIX

It was two-thirty in the morning, and Johnny and Carlo were on the move again.

"Can you believe this place?" Carlo was in the passenger seat, as usual, as they rode through the darkness. "Freakin' mountains and trees and cows and corn, that's all there is. The food sucks. Could you believe that spaghetti we ate last night? The sauce was ketchup with a little hamburger, the pasta was so overcooked it was like glue. And these people, man. Not an Italian in sight. I ain't seen a Jew or a black dude in a week, not that I miss them, but this is weird. No Catholic churches. Everybody's named Smith or Jones."

"Yeah, it's white bread," Johnny said. "Cracker white bread. The way they talk makes me want to puke. I never heard anybody make a two-syllable word out of yes. Yay-yus. And beer? Bee-yer. I swear to God I'd either die of boredom or shoot myself if I had to live here."

"That club was the worst I've ever been to," Carlo said. They'd driven to Johnson City on their way back from killing Luke Story. It's a college town, home to East Tennessee State University, and they thought they'd find some action, but it was summer and most of the students had gone home. "Did you see the way they looked at us? Like we were aliens or something, from outer space."

"I know. I wonder if they have tanning beds here. Everybody's so *pale.* They look like ghosts."

Johnny turned left onto Buck Mountain Road. The windows were down to let the smell of gasoline escape; the breeze flowed across his face and arms. The night was warm. Only a couple of miles to go.

"Ready?" Johnny asked. "We'll be there in a couple of minutes."

Carlo held up a lighter. "Am I breathing?"

"Wake up, girl! Something bad's going on!"

Charlie came out of sleep to hear the roar of an engine passing by her bedroom window. She sprang out of bed and ran to the window, but all she could see was dust and taillights. She heard the tires screeching as they pulled out onto Buck Mountain Road and disappeared into the soupy blackness of the night.

"Come on!" Jasper was shouting. "We got fire!"

Charlie cleared the back door to see fingers of orange flame crawling up the walls of both the barn and Jasper's shop. She sprinted toward the barn in her nightgown and bare feet. Gray smoke billowed toward the sky, the acrid smell of gasoline and burning wood attacked her. Light from the flames was flickering off the canopy behind the barn. She heard shrieking.

"Sadie! Oh my God, Sadie!"

Biscuit was running back and forth between the barn and the shop, barking ferociously. Jasper was about thirty feet ahead of Charlie. He'd hesitated at the barn

door, but now he disappeared. Charlie barreled headlong through the door after him. The heat inside the
barn was what Charlie imagined hell might feel like; the
roar of the fire consuming oxygen and fuel sounded like
a freight train.

Jasper was opening the door to Sadie's stall, surrounded by flames. He was shirtless and barefoot, wearing only a pair of boxer shorts. Charlie veered into the
tack room, grabbed a blanket, a halter and a lead line,
and sprinted to Sadie's stall. The door was now open and
Jasper was pushing her, but the terrified animal wouldn't
move.

"Take this!" Charlie yelled as she slipped the halter
over Sadie's ears. She held out the blanket. "Cover her
eyes!"

Jasper began covering the horse's eyes with the blanket while Charlie snapped the lead line onto the halter.
Her skin was hot and painful. She felt as though she was
being baked alive. A cross beam fell from the hayloft and
showered them in sparks.

"Gotta go!" Jasper shouted. "Gotta go gotta go
gotta go!"

Charlie pulled on the lead line and the horse
responded. They hurried through the stall door and
across the seemingly endless barn floor. The air outside
the barn was gloriously cool. Charlie led Sadie toward
the house and tied the lead line to a tree branch near
the back porch. She turned back toward the barn and
the shop, both raging infernos now. Jasper was standing twenty feet away with his back to her, his hands on
his hips. Charlie walked up and stood next to him, and

together, they watched two symbols of their heritage go up in flames. There was nothing either of them could do. The area was serviced by a volunteer fire department that was slow to react, and even if they'd called the minute they spotted the fire, it wouldn't have done any good. The old wood planks used to construct the buildings, the dry straw and hay, the chemicals in Jasper's shop, were all accelerants. The buildings were doomed the moment the fire started.

Charlie put a hand on Jasper's shoulder.

"Don't worry, uncle. We'll rebuild them."

She looked at her uncle's face, glowing in the light from the flames. His eyes were wet and angry. He dropped to his knees, spread his arms, and let out a feral wail that echoed off the nearby slopes.

"They're gone!" Jasper cried. "Momma and Daddy and Rachel! They're gone! Somebody's gonna pay for this!"

PART III

CHAPTER FORTY-SEVEN

Morning finally arrived, the volunteer firemen had finished drinking their coffee and left. Charlie had called them to make sure the fire didn't spread to the house and to document the scene for the insurance claim she planned to file. She wasn't at all optimistic about the reaction she would receive from the insurance company. She would tell them it was arson and they would immediately suspect her of setting the fire. They might pay the claim, they might not.

The barn and the shop were nothing but black, smoldering piles of ash. A couple of support poles stuck up out of the remains of the barn like burned bones. An arson investigator from the sheriff's department had showed up a little after seven. His name was Timmons, a short, thin, middle-aged rooster of a man who walked around the ruins at least a dozen times and kept running his hand across his shiny, hairless scalp. He seemed to be itching to dive into the ashes, but they were still too hot.

"So ye say ye saw 'em?" Timmons asked Charlie. They were standing about halfway between the house and the barn. Jasper and Biscuit were standing a few feet away.

"I saw their tail lights," Charlie said.

"So ye didn't see 'em."

"No, I guess not."

"But ye saw their lights?"

"Yes."

"So ye did see 'em, I reckon. Ye just can't *identify* 'em."

"Maybe you could get casts of their tire tracks," Charlie said.

"I do fires. Don't do tires. Hee-hee, that rhymes, don't it? Maybe I'll put it in a song. Timmons does fires but he don't do tires, doo-dah, doo-dah, Timmons does fires but he don't do tires, oh, doo-dah-day."

"Is there someone else who might be able to come and get casts?"

"I'll ask around when I get back," Timmons said. "Barn fire's all it is, though. Nobody hurt, livestock made it out. I don't reckon they'll be rollin' out the big guns for this one."

"That's comforting."

"So why you reckon they'd drive up like that?" Timmons asked.

"Probably because of the dog."

"So it was somebody that knows ye?"

"I don't know who it was."

"Well, it was somebody that knows ye well enough to know ye got a big ol' dog. Rolled in here near three in the mornin', threw a couple of bottles full of gasoline at each building, then tore on outta here. The smell and the shards of glass near the edge of the ashes gimme a pretty good clue. One of the boys at the department said he thinks it was probably that Clyde Dalton feller that's been stalking you."

"I don't think it was him."

"That so? Why not?"

"I just don't think it was him."

"Who else, then? Who else you made mad lately?"

"I don't know. I'm a lawyer. People get mad sometimes."

"I know a bunch of lawyers. Not a one of them has had their barn burned. Tell you what, I'll come back later and see if the ashes has cooled off enough for me to do a little sifting. Don't think it'll do much good, but maybe I'll get lucky and find something I can use."

"You ain't sifting nothing," Jasper said. He walked over and towered over Timmons, who looked at him curiously.

"What do ye mean? I can't find no clues if I don't sift."

"You already said it was gasoline. I could've told you that as soon as you got here and saved myself having to listen to your foolishness."

"But this is a crime scene. I got things I need to do."

"This is private property and I'm telling you there ain't going to be no sifting."

"Insurance company's gonna send an investigator if you file a claim."

"And I'll tell him the same as I'm telling you. This is my land, those are my ashes, and you or nobody else is going to touch them."

"Well if you just don't beat all."

"I didn't call you to come out here. One of them firemen must have done it. I don't want no investigation and I don't care about no insurance."

Timmons seemed to shrink into himself like a turtle.

"I reckon I'm done then," he said.

"I reckon so."

"Joe Dillard is coming up," Charlie said to Jasper as they watched Timmons drive away. "I called him because I feel like I need some advice. I'd like you to be there when I talk to him, but I hope you'll be a little more hospitable than you were to that investigator."

Joe arrived thirty minutes later. After she showed him the damage, Charlie served him coffee at the kitchen table. Jasper joined them. He'd barely said a word since the fire. Charlie could see that he was deeply wounded by the loss of his shop, and, she imagined, by the loss of his "special" mannequins. He was angry, too. She could see it in the set of his jaw, the curve in his brow, the harshness in his eyes.

"You know the old saying, 'Bad things happen to good people?'" Joe said as he lifted his cup to his lips. "You're a prime example."

"It's gotten out of hand," Charlie said. "You were right about the gold. It's been nothing but a curse. As soon as I found it, bad things started happening. First Clyde Dalton came along and then Jack got shot. Now my father had been murdered and someone has burned our barn and tried to kill my horse. Zane Barnes wanted it so badly, and look what's happened to him."

"With him being gone, the land is yours now," Joe said. "So is the gold. But it looks like someone else wants it. Maybe Barnes hired somebody and they turned on him."

"What am I going to do?" Charlie said. "I wish I could find whoever it is that wants it so badly. I'd give it to him or them or whoever it is. I swear I would."

"Maybe Clyde Dalton burned the barn," Joe said. "I don't know how he would be connected to Zane Barnes or why he would have killed him, but I guess stranger things have happened."

"It wasn't Dalton." Jasper spoke for the first time. "Dalton's gone."

Joe set the cup down and turned to Jasper.

"What do you mean?"

"I mean he's gone. He ain't gonna be coming around again."

"You and I don't know each other, Mr. Story," Joe said. "But I want to be clear about something. I'm not your lawyer, so the things you say to me are not protected by the attorney-client privilege. I don't intend to repeat anything that's said here this morning, but in case something comes up in the future, you should be careful what you say."

"I didn't say anything I'd take back," Jasper said. "I heard the man is gone, and I believe the person who told me. He didn't set no fire last night."

"Charlie, you asked me to come up here and talk. What is it you want to talk about?"

Charlie got up from the table and disappeared. When she returned, she was carrying something that was wrapped in a blanket. She plopped it down on the table, then disappeared again. She made four more trips.

"I want you to take these," she said. "I brought them in from the barn and have been keeping them under my bed. I don't want them in the house anymore."

"Is that what I think it is?"

Charlie pulled back the blankets, revealing five gleaming bars of gold.

"These bars represent more than two-and-a-half million dollars," she said. "Please take them."

Joe leaned back and drew a deep breath. "You know I'd like to help you, Charlie, but what would I do with it?"

"Put your grandchildren through college. Give it to charity. I don't care what you do with it. The sight of it sickens me now."

"Put it back, Charlie. However you got it out of the cave, just do the opposite. Put it back and leave it there. Give yourself some time to sort everything out."

Charlie sat down heavily in one of the chairs and covered her face with her hands.

"It isn't over," she said. "Whoever killed my father, whoever burned the barn wants the gold and they'll be back. Even if I take the gold to the cave, they'll be back. They think I'm the only person who knows where the gold is, and they'll come for me. I'm going to wind up like Zane Barnes. It's just a question of when."

"I think you and your uncle should invest in some security measures, some motion detectors, some alarms, whatever," Joe said. "Work out some kind of communication plan that allows you to check on each other regularly. Keep Jasper's dog close by. Maybe you should get yourself a pistol, Charlie. Do you know how to use a gun?"

"I'm a country girl. Of course I know how to use a gun."

"Do you have one?"

"I have two, but I'm not going to start carrying them around with me."

"Why not?"

"Because I'm not a killer. I'm a stupid, greedy young woman who became obsessed with the idea of being rich and I put my own selfish interests ahead of everything else. And now I'm paying the price. The best thing for everyone right now would be for me to take one of those guns you just mentioned and blow my brains out with it."

"You don't mean that," Joe said. "Listen, I've been where you are right now. I've blamed myself when bad things have happened, and there have been times I've wanted to just throw in the towel and quit. As a matter of fact, I *have* quit a couple of times. I've withdrawn, isolated myself in a little cocoon of self-pity and self-loathing. But I've learned to forgive myself when I make mistakes, and that's something you should try to do. So maybe you became a little pre-occupied with this gold. Who wouldn't? It's a fortune and it was handed to you with what you thought were no strings attached. You couldn't have foreseen the uproar it would cause. You couldn't—"

"You warned me," Charlie said. "You were the first person to use the phrase 'blood money.' You said bad things could happen, that people could get hurt. I should have listened to you."

"You haven't done anything wrong," Joe said.

"But what about now? What do I do now?"

"You keep your head on a swivel. You stay in close touch with me, with your uncle, with Jack. And you keep on going. That's all you can really do, Charlie. You just have to keep on going."

CHAPTER FORTY-EIGHT

Jordan Scott's trial was scheduled to begin in October, and despite everything that had happened, Joe had let it be known that he was still counting on Charlie to do a closing argument so compelling that the jury would find Jordan not guilty. Joe had been emailing her themes and phrases that he wanted her to use, but she'd been distracted and found it hard to concentrate for more than a few minutes at a time.

Joe left mid-morning to go to the cancer center in Johnson City where his wife was getting treatment. He went twice a week, every week, and sat with Caroline while she received the intravenous drugs that were keeping her alive. Jack had gone over to his aunt's diner to grab an early lunch before he went out and did an interview with a potential witness. Charlie was trying to concentrate on outlining her argument and looking over statements when she heard someone knocking on the front door of the office. It had remained locked since Clyde Dalton had shot up the place. Charlie got up and walked into the lobby. Standing outside the glass door were two unusual-looking young men.

"Can I help you?" Charlie yelled through the glass.

One of them was perhaps the largest human being Charlie had ever seen. He had black hair and eyes and muscles that rippled through the light jacket he was wearing. His hands were massive. The other one was smaller and also had dark features. He, too, was muscular, though nowhere near as muscular as the big one.

"We need a lawyer," the smaller one said. "Got a little trouble."

"What kind of trouble?" Charlie said.

"It's a little embarrassing yelling through the door like this," he said. "Mind opening up?"

Charlie was reluctant, but it was a potential client, so she unlocked the door. The small one introduced himself as Johnny and the big one said his name was Carlo. Charlie led them into Joe's office because there were extra chairs in there. She took a seat behind Joe's desk.

"What kind of trouble did you get into?" she said.

"I said it was a little trouble," the one who called himself Johnny said. "But that isn't really true. We got big trouble."

"Do you have a warrant? Any paperwork?"

"No."

"Okay ... why don't you just tell me what happened?"

"Somebody has something that belongs to us. We want it back."

"I don't understand. I thought you—"

"Did I tell you my last name? It's Russo. That mean anything to you?"

A wave of fear, cold and remorseless, swept over Charlie. Her mouth went dry. She couldn't have screamed if she'd tried. Her legs were suddenly trembling. She looked at both of them, alternately, and realized she was looking directly into the face of death.

"How's your horse, anyway?" His eyes bored into her. The big man got up, walked over and closed and locked the office door.

"This is how it's gonna be," Johnny Russo said. "You're gonna tell us where the gold is. If you don't, we're gonna rain fire down on you like you ain't never dreamed of. We're gonna kill everything and everybody you know, starting with that lawyer who left a little while ago. That other guy that left just a minute ago? He a friend of yours? Dead. Your uncle? Bye, bye. We'll crush his head in a vise the same way we did your old buddy Barnes, and we'll make you watch. If that don't do it, we'll start cutting you up, piece by piece. Carlo here likes to inflict pain. The first thing he'll do is cut your nipples off. After that, he'll cut off one little piece at a time until you either tell us or you bleed to death."

"I ... I can't." Charlie's voice was raspy. She could feel perspiration beneath her arms.

"You *can* and you *will*. Right now."

"I can't tell you where it is. It's in a cave in the mountains. You'd never find it. I'd have to show you. I'd have to take you there."

"Fine. Let's go."

"How do I know you won't just kill me after I show you?"

"You don't."

"Then I'm not going anywhere."

Russo turned his head to Carlo, who was standing near the door.

"Go over to that diner and wait for the pretty boy to come out. Shoot him in the head as soon as he clears the door."

"No," Charlie said. "Don't. Don't hurt him. I'll go with you. I'll show you where it is."

CHAPTER FORTY-NINE

"Two things," Charlie said as she pulled her pick-up onto the street. "We need a flashlight, and I have to text my uncle."

Her fear had subsided slowly. She felt it morphing into anger as she realized she was probably looking at her father's killer.

"Why do we need a flashlight?"

"Because it's in a cave. I told you that."

"No way on the uncle," Johnny said from the passenger side. Carlo was in a car behind them.

"I text him every thirty minutes. All it says is, 'ok.' If he doesn't get a text from me, he's going to call. If he calls and I don't answer, he'll get ahold of the police and they'll be all over the mountain by the time we get there."

"You're lying."

"I'm not. Here, look at my outgoing text messages." She offered her phone to Russo.

"I don't want to look at your phone. And you ain't texting nobody."

"He'll call."

"So he calls. You tell him you forgot. You tell him everything's fine. Why do you text him every thirty minutes, anyway?"

"Somebody killed my father. Somebody burned our barn and Jasper's shop. But you wouldn't know anything about that. My horse is fine, by the way. We got her out."

"Too bad," Johnny said. "I hate horses."

"So you killed my father."

"I didn't say that."

"But you did."

"I didn't kill him."

"Then that animal behind us killed him."

"Carlo ain't no animal."

"But he killed him."

"Shut your mouth. You talk too much."

Charlie's cell phone rang.

"I told you," she said. "It's my uncle."

Johnny produced a gun from beneath his jacket and pointed it at her stomach.

"You tell him what I said. One wrong word and I'll shoot you in the gut."

Charlie pushed the button on the phone. "Sorry, Jasper," she said. "I forgot. No, no, everything's fine. Everything's perfect. No, I'm in the car. Just running a couple of errands. Yes. How about you? Biscuit? Good. All right. Half-an-hour."

"Biscuit? What was that? Some kind of code?"

"Biscuit is his dog's name. Listen, I'm not kidding about the flashlight. We have to have it."

"Stop at a store and I'll send Carlo in. I swear to God if you're jerking me around you'll suffer for it."

Charlie stopped at a Wal-Mart in Elizabethton and she and Johnny waited while Carlo went inside.

"How are you planning on getting up there?" Charlie asked.

"Where?"

"To the cave. I had to hide my horse so you wouldn't kill it, so we can't take her, and I can't walk up the mountain in these shoes."

"It's somewhere on Barnes' old place, right?"

Charlie nodded.

"There's a four-wheeler there. We take it."

Charlie shook her head.

"What?"

"You have no idea what you're dealing with."

"What do you mean?"

"There's two thousand pounds of gold up there. The terrain is rugged. The cave is huge."

"You just get us there. Let me worry about the rest."

CHAPTER FIFTY

Jasper's lungs were burning as he jogged up the mountain. Peanut was in trouble. That was certain. She hadn't texted him when she was supposed to, and when he got her on the phone, she called him "Jasper." She called him "uncle," never "Jasper." And the word was supposed to be "okay." Everything is "okay." She said "fine" and "perfect." They'd talked things over for two hours after Joe suggested they work out some kind of emergency plan. Peanut's biggest fear was that whoever had been terrorizing her would grab her up and torture her until she told them where the gold was. Jasper wondered how they got to her.

She said she was in the car, which, he hoped, meant she was leading them to the cave. They'd also talked about the best way to handle it if whoever was behind all this got her into the cave. The plan was risky and imperfect. All Jasper had to go by was the memory of the map Peanut had drawn for him and the description she'd given him of the cave. He knew he could find it, but he didn't know if he could find the stream at the bottom. He hoped Peanut could keep her head. He hoped she was coming to the cave. He hoped he got there first. He hoped he'd done the right thing by leaving the dog locked up in the house. And he hoped he could shoot straight with the unfamiliar compound bow that was hanging across his back. His old re-curve, the one he'd used to kill Clyde Dalton, was destroyed in the fire.

It was only a little over a mile as the crow flies to the cave, but crows didn't fly along the surface of the mountain. Jasper jogged through draws and scrambled up steep slopes. He waded across the creek and climbed another slope. He cleared a ridge and the hourglass rock came into view, right where he thought it would be. He stopped and tried to catch his breath, tried to listen to the sounds of the mountain. There was no one in sight. He hurried down through the rocks and crossed the creek again. The rock loomed above him like a broad-shouldered sentry. He climbed the last few feet and saw it. The mouth of the cave, nearly hidden by vines. He stood in the opening and peered into the darkness, straining to hear some human sound.

There was none.

He flipped the switch on Peanut's high-powered spotlight and walked into the black.

CHAPTER FIFTY-ONE

Charlie was sandwiched between Johnny and Carlo on the four-wheeler. Johnny was driving with Charlie pointing the way, while Carlo was sitting on a metal rack, facing backward. The thought struck her that the morning was very much like the one on which Roscoe Barnes died. The sky was a deep blue and clear. It was warm with a soft breeze blowing. She wondered whether she was experiencing the majesty of the mountains for the last time. She wondered whether Jasper had figured out she was in trouble, whether he'd have time to get there before they killed her.

She was certain they'd leave her dead once she showed them where the gold was hidden. Why wouldn't they? She knew what they looked like. She knew Johnny's name and knew Carlo's first name. Johnny hadn't actually admitted to anything, but she knew these two were responsible for at least two deaths and an arson. There was something inhuman, animalistic, about Johnny and Carlo. Carlo hadn't said hardly a word, but she could feel the predator in both of them. She was their prey. Once they got what they wanted, they would kill her, discard her, and never give it a second thought.

She'd guided them slowly up the mountain and had directed Johnny away from the cave for as long as she could. Along the way, she'd questioned herself again about the way she'd handled things, about whether her greed had cost Luke his life. She could have done what Joe suggested, turned the gold over to the court and let the court case run its course. She could have worked out some kind of settlement with Barnes. She could have gotten the police involved early on. But she hadn't done any of those things, and now, well, now she was facing the consequences of her decisions. A part of her was almost relieved. Even if she ended up dead, at least she wouldn't have to be afraid anymore. And if they killed her, took the gold and left, Jasper would no longer be in danger, nor would Joe or Jack or Sadie or anyone else.

The hour glass was in front of them. Charlie pointed.

"There. Behind that rock."

They got off the four-wheeler. Charlie removed her shoes and set them on the seat. She looked at the others and the thought struck her that all three of them looked entirely out of place, they in their athletic wear and she in her business attire. Under different circumstances, she would have laughed.

"Give me the light," she said to Johnny.

"I'll carry the light."

"I have to go first. I need the light. You're both carrying guns. If I try to get away, shoot me."

Charlie snatched the flashlight from Johnny's left hand. His pistol was in his other hand. Carlo was carrying one, too. They weren't nearly so cocky up here on the mountain. Their eyes were darting around from the mouth of the cave to the boulder to the mountain to the four-wheeler.

"Watch out for bats," Charlie said. She turned and walked into the cave.

The smooth rock was cold beneath her feet as Charlie worked her way carefully through the first tunnel. The men behind her remained mute. When they came to the spot where the cave opened up into the first huge chamber, Charlie flashed the light around.

"We have to go to the bottom of this, then through another tunnel," she said.

"No way," Johnny said.

"Do you want it or not?"

There was no reply, so Charlie started winding her way downward through the formations. Now that she was in the cave with strangers, with people who she believed would do her harm, she felt almost comfortable, as though the cave was an old, familiar friend.

"I feel like I'm in hell," she heard Carlo say.

"Maybe you are," Charlie whispered.

A few minutes later, they were in the second tunnel, then in the bottom chamber.

"Wait, what's that?" It was Johnny.

"A still. It belonged to the man who kept the gold."

Charlie was trying to feel Jasper's presence. Was he there? Did he find it? Did he make it in time? If he was hiding somewhere in the darkness, what would he do?

The flashlight reflected off the stream. They were at the end of their journey.

"It's in there," Charlie said, shining the light on the spot where the stream flowed beneath the rock. "You have to walk down into the stream and wade in. It's about fifteen, twenty feet back. It opens up into a smaller chamber. The gold is on a ledge, in wooden crates."

"Lead the way," Johnny said.

"No. This is as far as I'm going. I've showed you where it is. Let me go."

"You're not going anywhere," Carlo said. He moved around Johnny, closer to her.

The chamber suddenly filled with a blinding light, coming from Charlie's right. Carlo and Johnny both turned and raised their guns. Carlo grunted and staggered back a step. Both of them started firing. Gunshots ripped the silence in rapid succession. Charlie backed away a step, looked at Johnny, saw him turning his gun toward her.

She ran two steps, sucked her lungs full of air, and dived headlong into the frigid water. The flashlight was still in her hand. It flickered and went out. She kicked furiously, knew she was already underneath the rock face, knew she was going toward the outside of the cave. How far was it? Blackness and cold covered her. It was as though she'd entered a freezing womb.

She saw it, a dim yet unmistakable glow, but it seemed so far away; she kept kicking. The light was growing brighter, but at the same time, her chest was tightening, her throat constricting. How much farther? She felt light-headed. The thought that she wasn't going to make it entered her mind. She didn't care. Dying wasn't so bad.

Suddenly the light was above her. She broke the surface gasping and choking, gulping in air between fits of coughing and gagging. She got her feet beneath her, found her balance, and stood. The water was thigh deep. She looked up and saw the rock face, knew where she was. She took two steps toward the stream's edge, stopped cold.

Uncle.

Charlie crawled out of the water and started running toward the cave entrance. She'd run close to a hundred yards when she realized the flashlight had gone out. It was still in her right hand, lifeless. How could she ever get back in there without light? She couldn't. She stopped and turned back toward the stream, back toward the cave, back toward the stream.

"Oh, god. What do I do? What do I do?"

She looked at the flashlight closely. It was cheap, a plastic case, but the bulb didn't seem to be burned out. She unscrewed the cap, poured the batteries out into her palm. She started rubbing them on her skirt, but it was soaked. So was her blouse, her vest. Everything was soaked.

She looked around. There was a stand of laurel bushes near the stream. She ran back and dropped to her knees. The top layer of leaves that had been shed by the bush was relatively dry. She scraped a handful and frantically stuffed them into the case. She pulled them back out with an index finger and started blowing into the case. She took the batteries and rubbed them with more leaves, rubbed the contact point on the bulb. She reassembled the flashlight and pushed the switch with her thumb, held her palm over the lens to shade it from the sunlight. It worked. The light was glowing.

Charlie got off her knees and ran to the cave. The beam from the flashlight was dull, but it was better than nothing. She hurried down the first tunnel with the light bouncing and her heart pounding. When she got to the end of the tunnel, to the top of the cathedral, she saw an intense light at the bottom close to where she knew the second tunnel opened up. She turned her flashlight off and instinctively went to her knees.

A long minute, maybe the longest of her life, passed. There was no sound. She was frozen in time, like an insect in amber. Then the light moved, almost imperceptibly. Moved again, just a bit.

Charlie stood slowly. She turned the flashlight on, pointed it at the ground, and started moving again.

"Uncle?" She said it softly.

"Uncle?" A little louder.

She heard a groan. Jasper's voice.

"Uncle!"

Down the slope she went as fast as damp feet against slick rock would allow. When she got to him, her light revealed a long, dark streak leading back into the tunnel.

Jasper was on his stomach, pushing the spotlight in front of him. As Charlie knelt, he rolled onto his back.

"You made it," he said. "I knew you would."

"What is it? What happened?"

"I gave 'em a little too much time." Jasper's face was white. "A ricochet got me in the leg. Must've cut the femoral. Losing a lot of blood."

"Are they ... ?"

"They're dead."

"Come on. Let me help you up. We have to get you out of here."

"Too late."

"Don't say that. You'll be fine. You'll be okay."

Jasper reached up with his right hand and ran his fingers through her hair, down her cheek.

"You're safe now. You're free."

"I said don't! Don't quit! Don't quit on me!"

Charlie felt tears welling in her eyes. She willed herself to keep her composure.

"Just bad luck is all," Jasper said. His voice was just above a whisper. "You take care of that hound of mine. There's money in the mattress in my bedroom, Peanut. Plenty of it. I want you to use some to hire a man named Wilbur Stoots to blow this cave shut. Put all the gold back and blow it shut. Seal it off forever."

Charlie bit her lower lip as tears ran down her cheeks.

"Please don't go," she whispered. "Please."

He sighed deeply, lifted his head. Charlie slipped her hand behind his neck. "Don't put me in the ground," he said. "Promise you won't put me in the ground. Take me to Riley and tell him to burn me. Put my ashes with Rachel."

Charlie nodded, unable to speak. Jasper's eyes fluttered. He took a long breath and looked directly into her eyes.

"I always loved you, Peanut. I should've told you."

And then he was gone.

CHAPTER FIFTY-TWO

Charlie sat next to him with his head in her lap for a long time, crying. She watched for signs of life early in the vigil, but before long the realization set in. There would be no signs. It was over.

She picked up the spotlight and walked back down into the cave near the stream. Carlo's body was sitting against the cave wall. Charlie looked at him for a long time. There was a large, dark spot of blood on his chest, another in his throat. He'd apparently managed to pull himself into a sitting position with his back resting against the cave wall. His eyes were open, staring down at his hands, which were curled in his lap.

Johnny Russo was floating face down in the stream. Charlie knew she had a legal obligation to call the police now. The bodies would need to be disposed of, questions would need to be answered. The police would open an investigation, and when they discovered that these two bodies led to Zane Barnes and Luke Story and Roscoe Barnes and ultimately, a hundred bars of gold, it would become a circus. The Tennessee Bureau of Investigation, the Federal Bureau of Investigation, every state and local police officer who wanted to try to stick his nose in the spotlight would want a piece of this one. The media attention would be insane.

The cops would question, analyze and second-guess every thought she'd had, every decision she'd made. They would search her house, accuse Jasper of murder, ask why she hadn't involved them earlier. She decided at that moment she wasn't going to deal with their scrutiny or their judgments. She shined the spotlight around and found Jasper's bow and five arrows, two of them bloody. She thought there was probably another arrow or two in the stream. If they were in there, they would stay there. She waded into the water and grabbed Johnny's ankles, dragged him out of the stream. She didn't want him floating beneath the rocks and popping up outside somewhere. Then she rifled his pockets for the key to the four-wheeler.

Jasper's blood was black and thick on the rock floor where he'd dragged himself toward the entrance. She went back to him, ran her arms beneath his shoulders and started dragging him out. She wished there was a more dignified way, but there just wasn't. She dragged him ten feet. Rested. Dragged him another ten feet. Rested. Finally, she got him back to the four wheeler. She laid him face down across the seat behind her, started the four-wheeler, and drove slowly home.

She finally managed to get Jasper's body into the house and laid it on his bed. Biscuit almost tore the back door off the hinges when Charlie climbed the steps, but the dog quickly became silent when the door opened and he inspected Jasper. Charlie found a soft, white, silk sheet that had belonged to her grandmother and wrapped it around him. She went into her bedroom and changed clothes, went outside and backed Jasper's truck up to the porch. She spread a blanket on the floor, rolled Jasper onto it carefully, pulled him outside, and put him in the bed of the truck.

Riley Potts was an old friend of Jasper's who lived on Spivey Mountain in Unicoi County. He, too, was a taxidermist and a hunter. Charlie had been to his house a few times when she was younger, and Riley had come by to drink coffee and talk with Jasper several times.

Riley's place wasn't much more than a plywood shack. It sat back in a cove about halfway up the mountain. Charlie blew the horn when she got close to the house. Five matted mutts came tearing around the corner, all of them barking. Riley walked out the front door. He was wearing denim bib overalls over a white t-shirt. He waved when he saw Jasper's truck and quieted the dogs.

Charlie pulled up close to the house.

"Well, I'll be dogged. Charlie, I hain't seen you in a coon's age."

"I need your help, Riley."

"What's wrong? Whar's that uncle o' yourn?"

"He's in the back."

Charlie got out and pulled back the blankets she'd wrapped around Jasper. She lifted the silk sheet from his face.

"I need you to take care of him for me," she said, choking back tears. "He said he didn't want to go into the ground."

CHAPTER FIFTY-THREE

I watched through the window as Charlie climbed out of her truck and walked toward the entrance of Buddy's Diner in Elizabethton. Neither Jack nor I had heard from her in days. We'd called her, texted her. We'd gone to her house and found it empty. No Charlie, no Jasper, no horse or dog. I called the Carter County Sheriff's Department and reported her missing, but as soon as the word got out that they were looking for her, an investigator at the department called me and said Charlie had contacted him by phone. She told him that after everything that had happened, she just needed to get out of town. She was fine, she said. She had called me late the night before and asked if I would meet her, without Jack, at the diner early the next morning.

The familiar smell of bacon frying and coffee brewing filled the diner. Quiet voices chatted about sports and disasters and politics. I was sitting in a booth, and she walked in and sat down across from me without saying anything. She looked exhausted. Dark circles had formed beneath her eyes and her face was pale and puffy. A waitress appeared immediately and she ordered a cup of coffee.

"Not hungry?" I asked.

"I'm having trouble eating," she said.

"We've been worried about you, Charlie. What's going on?"

"I'm not going to cry," she said. "All the way over here, that's what I've been telling myself. I'm not going to cry. I've cried so much over the past few days I don't think I have any tears left in me."

"Why? Why have you been crying? What happened?"

"They killed Jasper. They killed my uncle."

I sat there, stunned, while she told me what had happened the day she disappeared from the office. She told me about the young men, Johnny Russo and Carlo, who had come and forced her at gunpoint to the cave, about her communication with Jasper, about the battle that killed him. She said Russo and Carlo were in the cave, along with all of the gold, and that she had had Jasper's body cremated and spread the ashes among the ashes of his shop, the shop that had been burned down by Russo and Carlo.

"That's where he would want to be," she said. "There with his wife and my grandmother and grandfather."

"I don't understand," I said.

"You don't need to understand. He's where he would want to be."

She said she had taken the five bars of gold that were at her house back to the cave, tossed them inside, and then hired a man to dynamite the entrance.

"It's over now," she said. "Nobody will ever get to it."

After the entrance to the cave was sealed, she said she loaded her horse up into a trailer, loaded Biscuit into her truck, and went camping in the mountains of North Carolina.

"I needed to get away," she said. "I needed to think."

She spoke in the disaffected manner of one who had suffered a great trauma. Her voice was flat and cold, her demeanor dull and lifeless. I wanted to wrap my arms around her and hold her, to tell her that everything would be all right, to reassure her somehow, but I knew it would be pointless. There was only one thing that would heal her, and that was the passage of time.

"What about the police?" I said. "You aren't going to tell them what happened? Shouldn't the bodies in the cave be taken care of?"

"They got what they deserved," she said bitterly. "They killed my father and my uncle. They burned down our barn and my uncle's shop. They killed Zane Barnes. They wanted the gold, and now they have it. They'll be close to it forever."

"Won't someone come looking for them? Did they say where they were from?"

"I heard them mention Philadelphia," she said, "and I don't care if someone comes. They won't find them."

"I'm sorry," I said. "I'm so very, very sorry. What are your plans, Charlie? What are you going to do now? You need some help and support, and I want you to know that I'll do anything, anything I can to help you."

"I'm leaving," she said. "I can't stay here. It's too much. The house, the memories, the guilt, it's just too much to bear."

"Where will you go?"

"I don't know. West, maybe. Someplace with big skies. I want you to tell Jack goodbye for me, and I want you to tell him I'm sorry."

"You don't have anything to be sorry for."

"Tell him, will you?"

"I will. Do you need anything? Money?"

"No, thank you, I'm fine. My uncle said something to me once that I've been thinking about a lot lately. He said 'What's past is past, but that don't mean it's gone. You can't just wipe the board clean.' And he was right, you know? I'll never be able to wipe the board clean, but maybe if I put some distance between myself and this place, these memories, maybe I can blur everything enough to be able to live with myself again."

"When are you leaving?"

"This morning. I'm packed. All I have to do is load Sadie in the trailer and start driving. I guess I won't be around to help you with Jordan's trial. I'm sorry."

"I've tried cases by myself before. Don't worry about it."

"I've thought about Jordan a lot, too. About how people make decisions and then have to deal with the consequences. I made some bad decisions, and I'll have to deal with them for the rest of my life. Jordan made a decision, and maybe it wasn't a good decision, but he shouldn't have to spend the rest of his life in jail. How does it look for him? How do you think it will go?"

"You never know what a jury will do, but we got a huge break two days ago. The feds arrested Howard Raleigh and Raymond Peale on racketeering and conspiracy to commit murder charges. I thought the prosecution might think twice about going ahead with Jordan's case, but I talked to the district attorney yesterday and he said they're still going to trial. Typical prosecutorial pig-headedness."

"Good luck," Charlie said. "I know you'll do a great job."

"Will you ever come back?" I said.

She shook her head. "I don't know. I don't know what the future holds for me."

"Please tell me you'll stay in touch. That you'll let me know where you are and how you're doing."

"I will. I'm not making any promises about how soon it will be, but I will."

"I'll miss you, Charlie. Jack will miss you."

"I'll miss you, too. You've been good to me."

She slid out of the booth and stood.

"Goodbye, Joe," she said.

"I'll talk to you soon," I said, and I watched her walk out to her truck and drive away.

CHAPTER FIFTY-FOUR

(OCTOBER)

I walked into the district attorney's office in Blountville at eight-thirty in the morning and was greeted somberly by Griffin Dykes. Dykes was the district attorney general for Sullivan County, which made up the entirety of Tennessee's Second Judicial District. He was in his late fifties, serving his first term after having spent twenty years slugging it out in courtrooms as an assistant district attorney. His short hair was mostly gray now, his eyes brown and intense. His slim physique reflected his passion for running in marathons. He was wearing a charcoal gray suit and a starched, white shirt. I respected Dykes and had tried more than a dozen cases against him earlier in my career. He was a serious man, meticulous in his preparation, and I'd always found him to be fair-minded and reasonable.

"Just the two of us?" I said as we shook hands.

He nodded and motioned to a chair in front of his desk. It was Friday morning. Jordan Scott's trial was scheduled to begin the following Monday. Dykes had called me the day before and asked me to come over "and have a conversation." I knew he wanted to make a deal. I sat down across the desk from him.

"Can I offer you anything?" Dykes said. "Coffee, water?"

"Got any whiskey?"

He reached down and opened a drawer, pulled out a bottle of Glenlivet scotch and two glasses.

"I was kidding, Griffin," I said.

"I'm not," he said.

He poured two fingers into each glass, slid one of the glasses across the desk to me, and raised his own.

"What are we drinking to?" I asked.

"To reason."

"To reason," I said, and I took a small sip. Griffin drained his glass and set it on the desk.

"This matter we're about to try," Griffin said, "has caused me to lose more sleep than any case in my career. I choose to regard my role as district attorney in an idealistic fashion. I was elected to represent the people of this district in the prosecution of criminal cases, and I do my very best to serve them to the best of my ability."

"I know you do," I said.

"You've dealt with difficult cases before, and so have I, but this one ... this one troubles me. I find myself in the position of trying to convict a man of murder when I would rather give him a medal."

"I vote for the second option."

"Please, don't be cavalier. This is a serious matter, Joe. I'd like for you to help me resolve it in a way that will be ... palatable for all concerned."

Since the arrests of Howard Raleigh, Sheriff Raymond Peale and Chief Deputy Matthew Bacon, a steady stream of information had been made available to me through various sources, primarily Leon Bates. I had reports and notes of complaints made against Todd Raleigh, documentation of the results of internal investigations, copies of anonymous memos written to the sheriff by people in his department who were concerned about Todd Raleigh and the effect he was having on the department's reputation and morale, and even recordings of conversations made secretly by Matthew Bacon after he became an FBI informant. Griffin Dykes was unaware of all the information I possessed, and, as a criminal defense attorney, I had no obligation to tell him about it. I would spring it on him during the trial if the circumstances allowed and the judge ruled it admissible. I was sure that Griffin had access to the same information, but he had no way of knowing that I'd been able to get my hands on it.

"I know how serious it is," I said, "and I apologize if I was cavalier. But I think I can help you, Griffin."

He raised his eyebrows and poured another two fingers of scotch into his glass.

"Is that so?" he said. "And how might you be able to help?"

"Let's just go through the trial together. We'll make our opening statements. You'll say Jordan was acting as a vigilante, that he pre-meditated the killing, that he shot Todd Raleigh as Raleigh was trying to run away, and that he deserves to be punished. I'll counter by arguing that Raleigh was committing a rape and that Jordan stopped it, that he was within his legal rights to use deadly force in defense of the girl who was being raped. And then the real show will begin. You'll call the first responders, the deputies and the EMTs, to describe the scene and to establish the position of Raleigh's body to prove that he was moving away from Jordan when he was shot. Then you'll call the medical examiner to establish the cause of death. Once you get there, you're going to start running into problems. You can put the gun in evidence through one of the first responders, but in order to prove pre-meditation you're going to have to prove that it belonged to Jordan's father and that Jordan took it from him and had been carrying it for more than a week. How are you going to do that? By calling Duane Scott to the witness stand? That isn't going to go well. And it won't go well if you call the rape victim to try to solidify the point that Raleigh was running away. She'll be a tough witness for you because she's on our side. I'm sure you've talked to her. I have. Several times.

"To further your theme of pre-meditation, you'll have to call Jordan's friends, coaches, family. They're on your witness list, but I know you don't want to call any of them because they all love him and every single one of them will do whatever they can to hurt your case and help ours. When I cross-examine them, I'll make sure they let the jury know how they feel about Jordan. Most, if not all of them, will mention that Jordan changed after his girlfriend was raped and committed suicide, and I guarantee you that someone will blurt out the fact that Holly accused Raleigh of the rape, that they went to the sheriff's department, and that they were stonewalled. Not only were they stonewalled, but Matt Bacon, the chief deputy at the sheriff's department, blatantly accused Holly of lying so she could file a lawsuit and make herself rich. Once that cat gets out of the bag, you can bet I'm going to press the issue. I plan to call Matt Bacon and I think the judge will let him testify because the jury has a right to hear our theory of motive since we're going to admit to the shooting. Once Bacon gets on the stand, it'll hit the fan. I'll be trying to get in evidence of the conspiracy to murder Jordan the night they let him out of the jail and what pieces of trash Howard Raleigh and Raymond Peale are and you'll be objecting and hollering that it's all irrelevant and the judge will be hammering away with his gavel and the jury will be sitting there wondering just what in the hell is going on. I'll make them so angry at Todd Raleigh and Howard Raleigh and Raymond Peale and Matt Bacon that they'll be liable to form a lynch mob and find a rope. And then I'll—"

"Enough," Griffin said. "Take another sip of your drink and calm down."

"You're in a difficult position," I said. "I understand that and I sympathize. I've been in a few myself over the years. But, like you, I have a client to represent. You're representing the people of your district, and I'm representing one man."

"Who shot and killed someone in a public park in broad daylight."

"Yes, who shot and killed someone in a public park in broad daylight. But there were circumstances, and you know as well as I do what they were. So we can either go in there on Monday, try the case, and see where the chips fall, or we can work something out. I like my chances at trial. You're feeling uncomfortable about yours or I wouldn't be sitting here sipping on this fine whiskey. So make me an offer."

"Second-degree murder, minimum sentence as a mitigated offender," Griffin said. "He agrees to a thirteen-year sentence and is eligible for parole in less than three."

"That's probably what this is, legally, because Jordan acted after extreme provocation. And it's a generous offer, a fair offer, but I can't agree to it. I just can't do it. It'll follow him for the rest of his life. I'd rather roll the dice at trial."

"Don't you think your client should make that decision?"

"We've discussed it many times. I thought it might come to this, so we've talked over all the options. I know what he'll accept and what he won't."

"What will he accept?"

"Criminally negligent homicide, time already served, you agree to judicial diversion. He serves two years on probation and then it gets expunged."

"And how do I explain my agreement to reduce a first-degree murder to a negligent homicide to the people of the district?"

"How about telling them the truth? Hang out the sheriff's department's dirty laundry for everyone to see. Use Peale and Raleigh and Bacon as scapegoats. People can handle the truth, Griffin. I don't understand why politicians and government officials can't grasp that concept."

He poured himself another scotch, and I noticed his cheeks were beginning to take on a pinkish glow. I watched the brown liquid drain from his glass down his throat. He set the glass down firmly.

"All right," he said.

He stood and stuck out his right hand. I shook it firmly.

"So it's done?" I said.

"It's done."

CHAPTER FIFTY-FIVE

I was grilling steaks on my deck Monday evening following Jordan's plea. The judge accepted it, agreed to judicial diversion, and Jordan was released in the afternoon. I had invited Jordan and his parents, along with his brother and sister, out to have dinner with Caroline and me. Jordan was subdued, but I could tell he was relieved to have this particular chapter of his life behind him.

My cell phone rang just as I pulled the last steak off the grill. I looked down and saw it was Jack, who had returned to Nashville in August to resume his studies at the Vanderbilt law school.

"How did it go?" Jack said.

"Went fine, without a hitch. We got pretty much everything we wanted."

"Congratulations."

"Thanks. I wish you could have been here. And I was thinking earlier that I wish Charlie had been here, too. I've been thinking a lot about her lately. I miss her. I wonder where she is and how she's doing."

"She's doing fine," Jack said.

"What? Have you talked to her?"

"She sort of showed up here a couple of days ago. We've been spending quite a bit of time together. As a matter of fact, she's standing right next to me. Would you like to talk to her?"

"Sure," I said, feeling a smile cross my lips, "put her on the phone."

Thank you for reading, and I sincerely hope you enjoyed *Blood Money*. As an independently published author, I rely on you, the reader, to spread the word. So if you enjoyed the book, please tell your friends and family, and if it isn't too much trouble, I would appreciate a brief review on Amazon. Thanks again. My best to you and yours.

Scott

ABOUT THE AUTHOR

Scott Pratt was born in South Haven, Michigan, and moved to Tennessee when he was thirteen years old. He is a veteran of the United States Air Force and holds a Bachelor of Arts degree in English from East Tennessee State University and a Doctor of Jurisprudence from the University of Tennessee College of Law. He lives in Northeast Tennessee with his wife, their dogs, and a parrot named JoJo.

www.scottprattfiction.com

ALSO BY SCOTT PRATT

A CRIME OF PASSION

By

SCOTT PRATT

This book, along with every book I've written and every book I'll write, is dedicated to my darling Kristy, to her unconquerable spirit and to her inspirational courage. I loved her before I was born and I'll love her after I'm long gone.

"You are the exclusive judges of the facts in this case. Also, you are the exclusive judges of the law under the direction of the court. You should apply the law to the facts in deciding this case. You should consider all of the evidence in the light of your own observations and experience in life."

Tennessee Criminal Pattern Jury Instructions – Section 1.08

"Statements, arguments, and remarks of counsel are intended to help you in understanding the evidence and applying the law, but they are not evidence. If any statements were made that you believe are not supported by the evidence, you should disregard them."

Tennessee Criminal Pattern Jury Instructions – Section 1.07

PROLOGUE

The redhead stared across the desk at the lawyer, her blue eyes smoldering. She had requested an after-hours meeting so everyone would be gone. It hadn't quite worked out that way – high-priced, big-city lawyers worked late – but there were only a couple of people left in the sprawling, twenty-fifth floor office suite that over-looked the Cumberland River and downtown Nashville, so they had plenty of privacy.

"How much have I paid you over the years, Carl?" she said with an edge in her voice.

The lawyer shrugged and held her gaze. "Not enough for me to get involved in a murder conspiracy."

"Nobody is asking you to get involved," she said. "All I want is a contact. A point of entry. A name. The name of a company. Just get me something. I'll take care of the rest."

"I should probably make you aware at this point that the attorney-client privilege does not extend to situations in which the client attempts to involve the attorney in a crime."

"Damn it, Carl, have you gone deaf? I just said you don't have to get involved! Do you know what would happen if I went out on the street with something like this? I'd wind up hiring some inept thug for fifteen thousand dollars. Or worse, I'd hire a cop and find myself in jail."

"Then don't do it," Carl Browning, a fifty-year-old, balding, bespectacled senior partner at Allen, Parks, Browning and Cummings said. Browning had represented Lana Raines-Milius, the redheaded former country music diva, for eight years. Lana could be difficult, but there were also some occasional benefits that Browning found unspeakably delicious.

"I have to do it," Lana said.

"Why?"

"He *deserves* it. He's screwing a child."

"Why don't you just divorce him?"

"Because it would take years and the only people who would benefit would be people like you."

"I don't handle divorce cases, Lana."

"I can't believe this hasn't come up before," Lana said. "In all the years you've practiced law, all the rich, high-powered clients you've worked with, you can't tell me that you've never had anyone approach you with something like this."

"I didn't say that," Browning said. "What I said was I'm not going to involve myself in a murder conspiracy."

"So it's come up," Lana said, just a hint of a smile beginning to cross her lips.

"Maybe. Once or twice."

"And you know where to go."

"I might."

Lana stood and walked to the office door, locked it, and turned back toward Browning. She walked slowly around his desk, unbuttoning her blouse as she moved. She stopped a couple of feet from him and slipped out of the blouse, laid it on the desk. The lawyer rolled his high-backed chair away from the desk and turned to face her. She took a step closer and kneeled.

"You know what kind of resources I have," Lana said softly as she reached for his belt buckle. "But I also want you to know that I'm willing to do whatever it takes to get this done and get it done right. Quick and clean. In and out. Nobody will ever have to know a thing."

Lana slowly unzipped the lawyer's fly and licked her lips seductively.

"Just one little name," she said, as her mouth opened and she leaned in toward him. "Just one little name."

CHAPTER ONE

The call that led me to the world of Paul and Lana Milius came on Christmas Eve.

The family had gathered. My son, Jack, and his girlfriend, Charleston "Charlie" Story, were home from Nashville for the holidays and were staying with my wife, Caroline, and me. My daughter, Lilly, her husband, Randy, and their son, Joseph, were also at the house, along with my sister, Sarah, and her daughter, Grace. We were doing what people do at Christmas. We'd eaten a nice dinner that Caroline and I had cooked, we'd exchanged gifts and we were sitting around drinking wine, listening to Christmas music, laughing and playing with the kids when my cell rang. I wouldn't have answered it had I not seen "Leon Bates" on the screen. Leon had been the sheriff of Washington County, Tennessee, for a long time and as far as I could tell, he would remain the sheriff for as long as he wanted. He was a rare breed, an excellent law man, an even better politician, and a truly decent human being. He and I were close friends, but he didn't routinely call me on Christmas Eve.

"Merry Christmas, Sheriff," I said.

"Merry Christmas to you, brother Dillard," Leon said in his smooth drawl.

"What's Santa going to bring you this year?"

"Ah, probably a bag of hair or a box of rocks. Maybe both. I ain't been a very good boy."

"I find that hard to believe," I said. "You're a pillar of the community, a seeker of justice, a towering hunk of righteous, manly man—"

"You been drinkin' a little there, brother Dillard?"

"Yeah, I'm working on my third glass of wine, so I'm about half in the bag. What's up, Leon? What has caused you to reach out to me on this very special holiday evening?"

"I called to see if you'd be interested in getting rich."

"Rich? As in wealthy rich?"

"As in a million dollars rich."

I got up and walked out the door onto the back deck. The air was cold and crisp, the sky clear and full of brilliant stars.

"If you're serious, Leon, you have my undivided attention."

"Never been more serious in my life. Did you hear about that little ol' gal – country singer – that turned up dead in a hotel room in Nashville back in October? It was all over the news."

"Yeah, yeah. Kasey something ... Cartwright? Kasey Cartwright. She was from Boones Creek or Gray, wasn't she?"

"That's her. Pretty thing, voice like a nightingale. Wrote good songs, too. I saw her in concert when I was in Nashville back in September. One the best guitar pickers

I've ever seen. Played the banjo, the fiddle, the piano. Her dying at such a young age was a damned shame."

"I heard something later about an overdose. I thought they ruled her death an accident or maybe a suicide."

"There wasn't any overdose. That was just gossip reporters being gossip reporters, making stuff up. They ruled it a homicide after they did an autopsy and found out her hyoid bone had been crushed. Surprised you didn't hear that. There's been a lot of speculation about who did it, but turns out they made an arrest earlier today."

"Who got arrested?"

"Man by the name of Paul Milius. Ever heard of him?"

"Can't say that I have."

"Owns a company called Perseus Records, the record company that pretty much owned Kasey Cartwright, at least the professional part of her anyway. Nice enough man. I talked to him a few times at political get-togethers in Nashville and we wound up hitting it off so well that he invited me down to his house a couple of times. Paul discovered Kasey Cartwright at some county fair down around Newport back when she was fifteen is the way the story goes. Signed her to a record deal and started building her career. Turned her into a big star. Would have turned her into a superstar if she'd lived."

"Which means he turned her into a cash cow. Why would he kill his cash cow?"

I heard Leon's signature chuckle. It was throaty, both pleasant and infectious.

"That's why I like you so much, brother Dillard," he said after a few seconds. "There you are sitting at the house on the night before Christmas, half in the bag, as you put it, and I lay out a little scenario for you and you cut right to the chase. Why *would* he kill his cash cow? That's a question that's being asked all over Nashville as we speak. And I mean *all over* Nashville. Paul Milius is worth hundreds of millions of dollars, and hundreds of millions of dollars will buy you a lot of powerful friends in the capitol city of the great state of Tennessee. Those powerful friends are all wondering the same thing, and apparently Paul Milius is screaming to high heaven that he didn't do it."

"Speaking of cutting to the chase, what does this have to do with me?"

"Milius's wife wants you to help defend him," Leon said.

"Why? She's never heard of me."

"Okay, I'll give you that. You're probably right. I doubt that she'd ever heard of you until recently. But some friends of hers have heard of you, and they want you to defend him."

"What friends?"

"Me, most importantly. I've been making friends in high places in Nashville for years and years, and like I said a minute ago, Paul and Lana Milius are among those friends. Paul is in jail right now. I just got off the phone with his wife, Lana. She says he's in shock, which is understandable, especially if he's really innocent. She wants him to have the best lawyer they can get. I know you think of yourself as a ham-and-egger, but you've built quite a reputation. Getting yourself appointed district attorney after Mooney tried to kill you, then all that with John Lipscomb and those boys from Colombia, then rescuing the little girl that was kidnapped—"

"Don't remind me of all that bad stuff, Leon. It's Christmas." I was a touch wounded that he'd called me a "ham-and-egger." I didn't think of myself as a high-powered game changer, but I thought I was maybe a touch above a ham-and-egger.

"I was right there with you in the middle of all of it, and I don't regret a thing," Leon said. "But we're getting off track here. I've told Paul and Lana about you and they want to hire you. They've had their company lawyers advising Paul up to this point – which wasn't none too bright, if you ask me – and I think the advice was bad. Paul's talked to the police a couple of times and he voluntarily gave them a DNA sample.

"That's not good, Leon. Do the cops have a DNA match?"

"My contacts at the Nashville PD say they do. A small piece of skin that was wedged between the victim's teeth. Turns out that skin belonged to Paul, but he still swears he didn't kill the girl. His wife believes him. Hell, I believe him. We want you to go down there, run the case, and then handle the trial if it gets that far. I told them you wouldn't do it for less than a million retainer, non-refundable, plus expenses. Paul Milius can pay that out of the cookie jar on top of his refrigerator. He can also afford to post whatever bond you can talk a judge into setting."

"My wife has cancer, Leon. I can't go to Nashville."

"I thought she was doing well."

"She is, but that doesn't mean I'm going to run off three hundred miles away and do a murder case that could take a year or more."

"Demand a speedy trial. Get the judge to try him quick. And you can negotiate with Paul. He has a private jet. I've been on it. Make him fly you down there and back whenever you want. You can get Nashville lawyers to do the legwork for you. Hell, brother Dillard, you're a good negotiator. You can get whatever you want out of Paul."

"You really told them a million?"

"I swear on the memory of my sweet momma."

"And you think they'll pay it?"

"I wouldn't be talking to you if I didn't."

"You know, the biggest fee I ever got from a client was two hundred and fifty thousand dollars from Erlene Barlowe back before you became sheriff. This would make that look like peanuts."

"Erlene told me how much she paid you, plus she said she paid you another good lick to get *her* out of trouble. She doesn't begrudge a dime of it."

"You still seeing her?"

"She's in the kitchen making banana pudding. You want to holler at her?"

"Another time, Leon. Tell her I said Merry Christmas. Let me sleep on this."

"I told 'em you'd want to think about it a day or two, but don't take too long. They're a pretty itchy bunch."

"I'll let you know something within forty-eight hours."

"Sounds good. Merry Christmas, brother Dillard. I hope Santy Claus brings you a bushel and a peck of everything you want. Plus a million smackeroos."

CHAPTER TWO

When I went back into the living room, everyone was watching Sarah's three-year-old daughter, Grace, as she gave an impromptu performance of "The Dance of the Sugar Plum Fairy" in front of the Christmas tree. Caroline was sitting on the couch with her long legs crossed. She was wearing a red Christmas sweater and a white skirt. She had a glass of white wine in her right hand and a look of contentment on her face. As I stood there looking at Caroline, I was reminded of how lucky I was to have her and how fortunate all of us were that she was still among us. Her battle with metastatic breast cancer had turned into a trench war with Caroline dug in on one end of the field and the disease dug in at the other. Caroline and her doctors lobbed medications like Fasolodex, Femara, Zoladex and Zometa at the enemy, while the cancer simply dug in deeper and waited for a sign of weakness, anything that would allow it to strike or to mutate. It was a difficult and uncertain existence of all of us. She had made it more than a year since the terrible diagnosis that her cancer had metastasized to her bones had been delivered. She'd fought through a terribly difficult round of radiation, through pain, nausea, fatigue, dry mouth, weight loss. She was doing well under the circumstances, but fear was always there, lurking like a monster in the closet. When would the cancer break out again and spread to her liver, her kidneys, her heart? Would the doctors be able to control it again? And always the ultimate question: how long did she have? The statistics gave her another year. Her doctor at Vanderbilt said she could live much longer, but none of us knew. We'd tried to "live like she was dying," as the Tim McGraw song says, to enjoy each day, each moment, to its fullest, but we'd found it impractical. We'd discovered that living the way we had always lived worked best for us, and we wanted it to last as long as possible.

"Who was that?" Caroline said to me after the dance was finished and the applause died down.

"Leon Bates."

"Leon? On Christmas Eve? What did he want?"

It probably wasn't the most appropriate time to discuss it, but I knew that eventually everyone in the family would weigh in on the subject. Since Leon wanted a decision quickly, and since the family was gathered and the mood was light, I decided to forge ahead.

"He wants me to take a murder case in Nashville. The retainer is a million dollars."

The news brought a collective gasp and a thirty-second silence.

"Is it Paul Milius?" Jack said. He was sitting on an overstuffed chair next to the couch with Charlie curled up on his lap.

"How did you know?"

"Ever heard of Facebook? Twitter? They're forms of social media that have been around for quite some time now. They're sometimes used to spread news very quickly."

"Wise ass," I said. I looked around at the rest of the group. "Yes, Paul Milius. Owns a record company in Nashville. He's accused of murdering an eighteen-year-old country singer named Kasey Cartwright back in October."

"The girl from here?" Caroline asked.

"Yes. They apparently arrested him earlier today. Leon said Milius and his wife want me to defend him, and Leon made it pretty clear that *he* wants me to defend him. Leon said it doesn't make sense that Milius would kill a girl that was making him a fortune and he says Milius is insisting he's innocent. Leon told them the fee would be a million up front plus expenses and they apparently were okay with that figure. They want an answer within forty-eight hours." I looked at Caroline. "What do you think? Do I call Leon back and tell him no or should we consider it? It's a lot of money."

"How long will it take? A year?" she asked.

"Depends on which judge we draw and what his or her docket is like. It also depends on Milius. I can move for a speedy trial if that's what he wants, but you know how it is. Most defendants want it to drag on as long as possible hoping a key witness will die or evidence will get lost. It could take longer than a year."

"How much time will you have to actually spend in Nashville?"

"I don't know, babe. Leon says Milius has a private jet and I can negotiate being home as much as possible. Charlie and Jack are both living there so I can associate Charlie – if she's willing – and let her handle a lot of the pre-trial work. I can hire other lawyers from Nashville if I need to. If it winds up going to trial, which it probably will since he's paying out so much money, then I'll have to spend some time down there. But at this point, I don't have any way of knowing how long the trial will take because I don't know anything about the case."

"What if Caroline gets sick?"

The question came from my sister, Sarah, who was sitting near Caroline on the couch. She was the only adult in the room who was completely sober because she'd had so many problems with drug and alcohol abuse in the past that she didn't allow herself to drink. She didn't mind, however, that the rest of us imbibed occasionally.

"She's already sick," I said. "And that's why we're talking about it. If it wasn't for the cancer, I don't think there would be much question as to whether I'd take a case like this."

"What if she gets worse?" Sarah said.

I shrugged my shoulders and looked at Caroline.

"I hate to put this on you, but it's your call," I said. "If you don't want me to go, I won't, and I won't regret it in the least. If you want me to do it, I'll do it."

"That isn't fair, Dad," my daughter, Lilly, said with a slight slur. Lilly was the pacifist in the family. She avoided confrontation like she avoided communicable diseases, so I was surprised when she spoke up, but like the rest of us, she'd been drinking.

"Why is it not fair?" I said. "She's the one who has cancer. If she doesn't want me to take the case, all she has to do is say so. I'm willing to abide by whatever decision she makes."

"Just tell them thanks but no thanks," Lilly said. "If the circumstances were different, if Mom wasn't sick, then we could have a discussion about whether you being away for what could be an extended period of time would be a good idea. But she *is* sick, and I think it's selfish and egotistical of you to even consider it."

I felt my jaw drop involuntarily and took a sip of wine.

"Wow," I said. "Selfish and egotistical? Because I have the audacity to consider earning a million-dollar fee that will go a long, long way toward providing for my family for many years to come? That's a bit harsh, don't you think?"

"You don't have to 'provide for your family' anymore," Lilly said, using her fingers to place quotation marks around the phrase. "Randy and I are fine. I have a good job and he's in medical school. Jack is about to graduate from law school. All you have to worry about is you and Mom. You guys have money, don't you? Do you really need a million dollars?"

"Did you hear what you just said? Are you listening to yourself? Who the hell doesn't need a million dollars?"

Caroline stood and raised a hand.

"Stop," she said. "I won't have raised voices in the house on Christmas Eve." She looked around the room at each of us with tears welling in her eyes. "I love all of you so much, and I regret that we have to go through this ... this *experience* with cancer. Lilly, I appreciate what you said and I understand how you feel. And you're right. Your father doesn't need to provide for you and Jack anymore. You've both done a wonderful job of being able to take care of yourselves. But you also know how your father is. I don't think him taking a case like this has anything at all to do with money. From what he said a few minutes ago, he smells injustice, and when he smells injustice, he wants to do something about it. It's an important part of who he is, what he's become. It's what he does, and I admire him for it. And as far as me getting sicker, getting worse, even dying, well, I just can't accept that we have to live our lives or make our choices based on such a huge uncertainty.

"I realize I might not be here next Christmas, and I know all of you think about it. It's there, always, in the back of our minds. But you know what? I might be here ten Christmases from now. I read all the time about women with metastatic breast cancer who are still alive after ten, fifteen years. The treatments are better than they used to be, and I'm young and strong and, for the most part, healthy. So I say we take the cancer consideration completely out of the picture and make a decision based on what we think is best for everyone in this room. Jack, I'm sure your dad will involve you in the case as much as he can since you're in Nashville, and the experience you'll gain in a high-profile murder case will be extremely valuable to you. Charlie, he's already said he'd like to associate you, which I assume will mean you'll earn a fairly significant fee for yourself and gain some valuable experience. Lilly, you and Randy and Sarah and the kids can keep me company when Joe is away. It'll give us an excuse to get together more often. And say what you will about money, a million dollars isn't an amount you can simply ignore. It could eventually benefit Grace or Joey or any children Jack might have. Your dad and I have been on both sides of the poverty line during our marriage. Back when he was in law school we had two children and were living off the measly salary I was making at a dance school in Knoxville. We got through it, but I have to tell you that given the choice between wealth and poverty, I choose wealth."

She paused for a few seconds and shook her head. "I don't think I've ever said that many words at one time in my entire life." She looked at me, smiled, and nodded her head several times.

"What?" I said.

"Go to Nashville," she said. "Go do what you do. Be a hero."

CHAPTER THREE

Alex Pappas heard his office door open, looked up, and his heart went cold. Lana was walking in. Lana Milius. Alex's boss's wife. The burned-out diva. The spoiled-rotten-woman-child who would slash the throat of a baby seal if she wanted to wear a seal skin coat. No, no. Lana wouldn't slash the throat herself. She'd find a way to get someone else to do it for her. But she'd wear the coat.

Alex had been working for Paul Milius for three years, and were it not for Lana, his would be a dream job. Being the personal assistant to Paul Milius was demanding but interesting, he made great money, and he lived in an incredible house on a spectacular estate. He liked Paul – he was a decent guy who lived a busy and fascinating life – but he didn't think much of Paul's choice of a wife. Lana had apparently been a big shot before Alex came onto the scene, a platinum-coated country music artist. She was still pretty, even beautiful, but whenever Alex saw her, only one word came to mind, a word that started with "b" and rhymed with itch.

"Hidy, Allie," Lana said in her best hick voice. She was wearing her standard around-the-house attire – a silk kimono, this one all purple and floral and cut low around her chest and high around her thighs. On her feet were black, open-toed sandals with four-inch heels and across her shoulders was a sheer, pink scarf. She looked like a French hooker playing geisha girl. This was an "I want something from you" outfit. Alex had seen it several times before. He forced himself to smile.

"Hello, Mrs. Milius."

"Why do you always have to be so formal with me, Allie? Don't you like me?"

She tossed the name "Allie" at him like a dart, and each time she did it, it penetrated just a bit deeper beneath his skin.

"I like you just fine, Mrs. Milius."

Alex watched uncomfortably as Lana walked behind him. She dropped one end of her scarf on his right shoulder and pulled it across his back as she continued to walk around his desk.

"I need a little favor from you, Allie," Lana said.

"What kind of favor?"

"Just a couple of minor things. Some computer work. Actually you can probably do everything from a phone. I need you to provide some information to some people using an encrypted email, maybe transfer some money to them."

"An encrypted email? Sounds clandestine."

"Ooh, I like that word. Clandestine. Yes, it's all very clandestine," Lana said as she sat down in a chair across from Alex's desk and crossed her legs. "I need someone who knows their way around the internet."

"I don't know, Mrs. Milius. I think I'd have to have a little more information—"

"Are you refusing a request from your employer?" Lana snapped.

"Paul is my employer," Alex said.

"*We* are your employer," Lana said. "Our corporation employs you and all of the rest of the people who work here. And guess who the president and chief executive officer of that corporation happens to be? Little ol' me. I'll bet you never thought about that, did you? Not that you *should* be thinking about things like that. As a matter of fact, right now, the thing you should be thinking about the most is how to please Lana Raines-Milius. You should be asking yourself exactly what she wants and exactly what you're going to do to make sure she gets what she wants."

Alex held up his hand, almost defensively. "Hold on, Mrs. Milius. You're not making any sense. Exactly why are you here?"

"See? There you go, right there," Lana said. "Now you've got it. I'm here because I need you to do exactly what I tell you for the next few days without saying a word to anyone. I'm going to provide you with some computer files and a pre-paid cell phone, and I'm going to give you access to some money. You're going to send the files to the people I tell you to send them to, you're going to talk to them on the telephone if it becomes necessary, and you're going to transfer money when and where I tell you to."

Alex eyes narrowed as he listened. He'd always suspected Lana was capable of some unseemly things, but he hadn't expected her to involve him.

"And if I refuse?" Alex said.

"Let's not even talk about that," Lana said as she uncrossed her legs, revealing that she wasn't wearing panties. She re-crossed them quickly as Alex's mind flashed to an old movie he'd seen. What was it called? *Basic Instinct.* "Let's talk about what's in it for you if you do what I ask you to do. First of all, there's this." The legs uncrossed again and Lana kept them that way for ten seconds while she stared directly into Alex's eyes. "Any time you want it. Oh, and there are these." She reached up slowly and pulled the kimono down to reveal her breasts.

"Mrs. Milius, please," Alex said. "No offense, but I'm not interested in having sex with you. It just wouldn't be ... it wouldn't be right."

"Well listen to you, the perfect little gentleman," Lana said as she pulled the kimono back up and crossed her legs. "You've been having sex with Tilly, haven't you?"

"I beg your pardon?"

"Don't play games with me, Allie. I know everything that goes on in this house and most everything that goes on outside it. You and Tilly have been seeing each other for six months. Don't tell me you haven't sampled the goods."

"My relationship with Tilly is none of your business."

"You're so cute when you're angry," Lana said. "Your cute little lips tighten up in a line and your pretty little jaw starts to twitch."

"I'd appreciate it if you'd leave now," Alex said.

"But I'm not finished. I haven't told you what else is in it for you if you do what I ask. I'll give you a half-million in cash on the tenth of October if everything goes the way I want it to."

"Then it can't be legal," Alex said. "You're asking me to do something illegal."

Lana held the scarf in front of her face and started waving it back and forth. "Legality," she said. "Morality. They're just words. Who's to say what's legal and what isn't? Who's to say what's moral and what isn't? I don't feel bound by any of that. I do what I think is best for me."

"Why don't you just do whatever it is you want done yourself?" Alex said.

"Because I don't want to take a chance on getting caught. It would be awful if I was caught. I could go to jail."

"But it's all right if I go to jail?"

"Better you than me," Lana said. Her tone suddenly turned from syrupy to icy. "I've tried to be nice, Allie, but you're making it impossible, so let me just tell you what will happen if you *don't* do what I want. May I borrow a pen and a piece of paper? Please, just a sticky note will be fine. That's it."

Lana rose from her chair while Alex slid an ink pen and a pad of blue sticky notes across the desk. She leaned over and wrote something on the top sticky note, pulled it off, and set it down in front of Alex. Then she did it again. And again. Lana straightened up and smiled while Alex gazed down at the three small pieces of paper. On each one of them was what looked to be a perfect forgery of his signature.

"You know that black Centurion credit card that Paul lets you use? Well, you've been using it an awful lot lately. Do you know where it is, by the way?"

Alex reached into his pocket and pulled out a set of keys. He opened a desk drawer to his right, took out a small, leather case. It was empty. He began to feel nauseous.

"Oh, my," Lana said. "It's gone, isn't it? Do you know you've run up more than two hundred thousand dollars in unauthorized credit card purchases in the past two weeks? You've bought some beautiful jewelry for Tilly, which the police will find if they happen to get involved. You've also bought some extremely nice things for yourself, things that will find their way into your closet when the police come. I called one of my lawyers and asked him what would happen to someone who had stolen two hundred thousand dollars from his employer and he said that person would go to prison for at least eight years. And you must be aware that Paul knows most of the judges in town. If he thought you'd stolen all that money from him, I'm sure he'd make sure you went straight to jail. You wouldn't pass go. You wouldn't collect two hundred dollars. You'd just go straight to jail for a long, long time."

Alex was so stunned he could think of nothing to say. He looked at Lana, open-mouthed.

"So you'll come over to our wing and meet me in my office then," Lana said sweetly. "Let's say about thirty minutes? I'll show you what I need done, and then maybe we'll have a little fun."

If you enjoyed the beginning of *A Crime of Passion*, you can purchase here via Amazon:

<u>A Crime of Passion</u>
Again, thank you for reading!

Scott